THE SORCERER
AND THE ASSASSIN

THE SORCERER AND THE ASSASSIN

STEPHEN O'SHEA

BRASH
BOOKS

ISBN-13: 978-1-954841-57-4

Published by
Brash Books
PO Box 8212
Calabasas, CA 91372
www.brash-books.com

To the memory of Peter Carson

CAST OF CHARACTERS

THE POWERFUL

Blanche of Castile: Queen Mother of France, mother of King Louis IX (Saint Louis), at Paris

Raymond VII: Raymond of Saint-Gilles, Count of Toulouse, Duke of Narbonne, and Marquis of Provence, at Toulouse

Robert de Sorbon: chaplain of Louis IX, founder of the Sorbonne, at Paris

Robert of Amiens: French seneschal (royal governor), at Carcassonne

Romano: cardinal, at Rome

THE INVESTIGATORS

Balian of Mallorca: alchemist, physician, polyglot, rumored to be a sorcerer, at Saint-Germain-des-Prés

Bertran: Southern sergeant and bodyguard of the investigators, at Chantecler

Jean-Paul: French sergeant and bodyguard of the investigators, at Paris

Martin of Troyes: Franciscan friar, confessor of Queen Blanche, at Paris

Matilda of Périgueux: cross-dressing, clairvoyant chatelaine, at Chantecler

Tancred of Périgueux: troubadour lord, brother of Matilda, at Chantecler

THE DOMINICAN FRIARS

Brendan of Killiney: master builder, at Toulouse

Giuseppe of Fiesole: provincial (leader) of the order, at Narbonne
Hildebrand of Alsace: inquisitor, at Toulouse
Humbert of Chartres: inquisitor, at Carcassonne
Jean of Béthune: abbot of the friars, at Toulouse
Pierre of Tours: inquisitor, at Toulouse
Pons of Bram: junior friar, at Toulouse

THE OTHERS

Alcuin: scholar, former tutor of Balian of Mallorca and Matilda of Périgueux, at Chantecler
Aiméry of Montauban: steward of the Count of Toulouse, at Toulouse
Anselm: Benedictine abbot, at Saint Germain des Prés
Astruguetus of Narbonne: Jewish merchant and patriarch, at Avignonet
Cara: peasant girl, heretic, at Auriol-Cabardès
Dame Marti: heretic, at Toulouse
Esclarmonde: head of the kitchens of the Count of Toulouse, at Toulouse
Fatima: Moorish servant girl of the Count of Toulouse, at Toulouse
Gaetan: bodyguard of Humbert of Chartres, at Carcassonne
Garsenda of Castelnou: *trobairitz* (female troubadour), at Toulouse
Guilhem: chamberlain of the Count of Toulouse, at Toulouse
Ibrahim ibn Abdullah: Muslim hermit, at Auriol-Cabardès
Ivo of Reims: bishop, at Toulouse
Judith of Narbonne: daughter of Astruguetus, at Avignonet
Pascal: renegade Dominican friar, at Carcassonne, turned baker, at Toulouse
Vidal: torturer, at Carcassonne

THE YEAR 1242

CHAPTER ONE

The insistent winter wind seemed to insinuate itself into every fold of cloak and tunic and reach right through to the bone. For the party of riders, the smiling South of the troubadours had given way to the brooding slope of the Black Mountain, to be descended gingerly. They picked their way down along a rocky track, their palfreys struggling to find purchase for their hooves among the fissures. Alongside the path, the harsh yellow of the broom shrubs shivered under a pale sun.

There were a dozen of them, dressed in the red and gold livery of the Count of Toulouse. Save one, the youngest of the group, fifteen-year-old Fatima. She gripped her pony's mane and turned her unblemished face to scan the valley below, hoping for a sign of settlement, a village, perhaps even a town, that might function as respite from this windswept upland. Her master, Aiméry of Montauban, steward of the Count of Toulouse, made a point of conducting an inspection of the count's lands at all times of year, and Fatima was expected to accompany him, to cook and clean as she did when at home in the castle.

Fatima disliked these forays into the country, even during the warmer months. The rustics stared at her, the youngest among them sometimes coming shyly forward to touch the dark skin of her hands. And though she had learned to smile and lightly brush them away, the attention made her feel like an outcast. Their fascination with her was so unlike the easy familiarity she enjoyed in the count's castle. In Toulouse daughters and sons of al-Andalus had settled in the city as guarantors of peace, and others, like herself, had been stranded there after the death of parents on their way to the northern fairs to sell their wares of Cordovan leather and Toledan steel. Fatima had no memory of her mother and father, but she often wondered about them. Who were they? What were their dreams? What would they think of the child they had left behind? Perhaps they would have hoped for better than the life she led beneath the echoing vaults of the Count of Toulouse's kitchens.

Fatima looked at her fingernails, crimson with pomegranate. Early mornings were spent scoring the red fruit, immersing it in water, then banging the husk to make the seeds fall into the mortar, there to be crushed by the pestle to render the pomegranate juice to flavor the meat and game. This red was far more palatable than the red of the Blood Month of November, when terrified sows and boars of the count's estates were herded into pens set up in the courtyard to be stabbed and cut open. Squeals, moans, screams—a pitiful cacophony. The twitching carcasses would then be strung up by their hind trotters, the bristles of their hides scorched away by bunches of flaming straws, and at last butchered. Fatima crouched below the gibbet, wooden bucket in hand, catching the freely flowing blood and offal, which she then turned into the *butifarra* so prized by her masters. Yes, her parents would indeed be ashamed.

Much as she questioned her lot as a servant, it was all that she had ever known. Compared to jolting down this rugged hillside today, her life of toil in the count's castle seemed like a haven. There was always the easy banter with youngsters her own age, the flirting with the fresh boys behind the hayrick, the promise of a hot meal every evening.

Fatima's pony slipped on the shale, interrupting her reverie. Just as well, for the leader of Steward Aiméry's armed sergeants had called for a halt. She strained to see the reason for the delay. Another group of horsemen was toiling its way up toward them, single file, heads bent into the wind. One of those heads was

4

tonsured, the bald pate exposed to the elements. Its owner was perched unsteadily atop a mule, the hem of his long black habit grazing the rocks along the path. A Dominican friar—Fatima had seen these strange fellows in Toulouse. The presence of Dominicans usually spelled mischief or worse, as they were known as capricious enforcers of God's will. Intrigued, the girl urged her pony forward to hear what it was that the creature might desire.

"Auriol-Cabardès?" Steward Aiméry was exclaiming, generations of aristocratic disdain for the clergy dripping from his voice. "My dear Brother Humbert, your God must have led you astray. The village of Auriol lies over there, to the west, not a league away." Aiméry gestured grandly with a gloved hand in that direction. "But climb no further. You have reached the height of the village. You will know you are near it when the land becomes a plateau. No need for divine guidance."

Brother Humbert of Chartres held the steward in a level gaze. The fierceness of his faith glowed from his dark eyes, his gaunt features betraying a piety tinged with mortification. Humbert would not humor this man of the South with a reply. He had grown accustomed to the insolence and godlessness of these accursed Southern noblemen, still smarting from the sound beating they had suffered at the hands of the French Northerners over the past twenty years.

Steward Aiméry spurred his steed to one side of the track, making way for the Dominican friar and his party to proceed. But the steward's movement revealed the rest of his retinue, including Fatima.

Humbert sat back on his mule as if struck. He would never have expected one such as she to find employ in the service of Toulouse.

"What strange company you keep, Steward Aiméry," Humbert finally said in a voice redolent of the mellifluous tones of the rainy North. "Am I mistaken or is that not a daughter of Balthazar? Of the three magi, the only one to be as black as sin?"

All eyes swiveled in her direction. Fatima stared at some dry twigs of thyme on the ground, silently cursing the curiosity that had impelled her to spur her pony forward. Curiosity had landed her in trouble before, peering around a corner to see what she shouldn't, straining to hear a whispered exchange, and once, in her master's armory, even hefting a sword she had no business touching—an infraction that had cost her a dozen lashes of the count's *cravache*. To worsen matters, a freshening breeze seemed to toy with her modest cloak so as to leave her open to Brother Humbert's unwelcome gaze. A stronger gust blew back her hood, revealing her tight, dark curls, so dissimilar to the compliant plaits of her white sisters.

"Friar Humbert," the steward responded with some impatience, "this loyal servant has been a member of Count Raymond's household since childhood and is now grown into a capable and commendable wench to whom I entrust the feeding and care of my party whenever we must needs travel to serve our lord." He might have added that this girl, this Fatima, betrayed a nobility of movement and demeanor unusual for one in such a lowly station in life. But Steward Aiméry held his tongue.

Humbert looked unconvinced. "Our provincial will be notified," he said in a low voice. "We take a dim view of such impieties. Need I remind you, sir, that above all else we are servants of Christ?"

"And a good day to you too, Brother." The contempt in the steward's voice was no longer accompanied by even the ghost of a smile. He eased his heels into the flanks of his chestnut palfrey and signaled his escort to resume their descent. The interview was over.

As Fatima came closer to the Dominican, she resolved not to look away. Instead, she passed brazenly before the glowering friar, her eyes staring insolently into his. She noted the typical clerical mix of hatred and hunger dwelling there and, narrowing her gaze, willed herself not to blink. Only after passing him did she realize she'd been holding her breath. As the friar urged his mount toward the village of Auriol, Fatima glanced over her shoulder to look at the receding figure. The world, she thought, had no need of men such as him, and if ever she had the power to turn her beliefs into action, she would do what she could to cleanse his like from the Earth.

CHAPTER TWO

Brother Humbert could nearly smell the malodorous attar of her wantonness as she rode by, daring to lock glances with him, a man of God. He drew himself up in his ostentatiously humble saddle, hoping to regain the authority he had felt slipping away ever since glimpsing this Moorish daughter of al-Andalus.

"Gaetan," the friar said, addressing the strapping leader of his armed escort. "The day grows late. You are to take three men and ride ahead to Auriol. Round up all the villagers, tell them the word of Christ will be soon among them. If any of them dare disobey the summons, they risk their eternal soul."

Gaetan and his men galloped through the garrigue until they were out of sight, disappearing behind a knoll. Humbert reflected on what lay ahead: a village of the foul smelling and the filthy, totally unaware of how they were nesting in a bed of heretical pestilence. Three decades had been spent trying to eradicate the evil creed of the Cathars from the lands of Languedoc, thanks to the holy knights of the North and the sermons of the sainted Dominic, but no matter how many of the Southern vermin were killed by the flash of the sword and the flame of the fire, there always remained some who clung to the noxious faith of their fathers. Ignorant? Stubborn? Diabolical, more likely.

Humbert spurred his mule to a trot, eager to root out these foxes in the vineyards of the Lord. A week previously his spies had come to him in Carcassonne and told him that Auriol-Cabardès was a hotbed of the heterodox, isolated from the influence of the church in the more hospitable reaches of the valleys far below the

Black Mountain. Humbert looked murderously at the tendrils of gray smoke now visible in the middle distance—the cooking fires of these wretches.

He had sacrificed his studies in Chartres to join the order of Dominic, to effect change in the world, to rescue the laity from its embrace of the flesh. And when, shortly after Dominic had died, his Dominican friars were appointed by the Holy Father to form something new, an *Inquisition*, to track down and exterminate heretics, Humbert knew he had found his true calling. He spent four years of study in the newly founded Dominican university at Toulouse, learning of the unspeakable beliefs and practices of these devils and the methods of correcting them through inquisition and torture. The villagers of Auriol would learn that he, the Inquisitor of Carcassonne, was not to be defied. Humbert smiled grimly as his mount waded into a throng of villagers in a paddock, their dirty faces upturned in anticipation.

He would give them something to remember.

He dismounted and climbed up on a trestle table that Gaetan had set up as an improvised dais.

"My children, my children," Humbert began sweetly, the French inflection of his Occitan almost seductive. "I have journeyed here all the way from Carcassonne to save you. For so great is the love of the church for all of you that even the most illustrious of its members"—he inclined his head in false modesty—"will make his way through the briars and the nettles to speak to you as a pastor."

The crowd before Humbert remained impassive. A moment of silence passed. The friar scanned the gallery of faces as if trying to divine where the heresy lurked. Humbert thought these peasants to be contemptible bumpkins—it was a wonder that he bestirred himself in the service of saving their befouled souls. If anything, he thought, they should be crowding around the trestle table for the opportunity of kissing his sandals or the hem of his black robe.

He recognized that he would have to speak in a way their limited reasoning could grasp, a preaching precept drilled into him during his time in Toulouse. He knew that many on the Black Mountain were shepherds. "Heretics are wolves in sheep's clothing," Humbert said loudly. "They endanger the entire flock."

He raised a great staff and waved it slowly back and forth over the heads of the crowd. Then he froze it over one man, who shrank back reflexively.

This was precisely the reaction Humbert was hoping for, a spasm of fear. But the fellow was an exception: the rest of the villagers remained unmoved, their tired eyes trained on Humbert as if inspecting a prize rooster for purchase. The friar could see that their dislike for him as a busybody equaled his dislike for them as apostates.

Humbert and his listeners shared a moment of uncomfortable silence. The Dominican took a deep breath. This was no time to deploy fancy Parisian rhetoric, not when faced with these oafs. "You have returned to the noxious embrace of heresy," he roared. "Your souls will roast in Hell for eternity."

Silence, again. Somewhere nearby a horse whinnied.

Humbert looked down for a moment. He had to make these villagers understand that he and his brethren in the Holy Office of the Inquisition knew all about their disgusting heretical practices. He had studied them, his stomach churning, in his years of schooling in Toulouse.

"You must repent. You are an abomination," Humbert shouted. "Your errors are too vile; you are sullied. Evil has taken root within you. You must reject the lascivious practices of the devils among you. Incestuous copulation. You lie with your brothers, your sisters, your mother, your father. Demonic debauchery of the flesh. Then you roast and devour the misshapen infants spewed out of such sinful congress."

He caught his breath and looked out over a sea of skepticism. A few heads turned to one another, smiles growing on faces.

Humbert grunted like a gored bull. He would have to inform them that he knew of the most despicable of their practices.

"You fornicate with cats. With cats. Have you no shame?"

"Caw! Caw!"

It was a young woman's voice, taunting.

"Dominican crow. Caw. Caw." His black habit had not gone unnoticed.

A wave of laughter rippled through the crowd. Everyone loved Cara. She was a spirited slip of a girl, a young beauty as yet untamed, and not one to be intimidated by a black-robed friar, no matter how important he claimed to be.

"Caw. Caw."

Cara smiled at her neighbors, her friends, her kinsmen. We are simple people, she thought, minding our flocks, tending our vines, with an Understanding of the Good that this silly Frenchman knows nothing about. We fornicate with cats? The crow is a madman. How can he believe such nonsense? She had heard tell that these Dominican crows were afraid to touch a woman, so they spent their time playing with one another. Well, more power to them. When her time came, she would choose a man worthy of her appetites, aching to be with her, a stallion to her mare. She felt the eyes upon her as she adjusted her simple tunic. Her golden hair shifted languidly in the wind. It was good to be alive and held safe in the hundredfold thoughts of the village.

Humbert's face betrayed no emotion at the cries of the heckler. He thought silently on what lay ahead. He knew these creatures to be a pestiferous boil on the Mystical Body of Christ. Either they would recant their error, or he would burn them alive.

"My children," he said, changing tack, a counterfeit sweetness in his voice. "You have two days to think over whether you will come to me of your own accord and beg absolution. If you do, I shall be merciful. You can come to me at any time, day or night, to make your confessions and request forgiveness. If you are a good and true Christian, you have nothing to fear. But you must also tell me who else among you is afflicted with the illness of heresy. I want names. Do not withhold any names because they are your friends or your kin. It is your duty to tell all. If you are found to have held back names, then you too will be punished."

After a long pause, he raised his right hand and performed a blessing. Sourly, he noted that some in the crowd did not cross themselves in response. During his training as inquisitor, he had been taught that these heretics reviled the symbolism of the Cross. More than a few of the villagers kept their hands at their sides.

"Two days, my children. You have two days," Humbert said softly. "Do not return to heresy, like a dog returning to its vomit."

Gaetan helped Humbert down from his perch. Although he was still young, long seasons of study and prayer and fasting had turned this warrior for Christ into a frail man. But what he lacked in strength he made up for in conviction. These insects would be squashed.

The crowd parted to make way for Gaetan and the friar. In the heavy stillness a persistent breeze could be heard rustling through a spinney of poplars. A shrike gave out a shrill cry in the dying sunlight as it impaled an insect on a thorn.

When the outsiders had finally passed into the village chapel, the people of Auriol dispersed. There was much to think about. Instinctively, wives sought out their husbands; children, their mothers. Hands closed over hands as families made their way back home in silence. Once indoors, the frantic, fearful discussions would begin, lasting long into the night.

Four hours later, the blackness was absolute, the stars brilliant, the night locked in the grip of midwinter. The village was quiet, save for the occasional yelp of a dog, and all had entered their first sleep of the evening. They would wake, naturally, at around midnight, perform some chores or perhaps make love, then go back to their second sleep, awakening only when the world was light once more.

In the dimness of the chapel, a straw bed had been laid out in the front of the nave for Brother Humbert. Gaetan stood guard outside the door, and the scribes and notaries had been given places in a nearby manger. The visitors had also entered their first sleep and now slumbered profoundly, wearied by the arduous uphill journey they had undertaken earlier in the day from Carcassonne. The men accompanying the friar were from the gentle Aude valley, unaccustomed to scaling the slope of the Black Mountain. Auriol-Cabardès had the distinct disadvantage of being nestled close to the summit of the escarpment. Humbert of Chartres, who had been raised in the placid plains and meadows of the Beauce, was even less accustomed to such rugged uplands.

An odd, muffled sound came from outside the door. Humbert opened his eyes on his pallet. True, in his sermon, he had said they could come at any time, day or night, but these heretics were such a damnable nuisance sometimes. With more resignation than anticipation he got to his feet, brushing away stray strands of straw from his cassock. It was true that people generally preferred betraying their neighbors under cover of night. Human nature must be manured with fear to yield a crop for the torturer. He moved toward the door.

It opened. Humbert squinted. Instead of Gaetan's being there, the silhouette of a large, robed man filled the doorframe. Definitely not one of the scrawny villagers. Behind the figure, on the flagstones, lay a shapeless lump of a thing in a spreading pool of darkness.

Gaetan.

In the starlight, Friar Humbert of Chartres had time only to see the faint flash of the blade before it was driven deep into the bridge of his nose.

CHAPTER THREE

It was a chill afternoon in the goodly Christian city of Toulouse, and Brother Pons of Bram, a burly Dominican friar, ran up the muddy street toward the Seilhan House, home to the Inquisition. Pons' haste commanded respect, and passersby parted to allow the big young man to continue on his way. In response to his pounding on the door, a bolt slid and the Dominican on guard in the threshold let him pass, reassured by his black-and-white habit.

Pons took the stairs two at a time. On reaching the upper floor he burst into the first room on the left.

"Terrible tidings," Pons said breathlessly. "Brother Humbert is dead. Murdered."

"Good Lord! When?" responded his superior, Brother Pierre of Tours.

"Yesterday. We've only just got word."

Brother Pierre gripped the arms of his chair.

"These people are plague-sore carbuncles."

A thin man with the pursed lips of the ascetic, Pierre of Tours did not like surprises. For a man of faith, change was an enemy; resistance, an insult. Pierre had almost rejected his elevation to the rank of Grand Inquisitor of Toulouse, an unheard-of act of defiance in the Dominican Order, on the grounds that the people of the Languedoc were an impossible, immoral lot, practitioners of obscene rituals at every new moon, justifying their unnatural lusts with a perverted creed that seemed to well up out of the accursed soil and infect every generation. The sainted Dominic himself had debated these Cathar heretics for years, tried to pull them out of their filth, all to no avail. It was only after much prayer that Pierre had been told by God to shoulder his cross and move to this land of infamy.

So, he had a dead inquisitor to deal with, struck down by the very heretics he was charged to hunt. The wretches had never gone this far before. In the early days of the Holy Office some ten years previously, several inquisitors had been given a rough reception in the towns and cities they visited, but no blood was shed.

"Where?"

"Auriol-Cabardès, on the Black Mountain."

"Never heard of it."

"It is a small village. Remote."

Pierre of Tours got to his feet and smoothed the folds of his robe. Clearly, he was to have no tranquility for many a day. He looked searchingly at his young aide.

"You're from the Languedoc, Brother Pons. The town of Bram, if memory serves. What's the reputation of this Auriol?"

A thoughtful expression crossed Pons' fleshy features.

"The people of the Black Mountain are said to be superstitious, believers in black magic. And they keep to themselves."

"Are they thought to be dangerous?"

"No more than anybody else up there. Every now and then there is a brawl over a stolen sheep or some other matter. And on the Feast of Saint Vincent, when the wine is passed around in his honor, the odd fistfight isn't that rare."

"But they're not a murderous lot?"

Pons shook his head.

"I want them all rounded up."

"The whole village? But, Brother Pierre, begging your indulgence, the whole village did not commit the crime."

Pierre's face clouded. Even his most trusted confederates would allow him no serenity.

"They are all complicit," he said fiercely. "All of them. Every man, woman, and child." They had all conspired to disturb his peace and quiet.

Pons' eyes widened as the grand inquisitor continued in a steady voice. "Tell the civil authorities that on pain of excommunication they are to dispatch a squad of armed men to arrest all the villagers. Then they will be brought in chains here to our prison."

Pierre noticed the dubious look on Pons' face.

"What is it?"

"Auriol is far from Toulouse. Carcassonne is much closer."

Pierre waved his hand as if batting away a fly.

"Very well, then. We will travel to Carcassonne to question them ourselves. Lock them up in the Wall."

CHAPTER FOUR

The Wall of Carcassonne, the name given the Inquisition's prison, lowered over the right bank of the river Aude, its mute stone façade a reminder of the dread power of church and Crown. Facing it, across the river, rose the Lower Town, the dwelling place of the prosperous burghers of Carcassonne. Half-timbered houses, warehouses, shop trestles—all teemed with the commotion of commerce. Behind the Wall, on a commanding height, stood the battlements of the Upper Town, its many turrets and towers brooking no challenge to authority. Unlike the county of Toulouse, Carcassonne and its surroundings belonged to the Kingdom of France. The royal seneschal resided in the Upper Town, as did his men-at-arms. In an act of munificence, the seneschal had granted the Dominicans their own tall tower in the line of massive stone fortifications. Whenever inmates of the Wall had to be interrogated by the friars, they would be led in shackles up the steep hill that separated the prison from the Inquisition Tower.

Master Vidal, a local man with a gift for inflicting pain, performed his trade with little ceremony. Stocky, bearded, in midlife, with a shock of bushy eyebrows that gave him a look of perpetual surprise, Vidal nodded as Pierre of Tours issued his instructions. The suspect today was a young woman of Auriol who had been taken captive three days previously with all her fellow villagers and imprisoned in the Wall. She was a willowy, fetching creature, Brother Pierre thought, so unlike the homely womanhood of the countryside. He had learned that the girl was a troublemaker.

"Now, Cara, my child," Pierre said, "are you going to tell me who murdered Holy Brother Humbert?"

The interpreter beside him asked the question in Occitan.

"I know not," Cara replied, her eyes darting around the gloom in search of something, anything, that was familiar. What is this place? Who is this crow?

Pierre told his translator to ask again, to tell her it was her last chance. If she persisted in her obstinacy, the question would be put to her more forcibly.

Cara answered in the negative once again, her voice stronger now.

"Master Vidal," Pierre said, "the strappado, if you please."

Vidal nodded and shuffled over to a worktable on which there lay a large coil of rope. He took it, then approached the girl. He grabbed her hands and pulled her arms behind her back. Expertly, he bound together her wrists. Cara's face expressed more puzzlement than fear. Why had they just freed her from manacles only to tie her hands up again? With practiced ease, Vidal played out a considerable length of rope from the other end of the coil and threw it high in the air. It sailed over a ceiling beam, then plummeted to the floor.

The interpreter had a queasy look on his face. This Cara was but a maiden, after all. A young scribe, seated at a table, watched in incomprehension. This was his first time in the Inquisition Tower, having been transferred from his post in the courts. The great leather-bound Inquisition register for the year lay open before him on a blank page, awaiting his Latin transcription of a confession. He had dutifully entitled the page: *Cara, puella Aureoli.* As bewildered as the girl, he pushed the register aside and looked closely at Vidal's busy work.

Whistling softly, Vidal found the other end of the rope and wrapped it around his waist several times, securing it with a rough knot. He then pulled on the dangling rope above him to make it taut. He and the girl were at opposite ends of a rope looped over a beam far above their heads.

Pierre of Tours wiped his lips and then nodded to himself. He would wring the name of the killer out of this slut, even if that meant maiming her for life. Consorting with heretics was just as evil as being one, and he wagered that this young beauty took a lead role in their nocturnal orgies, giving herself serially to every man, even to her father and brothers, shrieking out in satanic abandon as her body shuddered in ecstasy. He saw in her shapely form the sinful voluptuousness of womanhood.

"Master Vidal, elevate."

The stocky man pulled down on the rope, hand over hand, causing the girl to ascend into the air, the hands bound behind her back now painfully above and behind her head. She screamed.

"Ask her again."

The interpreter stepped forward and uttered a few words in a quaking voice. Cara, her eyes bulging, shouted an obscenity at the stony-faced inquisitor.

Pierre watched as his Occitan speaker sadly shook his head.

The inquisitor then looked at Vidal, who was stoutly holding his end of the rope. As she was not a particularly heavy load, he had no need of the carved footholds in the stone floor.

Pierre held up a hand, two fingers raised. Vidal nodded.

He let go of the rope. The girl fell. A split second later, he grabbed the rope and made it firm. There was a cracking of shoulders, a wild howl of pain.

Then Vidal did it a second time. The screams became a keening of despair. Cara's arms were almost out of their sockets. Why are they doing this? she thought through her agony. What kind of God do these demons worship?

The scribe got groggily to his feet, then bent over like a stick-man and threw up, his body wracked by convulsions. Pierre hurried over to him and grabbed the dark brown hair at the back of his tonsure. He looked into the young face, gray as ash.

"Pray with me, Brother Pascal," Pierre said softly. "Pray with me." He nodded reassuringly, then began, *"Pater noster, qui es in caelis, sanctificetur nomen tuum…"*

The youth joined the inquisitor in the Lord's Prayer, not daring to think of the girl agonizing overhead. When they had finished, Pierre let go of his head and returned to his place below the girl.

"Lower her, Vidal."

The girl, barely conscious, came to eye level with the inquisitor, her feet still hanging in the air. Pierre gripped her soft chin and jerked it upward.

"What say you, Cara, you little harlot?" Pierre said. His hand wandered down her neck and onto her left breast, then stayed there.

Cara roused herself and looked at him through her pain. He was a black vision of evil. She tried to shrink from him, arching her back, to escape his repulsive touch. Pierre pushed harder, his hand on her heaving breast unwavering. A slight, sickly smile flickered across his features. So, this was where the heretics first took their pleasure. An idea occurred to him.

"I will spare you, but you must share your favors with me."

Cara stepped into the abyss of his eyes.

"You … you … serve the Devil."

She spat in his face.

A tremendous blow struck her. An angry welt rose on her cheek. At least his hand had gone elsewhere.

"The bells, Vidal."

The torturer raised his forested eyebrows and then called to a far corner of the tower, where wooden shelves anchored in the stone wall held a variety of weights and tools. A young man sat on a stool before the shelving.

"Come on, son," Vidal said, "bring them over."

The youth struggled across the room, his arms distended from gripping ropes attached to the crowns of two large bells, each one almost a quarter as tall as a man. As they had no clappers they did not toll. They were designed to elicit sound, not make it.

Once before the girl, Vidal and the youth grabbed her ankles and made fast a bell to each foot. The great metal objects lay benignly on the ground, the girl oblivious to what had been affixed to her.

"Elevate, Vidal."

This time he slipped his feet into the grooves of the stone floor, the front of his clogs secured by good hard granite. Vidal strained to raise the girl and the bells. She screamed as the cartilage in her shoulders felt her weight doubled, if not trebled.

At about fifteen feet above the floor, Vidal immobilized her. She was like a fly, barely human, her modest tunic ripped open.

Vidal let go of the rope. Then grabbed it.

He fell backward; there was no counterweight. He heard the thud of bells and a strange whizzing sound of rope. As he sprawled on the floor, the rope came tumbling down upon him, and then two arms, detached from a torso. They struck him in the face. Blood flowed freely from one arm and soaked his beard.

He got slowly to his feet and saw the bells and the girl, armless, staring up from the hard stone, blood and brain oozing out of her ears. She made no sound, drew no breath.

CHAPTER FIVE

Pascal the scribe bolted from the chamber, his footfalls on the cold flagstones alternating with the sounds of his vomiting. This was his first time in the Inquisition Tower, and it would be his last. He raced down the spiral stone staircase. He did not become a friar only to become a murderer. He would leave the order.

Light poured in from an open doorway at the base of the tower. Pascal paused for a second, then emerged into the sunshine bathing the dusty courtyard of the seneschal's castle. He wiped the tears from his cheeks and hurried to the stables on the far side of the enclosure. The groom greeted him familiarly and agreed to take him to the barn where the friars kept their mules. This entailed walking through the horse stables first.

"Look here," the groom said affably. "A hobby. A fine horse. You don't see many of these in the South. Just came in today."

Pascal nodded absently and followed the talkative man farther along.

"Why would you need a mule now?" the hostler asked. "It'll soon be nightfall."

"Need to haul a load," he replied. He neglected to say that the load was himself and his meager belongings, plus a few scraps of food soon to be pilfered from the larder of the Dominican convent in the Lower Town. And that he would trust in God to flee this infernal city for good.

Soon he was riding through the Aude Gate of the fortifications, following the track down to the river and the Lower Town.

He turned to look at the Upper Town one last time and saw, in the upper mullioned window of the Inquisition Tower, the interpreter's face staring out.

The view from that vantage point took in the entirety of the Lower Town and the looming hogback of the Black Mountain in the distance. The interpreter contemplated the scenery absently, taking care not to turn away from it and be confronted with the bloody sight lying mutilated on the floor behind him.

Brother Pierre looked over at Vidal, who was pushing the girl's arms out of his way with an indifferent foot. The torturer caught the inquisitor's eye and shrugged.

"Take her out tonight," Pierre said, "and hang her from the bridge."

"Near the Lower Town?"

"Yes, Vidal. I want the people to see."

Satisfied, Pierre of Tours left the chamber and made his way in the light of sunset toward a church, hands clasped before him, lost in prayer.

Ever since the investigation into Brother Humbert's murder had begun some three days previously, Pierre had made it his custom to linger in the Upper Town and pray in the Cathedral of Saint-Nazaire. He would then descend to the Lower Town to join the other friars in the refectory of their convent. His brethren came to expect him to be late, his reputation for saintliness growing by the day.

Although not a Dominican church, Saint-Nazaire had a radiating chapel dedicated to Saint Dominic, who had performed many wondrous miracles in the diocese not thirty years earlier. Pierre's custom was to lie on the floor in front of the likeness of the great man and beseech him for another day's guidance in the ways of the Lord. The girl he had just put to the question had obviously been a heretic and thus deserved to die. It was a pity that death had come so quickly to spare her further torment.

Pierre prostrated himself on the cold floor, facedown, and sought Dominic's blessing. He had no doubt it would be forthcoming.

The creak of a door opening on its hinges signaled that another worshipper had entered the sanctuary. Pierre rose from the floor and adopted a kneeling position. His piety might be immodest, but he was modest in displaying it.

A snort sounded behind him, then a voice said, "Good. You have assumed the posture."

Pierre's eyes widened as he recognized the voice. He turned to confirm, but it was too late. A broadsword sliced through the air and cleaved his neck. The grand inquisitor's head bounced on the floor, eyes open, astonished.

CHAPTER SIX

In the early light of morning, a gray heron looked down on the city from its perch atop the scaffolding that hugged the cathedral under construction. The bird could see the shopkeepers on the Petit Pont, the sole bridge over the Seine connecting the Latin Quarter and the Île-de la Cité. The merchants opened their shutters and set up trestles to display their wares. The bustle of commerce, to which the bird had become accustomed in its home near the heart of the great city, was about to begin once more. The faint smell of charcoal and wood from hundreds of hearths still hung over the rooftops, to be renewed again at sunset when fires were relit to ward off the chill of a late winter night.

The heron launched itself into the dawn mist, its long neck retracted in a tight S shape for flight, and wheeled lazily above the bridge and the river, looking for a place to feed. A few ripples in the water upstream signaled some small fish, perhaps an eel or a frog, ready to be skewered by its long sharp bill and devoured as the first meal of the day. Within seconds the bird stood motionless on the muddy riverbank, three feet tall, a predatory statue. The telltale ripples on the water's surface had subsided, leaving the heron peering into an expanse devoid of promise. Its long legs took a few steps closer to the base of the bridge.

"Hey-oh. Hey-oh."

A human voice. The heron looked up and saw a man in a long green cloak. Suddenly a large hunk of warm bread landed with a *thud in the reeds. Greedily, the bird bent down and with a move-ment of its bill tore the bread apart and swallowed it.*

"Bon appétit, my friend. Bon appétit."

There came a sharp laugh, and then the man was no longer there.

CHAPTER SEVEN

"Balian of Mallorca. Balian of Mallorca."

The page's voice pierced the vaulted waiting room, causing it to bubble like a cauldron brought to a simmer. Muttered oaths were exchanged as a young man in a flowing green robe stood up from the long bench on the far side of the hall. His dark eyes gleamed with mischief underneath a swelling torrent of hair of the deepest black.

He made his way across the stone slabs to the page standing before the elaborately carved oak door, aware of the thoughts of all those staring at him. So, this was the diabolical Balian of Mallorca, the sorcerer of Saint-Germain-des-Prés. The man was said to speak every tongue in God's Creation, even the language of animals. Dozens of eyes bored into his back as he approached the great door.

It swung open to reveal a spare stone chamber with a throne at one end. The room was as austere as its royal owner, King Louis IX of France.

"Good of you to come, Master Balian." Robert de Sorbon, a churchman with a friendly expression, grasped his hand and led him forward. "It has been too long, has it not?"

Balian nodded, noticing the lines around Sorbon's eyes. A scholar, spending too much time raising money for the construction of his new school in the Latin Quarter. But also a courtier, with the hunted look of someone desperate to retain the favor of a regal patron.

Balian turned, then spied the throne at the far end of the chamber. It was occupied not by Louis, but by his mother, Blanche of Castile.

He took several paces forward, then genuflected.

"This is a great honor, Majesty," he said in the Castilian tongue. "I trust you no longer suffer from the ague for which I was summoned to your bedside some years ago."

Blanche surveyed him haughtily. He noticed a cane leaning against her armrest. Cherry, a fine wood for walking sticks.

"We are in Paris," she said in French, pointedly. "We are in France. And I am its queen."

Queen mother, he thought.

She nodded and he rose to his feet and looked at her guardedly. Blanche of Castile, the most remarkable woman in the kingdom, the most remarkable queen since her grandmother, the hellion Eleanor of Aquitaine. Widowed young, with an infant son, Blanche had fought the rebellious barons of France to a standstill until her boy came of age. Never one to diminish her accomplishments, she compared herself to the biblical Queen Esther, saving her people from destruction. She had even paid for a rose window showing the genealogy of Jesus Christ's family at the new church in Chartres.

"How may I be of service, ma'am?"

A chill silence filled the room. Blanche's lips were tightly shut, he saw, the grim rictus earned by a lifetime of scheming.

"How may I serve your son?"

"My son is sometimes too busy to attend to the affairs of his realm."

Balian remained silent.

"He is currently in the Cathedral of Notre-Dame … performing his penance."

Was that a curl of disdain on the old woman's lips? Balian had heard the stories, about the king's lying for hours on the cold stone floor of the recently completed nave. About the hair shirt worn underneath the royal finery. About the scars on his back, opened nightly with a flick of the switch. Then there was the Sainte-Chapelle that was being constructed next door to this royal residence. A bauble, Balian thought, a jewelry box for His Majesty's credulity. A vial of the Virgin's milk, the Crown of Thorns, a splinter of the True Cross, who knew what else King Louis believed he possessed? Relics purchased for two hundred thousand in Constantinople, he had heard whispered, much more than a king's ransom. Much more than it took even to build the chapel.

"It has become my unwanted lot to occupy myself with matters of the kingdom," Blanche said evenly.

Balian bowed his head, the better to hide the smile stealing over his face. Her unwanted lot? No one in France was unaware that Blanche knew how and when to twist the knife, and that she enjoyed doing so. It was said that in the early days of her widowhood she had taken as her lover a young prelate named Romano, a man as worldly and cunning as his royal mistress and now a powerful cardinal in Rome. If the rumor were true, and had they remained together, the brilliant couple of Blanche and Romano could have wreaked as much havoc as the Norsemen of yore.

"A great pity, Majesty."

Her basilisk eyes flashed at him for an instant, then regained their glassy impassiveness. He noticed her twisting a large ring on her left hand, as if considering what to say next.

"Balian of Mallorca. A man of the South."

He nodded.

"Balian... that's a name you don't often hear around the Mediterranean."

"My father was a great admirer of Balian of Ibelin, the man who defended Jerusalem."

"The man who surrendered Jerusalem."

A gulf yawned between them now. Blanche's chin quivered in indignation. A lifetime ago Balian's namesake, Balian of Ibelin, had negotiated a truce with the victorious Saladin and evacuated the holy city, leaving it to be absorbed into the lands of Islam.

"Majesty … Balian of Ibelin saved many lives—"

"And lost his eternal soul!"

The conversation had reached an impasse. The queen mother looked fixedly at Balian. Undaunted, he held her gaze.

"You were brought up among the Saracens."

"Our islands were not freed until recently, ma'am. By your kinsman, the King of Aragon, and by the Bishop of Saragossa."

This was the way to go, telling her things she already knew. He would not venture any other detail of his upbringing, not before this questioner. She resumed her silent inspection of him, her lined face now a mask of suspicion.

"How fares our good Abbot Anselm?"

The friendly voice was Sorbon's, gamely trying to deflect the queen mother's displeasure. Balian now understood what he had only suspected on entering the room: he was here at Sorbon's suggestion, probably without the king's knowledge. The queen mother did not approve of Balian either but was willing to appraise him. Sorbon, on the other hand, whom he had often seen hectoring the laborers at the college he was building, was almost a friend, certainly a kindred spirit. He looked at the kind face, saw again the cat's cradle of wrinkles surrounding the rheumy eyes. How difficult Sorbon's balancing act must be.

"He is quite well, Your Grace. As are the monks."

"You are kept busy, I trust? There are so many of them."

Like everyone else at court, Sorbon knew of Balian's peculiar arrangement with the Abbey of Saint-Germain-des-Prés. Balian had left his beloved South to come to the cloudy North five years previously, following his medical studies in Montpellier. His late father had done much to inculcate in him the need for tact and discretion in the practice of medicine. "Remember what they teach you," he had said, "if only to make sure you don't repeat their mistakes." In Balian's childhood, on the island of Mallorca, his father had taught him to be observant, to look around at the sights and sounds of the natural world, to draw conclusions based on reason, not superstition. A few years into his stay in Paris, the desperate Benedictines of Saint-Germain had sought him out in his small surgery near the church of Saint-Julien-le-Pauvre. When Balian reached the sickroom in the Saint-Germain abbey, he could see that the ailing Abbot Anselm had been bled by the monastic infirmarer almost to the point of death. Careful not to offend, but careful, too, to inspire confidence, he'd ordered the thirsty leeches removed. Then he'd had the monks administer hearty beef broths to their enfeebled superior and apply compresses soaked with cold well water to his burning brow. The fever either would break or would not; there was precious little else that anyone could do—this he knew but did not say. Happily, Balian's advice was heeded. On recovering, the abbot proposed to the physician the novel idea of moving his residence to an outdwelling on the monastery grounds beyond the walls of Paris and, in exchange for rent, taking care of any monks who fell ill. The young doctor hadn't thought twice about the offer; he could conduct his alchemical experiments well away from the censorious snoops who haunted the theology faculties.

"So, so many of them," Balian echoed. "It seems that every year the members of the novitiate grow in number. Little wonder that the abbey is a building site. They have to be housed."

Sorbon's face creased into a false smile.

"I will take a collation." The queen mother had risen suddenly and was already moving with surprising speed toward a side door, her cherry cane tapping imperiously on the flagstones.

Sorbon bowed to Balian and rushed after her. This woman of sudden appetites was not to be disobeyed.

Blanche paused in the doorway. On the old woman's face there was a hint of a smile, of glee almost. "You," she said to Balian, "will accompany us."

CHAPTER EIGHT

Eating in public was always an ordeal for Balian. He was repelled by the mix of cloying porridges and honeyed puddings that was served at even the noblest of tables. He had grown up under Muslim rule; his father, as he made sure not to mention to Queen Blanche or to anyone else, had been court physician to the Emir of Mallorca. Nothing passed the emir's lips until it was tested and tasted by his doctor. The cornucopia of Islam had long overflowed the Balearic Islands, imported from the splendid gardens of Valencia and Córdoba. Paris might be a jewel of the Christian continent, but its daily fare dulled it in Balian's eyes. When he had been given his country house in the fields of Saint-Germain, he determined to remedy the situation. If he longed for the cornucopia of his boyhood, then he would have to cultivate it himself.

And it was to a boyhood friend he had made his appeal: Moses ben Shaprut, now a prominent merchant of Granada, who voyaged north every year to attend the fairs in Champagne. Balian pleaded with Moses to bring to him the fruits and vegetables of Islam, as well as large quantities of olive oil and wine from the family estate Moses managed for Balian in the Roussillon, near Perpignan. Within a few seasons, the most unusual garden in the north of France was blooming with exotic vegetables, unknown to anyone but Balian and his tight-lipped groundskeeper. Artichoke, asparagus, eggplant, watermelon... a litany of earthly delights foreign to the French palate. Balian had made sure to wall off the garden from the eyes of the curious, but whenever anyone ventured to ask just what it was that he was cultivating, he would simply answer, "medicinal plants." And it was true, partly, as much of the garden teemed with the herbs and flowers needed for his tinctures and balms. But he had thought it prudent to keep his singular diet to himself.

And now the royal hand held a knife pointed at Balian. Agate, yes, agate, that was the stone in her large ring. And at her neck, a collar of lace. A manufacture of Bruges, the finest in Flanders. His mind raced, desperate not to hear what she was saying. Her black wimple was embroidered, as was the custom in Spain.

"My man does his tasting in the kitchens, as the food is being prepared," Blanche was explaining. "But as you are a physician ... we would like a second opinion."

"I would be honored," he said with a suaveness he did not feel. Masking his misgiving, he gamely took the knife from her. Skewered on the point of the blade was something circular, reddish, gray-brown, with blobs of congealed fat, like pearl buttons, trapped in a petrified eddy of bloodied flesh and offal.

"The hunt at Senlis on the Feast of Saint Hubert was exceptional this year," said the queen mother, animated at the sight of her guest's discomfiture. "All the beasts of creation set to flight. We are fortunate to live amid such bounty."

"The king himself killed the boar. Dismounted, with nothing but a spear," Sorbon added. "It was a magnificent creature, such spirit ... "

Balian's table companions watched as he brought the slice of boar sausage to his mouth. All his life he had known such food to be unclean. His mind alighted briefly on the artichoke of the previous evening. Thank you, Moses ben Shaprut. The flesh had been firm, pure, yielding to the palate in its mantle of olive oil, but this ... this revolting vomitus of gristle and guts ...

"The Holy Father's physician tastes all his food," Blanche said pointedly.

Balian saw Sorbon's eyebrows arch involuntarily. The doctor to the popes, as everyone at the table knew, was always a Jew.

Balian took a large bite and began to chew. He must not gag, or even look sour-faced, like a boy forced to eat his greens.

"Do you slaughter?" Blanche asked, enjoying his torment.

"The monks … " he said, his mouth full. The foulest days of the year, the slaughtering days of the Blood Month of November.

"Of course. You keep no sows. You have a milch cow, two goats, and four chickens." The precision of the queen mother's inventory was meant to convey that she had spies among the monks, who reported back to her on his unusual household. And that she knew his avoidance of pig husbandry was decidedly un-Christian. Balian feigned not to understand the implication, swallowing the vile mass in his mouth and promising to prepare himself a powerful emetic once back at home.

"A splendid victual, Majesty," he said at last, willing himself not to lunge at the goblet of wine in front of him to rinse the vile taste from his mouth. Even his nostrils seemed to have been conquered by some noisome porcine fog. "I appear almost to have survived it."

The queen mother gave out an almost girlish laugh, pleased at the remark. "You will be one of us yet, Master Balian," she said quickly in her native Castilian. "We will see to that."

Balian inclined his head. "To live amid bounty, there must be all manner of beasts."

When he looked up, he saw the old woman slowly chewing her slice of sausage, looking at him with icy respect. Robert de Sorbon smiled broadly. He had not been wrong to gamble that Balian of Mallorca might be the man Blanche of Castile was looking for.

CHAPTER NINE

Pascal opened the door of the bread oven and leaned down to see if the loaves had risen. He felt the blast of heat on his face, now permanently reddened after a month of baking bread for his uncle. The rounded wheat boules had indeed risen, so he grabbed his long bread peel and slid it under the loaves, then deftly removed them from the fiery embers to cool in a wicker basket at his feet. This batch was for the city's wealthy elite, the burghers who set great store in imitating the habits of the nobility, in dress, in speech, and, especially, at table. They turned their noses up at the lowly daily fare of rye breads consumed by the masses. Pascal deposited the last of the boules in the basket and paused to wonder at his good fortune.

Some four weeks earlier, Pascal had loosed his mule outside the fortifications of Toulouse, a gift to some unknown peasant, then made his way onto the cobblestones of the city. On his night flight from the horrors of the Inquisition Tower in Carcassonne, the young scribe had taken a risk and slept rough outdoors in a thick copse of cypress trees. Providence had smiled on him, and no marauder had found him to steal his small purse or do him harm.

In Toulouse's sinuous warren of streets, Pascal would have to find a new life. He was now a wanted man, a runaway friar liable to imprisonment in a Dominican jail should he be discovered. He needed a place to hide, a means to support himself, an occupation to chase away his terrible memories. There was only one place he could go to effect such a plan, and it was by no means certain that it would work out.

His uncle's bakery had not been hard to find. In the main street leading from the cathedral square, a parade of colorful shopfronts beckoned passersby, their ground-floor windowsills supporting trestles to display their wares and their upper stories featuring protruding shingle signs announcing each merchant's specialty. Aside from the heavenly smell that enveloped Pascal as he neared the bakery, there was also a shingle featuring two bread peels placed in such a manner as to suggest crossed swords, as if the baker possessed some sort of heraldic prestige. Pascal smiled on seeing this, knowing his uncle to be possessed of a sense of humor.

He pushed open the door. "Uncle?" he ventured. "Uncle Tomas?"

A voice came from the rear of the dark room.

"Go take a walk around the square. The next batch will be ready soon."

"No, Uncle," Pascal said loudly in the direction from which the voice had come. "It's me, Pascal, your brother André's son."

A large, sweating man emerged from the penumbra, rubbing his hands on a cloth apron.

"Pascal? What the hell are you doing here? I thought you'd become a crow and buried yourself in Carcassonne."

"I've left the order," Pascal said.

The older man clapped his hands together. "I always knew you were a bright lad. You'd want no business with those damned friars. Buggers drunk on incense."

Once the two men had embraced, Pascal explained that as a runaway from the convent, he had broken his vows and was thus in danger. If he were found, that is.

Tomas needed no further explanation. "So, you'll want to put on a bonnet to hide that silly ring of hair on your head and grow a nice bushy beard?"

Pascal nodded.

"And I'll wager that you need a roof over your head and a jingle of well-earned coins."

"I could learn the trade, become your apprentice, Uncle. And I could keep your ledgers, make sure that no sums go missing."

Tomas pursed his lips thoughtfully. "I suppose," he said more to himself than to Pascal, "I suppose I owe it to your poor father's memory … " He paused. "My boy Jaume is as yet too young to be working at the oven, and I'm not getting any younger, God knows."

The youth held his breath.

"Very well, then," Tomas said conclusively, "a baker you will be. And that's a damn sight more worthy a calling than being a bloodsucking crow."

CHAPTER TEN

Mercifully, the meal was over. Blanche, Balian, and Sorbon left the small dining room, but not before the queen mother admonished one of the servants about the rushes strewn on the floor. They must be replaced regularly, she said sharply, that is the whole point of them. To keep the odors in a room from accumulating, one had to renew the aromatics. Balian thought idly of his manservant mopping down the floors daily in his house, a practice meant to eliminate filth, not disguise it.

Once they were seated again in the spare audience chamber, Sorbon at last exposed the reason they had summoned Balian. He was to be entrusted with a mission that called for surpassing tact and discernment, thus suitable for a man of his many talents. Balian knew from his dealings with the great that such flattery usually preceded the outlining of an unpleasant and difficult commission. He was not wrong.

"The Holy Office is in an uproar," Sorbon explained. "Two inquisitors were murdered in the Languedoc. Humbert of Chartres on the Black Mountain and Pierre of Tours in Carcassonne."

Balian looked at the floor. It sounded like a good thing to him, a world with two fewer inquisitors.

Blanche and Sorbon kept their gaze on Balian, expectant. What did he make of these outrages? The expression on the old woman's face seemed to say, So what do you think, sorcerer? Or whatever you are?

Balian remained silent for a long moment, feeling their eyes upon him. He would have to choose his words carefully, for the subject of the Languedoc was fraught with peril. Too many terrible things had happened in the lands of the South.

"It must have been the work of some disgruntled faction," he said at last. "Some people in the South have been sorely tried these past few years."

An angel passed in the silence that greeted this remark. Balian had uttered an understatement of colossal proportions. For the past generation the people of the Languedoc had gone through a calvary of cruelty and rapine, much of it inflicted on commands issued from the chamber in which he now sat, with the taste of pig in his mouth. A crusade against heretics in the Languedoc had been launched by the pope, and the nobles of France had answered the call for twenty bloody years.

Although he had been just a boy then, Balian remembered the refugees from the terror coming to their estate near Perpignan, to which his father had moved when the emir banished him from Mallorca for having the temerity to request payment for his services. Balian's father shooed his son and closed the door to his study, but the boy later learned of the horrific story the newcomers had to relate. They came from a market town called Lavaur, where several hundred people had been marched down to the dry riverbed below the battlements and burned alive. Balian's ears filled with the wailing coming from the study, as his father frantically mixed a potion to calm his visitors.

"What you say may be true," Sorbon allowed, glancing nervously at the queen mother. "Certainly, the two friars slain in the winter may have been dispatched by this ... disgruntled faction."

"Heretics!" Blanche snapped. "Nests of them everywhere down there."

But surely, Balian thought testily, she had not summoned him here to hunt heretics?

"It has come to our attention that the murderers of the inquisitors might not be heretics," said Sorbon, his voice even. "There is something odd about the circumstances, something inexplicable."

Sorbon looked to Blanche for guidance. She touched the agate ring and nodded at the older man.

"The Holy Office is staffed almost exclusively with the brothers of the Order of Friars Preachers … the Dominicans."

The *domini canes*, Balian thought, the hounds of God.

"They are … they are new men," Sorbon said slowly, pausing in search of the right formulation. "Zeal is their byword. Their sainted founder is but twenty years dead, yet they have built scores of convents and churches the length and breadth of Christendom. They are men on a mission."

Sorbon sighed, rubbed his chin with a blotchy hand.

"Sometimes their interests and the interests of this kingdom do not coincide, and sometimes their temperament leads them to a certain rashness of action. It can cloud their judgment."

Sorbon rose to his feet. "The Dominicans are set on crushing heresy and avenging the deaths of their brothers. That is understandable. Yet among them are men who know no bounds; they will lash out at everyone and anyone in the Languedoc. Through their cruelty and single-mindedness, the innocent will be caught up in their nets, the people will become restive … "

"The Languedoc will rise in revolt," Blanche said less cryptically. "As it did three summers ago, when my Louis had to put down the leprous mobs in Carcassonne."

Balian looked from the prelate to the queen. So that was it. They wanted him to check the fury of the Inquisition and thus stop the Languedoc from revolting against the French king. A rather tall order.

"Someone must discover who is slaughtering the inquisitors," Sorbon said. "Before the Dominicans do irreparable harm."

Sorbon was at Balian's side now, laying a firm hand on his shoulder.

"You are a man of the South; you know these people. You have done many services for the barons of our Northern lands. In Brittany, Burgundy, and elsewhere. And you are schooled in many arts. If you value your... your unconventional life here in our kingdom, your house at Saint-Germain-des-Prés, your Saracen garden, your alchemist laboratory hidden behind a false wall... you will do your duty."

Balian betrayed no emotion, noting only the freighted detail used in describing his home.

"You must find the killers," Sorbon intoned. "And soon."

Blanche turned to him, wearing the slightest of smiles. Balian smiled back.

"This will be a costly undertaking," he said coolly.

Sorbon removed his hand from Balian's shoulder and sat back down, astounded at the effrontery.

Blanche's smile remained serene. Perhaps she, and not Sorbon, was the kindred spirit.

"Half on acceptance of the commission, half on its completion," she said. "And you will have as your superior Brother Martin of Troyes, my confessor, a holy Franciscan dear to our heart."

Martin of Troyes was a friar known to be as slippery as a serpent. "A Franciscan to meddle in the affairs of the Dominicans?" Balian said. "The two orders of friars are often at each other's throats."

Blanche snorted. "Martin is a capable man, more than able to meet any adversity. And you should mind your own business, Balian of Mallorca."

"Very well, then, I shall. Three thousand in total," Balian said. "It may take some time."

Blanche reached over and placed her steady hand on his. "Just see that it doesn't, my peculiar friend," she said in a low voice, "and we'll make it four thousand."

"Much cheaper than raising an army, Majesty," he said, rising to his feet, without so much as a by-your-leave. The queen mother and Robert de Sorbon looked on in amazement as Balian of Mallorca strode out of the room.

CHAPTER ELEVEN

As the mists of morning lifted, Tancred of Périgueux toyed with a small harp on the battlements of Chantecler, the castle on the river Dordogne that he had inherited from his brother. He was seated on a stone bench of the parapet, the light carping of the strings carrying over the lowing of the cattle being herded by drovers into an enclosed pasture. He was the lord of Chantecler, his elder brother having been fool enough to die four years ago, a nip given him by his best falcon setting off the calamity that did him in. A finger reddened, then a hand blackened, a greenish arm cut off, but too late—the poison reached his heart and extinguished it. The splendid property had unexpectedly landed in Tancred's lap, along with its tenant farmers and villeins. Chastened by his brother's misfortune, Tancred had turned to other, less dangerous amusements. Now his battles were no longer conducted in the jousting lists or falconers' woods, but in the bower, the banquet hall, the balcony, and, if all went well, the bed.

He plucked the instrument uncertainly, searching for the tune. His singing was just as tentative: "The doe is vouchsafed to the hart, the heart is promised to the ... the ... ?"

It was not going well.

The young man sighed and leaned back against the stone wall. He was almost intolerably handsome, muscular and trim, the chiseled features of his face culminating in a mane of waving gold. He needed no harp to make the ladies swoon.

"So this is where you're hiding."

The speaker, a slender girl of seventeen years, was as lovely as Tancred was handsome. Her emerald eyes sparkled, and long strands of fiery red hair flew across a smooth countenance, pushed there by a caressing breeze.

"Speak to me more kindly, sister," said Tancred with mock gravity. "I am undone. My muse has fled, my song goes nowhere."

"And to which lucky lady is the song addressed?"

"To you, Matilda, of course!"

The girl laughed and gave her brother a chaste peck on the cheek. Seeing him smile, she moved up and said in his ear, "You must come to the hall straightaway to see the stewards. They are awaiting you. As master of the house, you must attend to the ledgers."

His smile faded.

"Not to worry your precious little head, Tancred," she said. "I went over all the figures and they add up. We did exceedingly well with the harvest last year. All we need now is for you to affix your seal, m'lord."

He opened his mouth to protest, but no words came. He decided instead to follow Matilda dutifully down the steps to the great hall of the keep.

CHAPTER TWELVE

The pigeon left its master's hand and flew straight and true over the forested expanse of the Île-de-France, southward toward the sun. Far below, wreathed in smoke from humble hearths, small wattled villages with their fields and pastures flashed by, islands of habitation engulfed in a sea of woodland. A deer stood quietly in a small dale, head down, feeding on the mosslike grass, unaware that in a clearing less than two leagues away a pack of wolves sunned themselves in the pale light of spring.

The trees at last gave way to the flat open fields of the Beauce. The autumn harvest of rye and wheat had long ago been stored away, and now a few peasants could be seen plodding behind horses in harness, dutifully tilling the land ahead of the spring sowing. A few dark steeples stood out in random dignity on the horizon, softening the monotony and pointedly reminding the farmers of the divine.

A great ribbon of shimmering gray came into view. The Loire. Its surface roiled here and there, proof of its fathomless gift of salmon, lamprey, and sturgeon. Men and boys stood on the river-bank, poles and nets arrayed, performing their age-old communal task, singing as they hauled in the nets, a song that their fathers and their fathers' fathers had sung before them, as descendants of Saint Peter.

The bird alighted on a tall steeple near the right bank of the river, the highest structure for miles around. From its perch atop the Abbey of Saint-Benoît, the pigeon could survey its surroundings, the flotilla of small craft heading downstream to market at

Orléans, the great farm horses on the towpaths on the opposite bank straining to haul upstream barges laden with goods. From directly below, in the monastery's courtyard, came the cluck of chickens—and where there were chickens there was food.

The pigeon leapt from the spire and swooped down to the ground below. Grain had just been showered into the enclosure and its inhabitants were too busy feasting to notice the arrival of an interloper. Once satisfied, the pigeon took to the air again to resume its journey.

The Loire was crossed as the midday Angelus rang out from the belfry of Saint-Benoît. A mix of woodland and pasture lay ahead, great stands of towering oaks announcing the rugged uplands to come. Farther on, the cattle in the meadows became rarer, the villages fewer. This was the rough rocky heart of the country, covered with spiky pines and fragrant thyme. The warm South was now not far off.

As dusk gathered, the pigeon at last espied the dark water of the Dordogne carving its winding path past limestone cliffs. At a bend in the river rose the tawny towers of Chantecler. The bird banked, then plunged earthward, its destination a pigeonhole in the lowest tier of the castle's dovecote. With a noisy flapping of wings, the tired bird found its home in the tan structure and entered its cubby, tripping a string attached to a small green tab on the exterior of the dovecote. This signaled to the pigeon master that the bird had arrived from Paris, bearing a message.

CHAPTER THIRTEEN

"Balian of Mallorca arrives in Avignonet at Eastertide," Tancred said, striding through the solar room. Matilda, gathering her skirts, struggled to keep up with him. "His message said that he wants me to meet him there with my men. He's on the king's business."

"I would like to meet this Balian."

Tancred stopped.

"What?"

"I said I would like to meet Balian of Mallorca. I have heard so much about him. He is some sort of secret Saracen, isn't he?"

Tancred grasped her shoulders and frowned at her upturned face.

"Sister, will you never change? You are a daughter of Eve. This is men's work. You know it's not your place."

The green eyes flashed. Soon he would be telling her that he had found a fine match for her, some decrepit old baron back from crusading, with a few wisps of hair above and a paltry fewer below. Or of the consolations of the convent, since no respectable man would willingly consort with a redhead, no matter how great her beauty and her dowry. If she wanted to marry a virile man, she might well have to travel to the island of the Gaels, where it was said that all men and women had red hair, even the noblest of those savages.

"We can say that I am going to the Church of Saint-Sernin in Toulouse, to prostrate myself before the relics of Saints Saturnin and Honoratus."

Tancred looked at his sister, surprised at her store of learning. She caught the look.

"I have been taking lessons from Alcuin."

"Alcuin?! The servant?!"

"Tancred, if you ever roused yourself from your dreams of love, you would know that these walls enclose worlds. Alcuin is a learned scholar; he has taught me much."

"This is incredible."

"Not in the least. Master Alcuin was brought here by Father, when you were at your studies in Paris. There had been some ... some scandal at his former employ as the tutor of Marie of Angoulême. Father took him on here as a favor to her father."

Tancred let this sink in. Clearly, his household had a life independent of its master.

"And there is no scandal here, I trust?"

Matilda let out a laugh.

"Alcuin? Why, he is a graybeard. Just like you."

Tancred scowled. "And what about that week when you left Chantecler last year? And no one could find you? That was a bloody scandal."

"Really, Tancred, we've been through all this before. I have friends in our little part of the world. I like to visit them."

"I'd like to know what you were up to. You owe me that, as I am the lord around here."

She frowned. "An accident of birth, brother."

"I will not be defied in this way."

Her only answer was a broad smile that lit up her face like the sun on the surface of a mill pond. She was a fair creature, Tancred thought, perhaps too damned fair.

"You are not coming to Avignonet. The way is not safe. There are brigands abroad."

"But you shall protect me?"

"I travel with a small escort. I will raise more men if need be from our kin in Toulouse."

"This Balian says ride and you say how far?"

"He saved my life, Matilda." Tancred thought back to the dark room to which he had been carried when the fever had peaked. Then of the lurching ride on a horse-drawn cart to Balian's house beyond the walls of Paris, his form hidden under a blanket so the fear of contagion would not grip the city. And then the days of delirium, as a gentle hand administered all manner of medicaments, tasting of things he would never encounter again. And at last the convalescence, the shared laughter, the high spirits of young men, the friendship.

He had stayed at Balian's house in Saint-Germain-des-Prés throughout the summer, until the physician's lectures resumed on the Left Bank in the fall. But what he learned from the brilliant Mallorcan in those few months surpassed all that he would learn in the schools. It was a way of looking at things, of seeing the world. He never again felt at home with men of his station in life, with their acceptance of everything as it always had been. Their certainties, their superstitions, their self-sufficiency. When his father died, and his brother shortly thereafter, he had had to leave the schools of Paris to take his place as lord of the manor. But he had returned utterly changed.

"I grow bored of Chantecler. It is a prison."

"You have strange ideas for a maiden."

"There. You've shown it. You *are* a graybeard."

He turned and took the steps down to the great hall two at a time. She would not catch him, not encumbered with her skirts. Matilda gathered them up and moved listlessly back to her wardrobe. Would she always be subject to the tyranny of others, always a prisoner behind stone walls, a spectator on the battlements, gazing out at life in the wider world? In some ways she was worse off than her distant sisters among the villeins, who at least felt the sun warm their faces and the wind ruffle their hair. Before the room's crude looking glass, she paused for a long moment and surveyed herself. Then, in her mind's eye, she had a vision of Balian of Mallorca. Smiling and, of course, handsome.

To hell with her brother. She had her maid summon Alcuin.

CHAPTER FOURTEEN

A few days before Easter, Tancred and his party left Chantecler before dawn to ride through the no-man's-land between Guyenne and the Languedoc. There had been war not so long ago in these hills, the ever-irritating English king Henry, the feudal claimant to Aquitaine, insisting on his inheritance. King Louis had eventually made peace with him, letting his detested kinsman keep a huge swath of land that Louis thought should rightfully be his.

The clamor of war and siege had abated, to be replaced by the low moan of the wind blowing in from the great wide sea. The riders picked their way past naked vine stocks on the slopes, stripped of their leaves and ruthlessly shorn of their shoots, a vegetal army of the tormented, collectively arrayed in a regular battle order yet individually twisted, contorted in pain. To the sinner, the tortured vineyard seemed a prospect of damnation, a foretaste of the suffering that lay beyond the grave. To Tancred, the sight turned his thoughts to the warm claret that these stunted stocks would soon produce, to spark laughter and to loosen bodices. They were miracle workers, really, these little fellows, servants in the cause of love.

The horsemen from Chantecler crested a hill and saw, in the distance, the town of Avignonet. It stood on a slight eminence in the valley of the river Fresquel, its terra-cotta roofs glowing warm in the sun.

In the message delivered by his trusty pigeon, Balian had instructed Tancred to meet him here, halfway between

Carcassonne and Toulouse, in the town house of Astruguetus, a learned and wealthy Jew from Narbonne who had known Balian's father for many years, long before the French had come down to the South to spread misery. Once quit of Avignonet, Balian and Tancred would go to Toulouse together to meet the newly appointed grand inquisitor. Balian could work his customary magic and find out who was killing the inquisitors of the Languedoc, while Tancred would lurk in the background, to protect their interests and befriend the guileless. And, with any luck, woo and win a lady as yet unmet.

The reunion was raucous. Balian advanced toward the new arrivals from Chantecler, his long black and scarlet cloak just clearing the gravel of the courtyard. He looked more like a warlock than an emissary of His Most Catholic Majesty, King Louis IX of France. Astruguetus of Narbonne, stooped with age but possessed of a lively mien, followed him, similarly attired. Tancred laughed in delight.

"My good doctor, you look as though you've just transformed a base metal into a precious one," Tancred cried out in amusement.

"Welcome, brother. We may do that yet. But first we must turn darkness into light."

Balian's broad smile seemed to encompass everyone in the courtyard, most of whom gawked at the sight of him. He was clearly elated to see his old friend. He introduced Tancred to their host, who entreated them to go directly to the dining hall. Astruguetus would have his stewards make sure the riders of Chantecler were billeted in the village or in the various outbuildings of his estate. The same had already been done with the escort of French royal sergeants who had accompanied Balian on his journey down the Rhône.

When Astruguetus joined his guests in the hall, Balian was explaining that Brother Martin of Troyes, the friar who was his superior on this royal embassy, had elected to stay at the rectory

THE SORCERER AND THE ASSASSIN

of the local priest rather than take his ease in these more comfortable quarters.

"Not because he is vowed to poverty?"

Balian shook his head wearily.

"He would not accept the hospitality of a son of Abraham?" Tancred ventured.

Balian nodded. Some of these Christians, he thought, were dogged in their hatred of people unlike themselves.

Astruguetus pretended not to have heard Tancred's question.

"I assume your journeys have made you hale in appetite," the older man said.

"Quite so," Tancred replied. "Crossing all of those vineyards has given me a thirst as well."

Astruguetus clapped his hands. "My daughter will see to your needs. When she is not playing her lute, she attends to my table."

A raven-haired girl approached them, her eyes downcast and her bearing demure. As she raised the terra-cotta pitcher to pour the wine in their goblets, she raised her eyes too, and Tancred was struck with a bolt of their cobalt beauty. The instant was fleeting, but the girl seemed to flush, as if moved by the sight of their striking guest, his hair cascading gold over his shoulders.

Balian contemplated the two, aware of his friend's foibles. Tancred, lost in thought while watching the girl rustle from the room, failed to see Astruguetus raise his cup. Balian elbowed his companion.

"To the success of your mission," Astruguetus intoned.

"And to your continued prosperity," Balian replied.

The men took a long draft of the wine.

The wine revived Tancred. "But this is excellent! It's as if you have captured Helios in a goblet."

His host beamed with pleasure. "It is from my estate, on the Black Mountain, in the Cabardès. My men are expert at the task."

A look of confusion crossed Tancred's face. It was forbidden for Jews to own lands or have Christians work for them.

Astruguetus sensed the puzzlement. "The good lord Roger of Cabaret manages the estate for me. And I render him those sundry services that I can offer."

Balian ignored the drift of the conversation. "The Cabardès? Is that not where the village of Auriol sits? Where Inquisitor Humbert was murdered by the villagers?"

Astruguetus nodded. "A terrible business. The villagers of Auriol all lie tormented in the Wall of Carcassonne, all deemed guilty without a shred of material evidence save the body of the unfortunate friar struck down. A terrible business."

"You do not believe the deed was the work of a villager?"

The older man weighed his words before replying. "These ... these people, the people that the Roman Church calls heretics ... I have lived here many long years, and I have known many of them. I cannot see it. They are docile, docile as lambs."

Astruguetus sat back thoughtfully, wondering if he had said too much. The silence was broken by the whispering of linens.

"Yes, Judith."

"Father, there are two men outside. The elder claims to be an old friend of Master Balian's and prays an audience with the doctor privately."

Astruguetus and Balian started in surprise. Perhaps it was Brother Martin, who had changed his mind about whose company he could or couldn't keep. Tancred's face showed no surprise or even acknowledgment of the news; instead, his features were suffused with admiration for the girl standing in front of them. Judith, feeling his eyes upon her, shifted slightly in her place, which only heightened matters as the movement drew attention to her further perfections.

Balian bestirred himself, rose, and stepped off the dais. Judith made to accompany him.

"No, stay here, child. You must keep my friend Tancred company. He too is an accomplished musician; you two should have much to talk about."

Tancred watched Balian leave the dining hall. Such a dear, dear friend he was at such moments. The young lord turned his attentions to Judith.

CHAPTER FIFTEEN

B alian blinked in the semidarkness. Then he saw them.
   "Alcuin. Is that you? I don't believe it."

The older of the two newcomers stood in the guttering light of a pitch torch ensconced in the stone wall of the entranceway. The approach to Astruguetus' home was flanked by two such impressive walls, testament to the importance of the estate's occupants.

Alcuin moved forward to the finely wrought iron door in front of which Balian stood.

"Yes, it is I, Master Balian. If you don't believe it, then my being here has struck you as supernatural, perhaps?"

Balian barked out a laugh and then recited from memory: "The supernatural is that which has not yet been explained."

"Good. Good. You remember our lessons."

"How could I forget, dear magister? I have oft thought of you. Are you still in Montpellier?"

"These past few years I've been on the banks of the Dordogne, at Chantecler, in the employ of Tancred of Périgueux."

"Why, he dines within—"

"Which is how I knew you were here."

The two men paused, looked at each other, Balian puzzled, Alcuin serene.

"Then what is the nature of your business with me now, Magister?"

Alcuin raised his arm and beckoned his traveling companion to come forward. The young man advanced a step or two but remained beyond the flickering sphere of light.

"I am off to Girona," Alcuin began. "My cousin is the bishop there. He has asked to me to authenticate a relic... the pelvis of Saint Eulalia, found recently by a shepherd on a hilltop."

Balian smiled. "How will you know it's hers? Wasn't she put to death long ago? When the Old Romans ruled."

"The pelvis has performed miracles," Alcuin replied, his voice affectless. "And it is up to me to prove that it is, indeed, hers."

"And will you prove it?"

Balian's smile broadened; Alcuin ignored him.

"The jury consists of me and Armand of Marseille."

"How convenient! Did you choose him to adjudicate with you?"

"I did."

Balian chuckled. "And does your cousin the bishop know that Armand is your good friend?"

"He does."

Alcuin nodded slightly, his eyes closing for an instant. They both knew that if a relic proved popular, there would be a flood of pilgrims and their purses.

"If we are successful in authenticating a proof, then my cousin might very well see to a great change in... in my material circumstances. And I should then be obliged to absent myself from Chantecler for some time. So, I thought it wise to entrust to you my apprentice. He is but a twig of a lad, but he has been a quick study from his earliest days. Come, Mathias."

The young man took a step forward, into the half-light. Balian was struck by his youth, the wisps of red hair that escaped the brim of his cap.

"He has been taught everything that I taught you, Balian, but only more recently. You may find him useful. He may remember things you have already forgotten."

Balian looked at the boy with interest.

"The balm for a burn?"

"Aloe vera," the boy replied in a soft voice.

"For fever?"

"Coriander."

"Toothache?"

"Pellitory, the root."

"Melancholia?"

"Saint-John's-wort."

"Aches, in the bones?"

"Herbbane."

"And ... ?"

"Hemlock."

"Very impressive, young fellow," Balian exclaimed. "Your master may be right. I may have use for you in the days ahead."

Balian searched in a sleeve and extracted a pouch. "Come closer, son, and have a sniff of this. Can you tell me what it is?"

The boy moved fully into the light and gracefully inclined his head downward.

"Fenugreek," he said without hesitation.

But Balian had forgotten his question. He surveyed the boy carefully, the beardless chin, the flawless neck.

Alcuin cleared his throat. "So is the boy satisfactory?"

Balian paid him no attention. He looked into the boy's green eyes, then whispered, "I am a physician, you know."

"And I," the boy whispered in rejoinder, "am not ill."

The two held each other's gaze for an instant. The sparkling eyes settled the matter.

"Yes, he will do fine. I may need an assistant," Balian said, turning to Alcuin, who smiled back in complicity. "Now will you come join us at table, Magister?"

"No, no," the older man said quickly. "I have secured a place at an inn and am in no mind to meet with Lord Tancred. I will send him word in a few weeks when I know what the future holds."

After a warm leave-taking of their teacher, Balian and Mathias turned toward the town house. A silence fell between them.

"Would you care to join us for supper, Matilda?"

"No, Master Alcuin and I supped—"

The girl blushed deeply.

"Was my disguise that wretched?"

"Quite the contrary."

She smiled at his gallantry.

"But how did you know my name?"

"Paris. Your brother cried out for you when he was taken by the fever. He cares deeply for his sister. When he recovered, he spoke lovingly about you, Matilda. You are all he has left."

Matilda hung her head for an instant. Balian noticed the amber down on the nape of her neck.

"Does he know you're here?" Balian asked.

"Of course not."

"Would he send you home?"

"I would not go."

The two looked at each other once more. Her green eyes seemed to burn into him. But the sensation was not unpleasant.

"Why did you come?"

"Because I wanted to meet you. You, Balian of Mallorca. Almost all my life I have heard stories about you, about how Balian of Mallorca can do just about anything."

Balian flushed for a moment, then said, "You are a silly girl. How will you escape detection? Especially as your brother is in my party."

"I am not silly, Master Balian," she replied. "And I am not worried. As I said, I hear that you can do anything."

She smiled at him complacently, as Balian, with a look of resignation, conceded defeat.

CHAPTER SIXTEEN

It proved difficult, devilishly difficult, to transform this butterfly into a chrysalis, yet Balian's skills as an artificer rose to the challenge. Crushed poppy seed was rubbed vigorously onto Matilda's jawline and the backs of her hands. What had been immaculate and soft now had the appearance of a certain male coarseness. Other abrasives were applied to her brow, her cheeks, and the outlines of her nose.

Matilda looked carefully at Balian, aware, even if he was not, of the intimacy of what they were engaged in.

When he reached down to scrub her chin and throat, Matilda began to giggle.

"What is it?"

"You're tickling me."

Balian frowned and stepped back to survey his handiwork, holding a candle close to her face. Only time can erase beauty, and whether this would ever happen to Matilda was an open question. The creature was a glorious specimen, in full bloom, devastating and magnificent all at the same time.

"Stop batting your eyelashes, for God's sake. You look ready for a dance."

"I was just blinking," she said, smiling.

Eventually his hard work met with some success. He surveyed her closely for a last time and sighed. She looked like a very pretty boy.

"That will have to do," he said, sitting down on the straw bed beside her. At daybreak, he would darken her fair skin.

An awkward silence ensued.

At last, Balian asked, "Have you had enough to eat?"

She gestured to the empty platter on the table, its chicken leg gnawed to the bone. Balian had pleaded fatigue at Astruguetus' table and taken the plate to his room for her.

"Matilda, tonight you will have to sleep here."

Instead of starting in surprise, as he had expected, she said, "Of course. You can't very well lodge a boy in the room with your friend's daughter … And you wouldn't be able to explain why you decided to sleep in the stable tonight."

Balian was impressed with the girl's level-headedness, the virtue he prized above all others, surrounded as he usually was by the histrionics of ignorance.

"You shall take the bed, and I the floor."

Once again, she acquiesced sensibly.

Extinguishing the candles, he stretched out on the blanket he had spread on the earthen floor. In the quiet, he heard her removing her tunic, then what to his ears sounded like a long whisper, as if she were unspooling a roll of fabric. The unraveling was soft, rippling almost.

Balian scratched at his chin. What could she possibly be doing? He had a mind suited for solving mysteries, for reasoning out an answer, yet here he was entirely stumped.

His bewilderment must have been palpable, for when the sound ceased Matilda explained, "The strips wrapped to restrain my bosom … for the disguise … They were too confining."

Balian closed his eyes. Good Lord.

"Good night, Master Balian," came the voice again.

Understandably, the first sleep was slow in coming, and not only from the thought of his unbound companion close by. Balian began to question why he had agreed to take on this masquerade, why he had let himself be led into such a compromising situation. True, he needed an assistant, a shrewd second pair of eyes, and there was no doubt Tancred's sister was as clever as her brother was loyal. Of that he was now certain. But she would be found out eventually. Why had he done it? Was he really going to sneak a beautiful maid into the midst of the Dominicans of Toulouse? If the friars were anything like the monks of Saint-Germain-des-Prés, half of them loathed women and the other half feared them. A smile spread across Balian's face. He was beginning to like the idea.

He woke from his first sleep in the middle of the night and got groggily to his feet. The fire had gone out. In the darkness he could just make out the ewer of wine on the table. He poured himself a cup and drank. This would help him get back to sleep, for the cold floor had not been kind. Balian reached around and massaged his lower back. Not quite as young as he used to be.

Once his eyes had adjusted to the dimness, he glanced over at Matilda. She was wide awake.

"Come to bed, Balian."

She shifted on the straw to make room for him. The tenor of her voice was matter-of-fact. He had the king's work to do, they knew, so he couldn't very well be limping about with aching bones.

He lay down on the straw, careful not to touch her. Their eyes met. Matilda smiled.

"Good night, Balian."

He returned her smile.

"Good night, Matilda."

Balian shifted onto his back and looked up at the ceiling beams. He could hear the girl do likewise. He could also hear her breathing, how it was quickened and slightly irregular. A long moment passed as the two listened to each other in the silence.

"Have you a lady wife, Master Balian?"

"A long time ago. She died in her confinement. I ... I could save neither of them."

"I'm sorry."

Pilar. He never spoke about her. No one in Paris knew. He remembered Pilar that last year, when he and she had been so young and so alive to love, like two vines entwined. Pilar, a laughing Catalan beauty, that deep blue wildflower in her fair hair one day in the mountains, Pluto meeting Venus, and the eyes, the dark eyes, always ready to gleam with mischief and affection. His father hadn't approved; her family worked his lands. His son Balian could do much better, pursue his studies, find a helpmeet among the well-born. And then eleven months later, Pilar was gone, in the ground, her face across the table vanished forever. Balian wondered why he had told Matilda about her.

"Now you may ask one question of me."

What an extraordinary girl. She had asked it, so now so would he.

"Have you ever lain with a man, m'lady?"

There came a slight snort from her side of the bed.

"I came here to meet you, Balian of Mallorca, not to offer you my maidenhead."

They both laughed at this.

Balian closed his eyes, a smile forming on his face. He felt her arm fall across his chest, her soft body pressing against his.

"It's cold," she whispered.

He had never slept so soundly.

CHAPTER SEVENTEEN

The first wan stirrings of dawn were met by a soft chorus of birdsong. Fatima, damp broom and wooden bucket in hand, walked from the interior enclosure of Count Raymond's castle into an adjoining courtyard. In the dimness she could see that its cobblestones had been exuberantly soiled the previous evening by the passage of horses on their way to the stables. She set to work, gripping the broom of dried vine cuttings roughly secured by raffia twine. She vigorously wielded the broom on the uneven surfaces, guiding the waste to the drain in the courtyard's center. Although slight in build and small in stature, Fatima was possessed of surprising strength, capable of performing the demanding tasks the count's household had set her since her earliest days.

She dipped the broom in the bucket to lap up some more water. She liked this time of day and this moment of solitude. Soon enough she would be thrust back into the hubbub of her daily round of chores—cleaning, dusting, chopping, cooking—with the attendant gossip of the other servant girls, but for now Fatima had the world to herself and time to think.

The arrival of spring had done little to disperse the vague sense of foreboding hanging over the city. On market days, usually times for festivity and camaraderie, she could see misgiving written plainly on the faces of her fellow Toulousans, a drawn, pinched look as if sleep had been elusive and worry too burdensome. The winter had been so terrible. She shuddered at the memory of her encounter on the Black Mountain three months earlier, the baleful glare of hatred and lust from a friar on his way to a rendezvous with death. Then the news from Carcassonne, another inquisitor cut down, beheaded, in the sacred confines of the cathedral. She had not known this Brother Pierre, but she'd been told that if his successor resembled him in any way, then the church and its Dominicans were lying in wait, coiled up like the vipers of the hot months, ready to strike.

There might be a glimmer of hope, though, at least if Count Raymond's young chamberlain were to be believed. Having been appointed to the post on the demise of his father, the youthful official took pains to underscore the centrality of his dealings with the count, especially to the keenly intelligent Fatima, whom he had known since childhood. He was more than pleased to satisfy her innate curiosity with proofs of his own importance. Two weeks previously, he had informed her that he himself had opened a letter from Paris, bearing the seal of Queen Mother Blanche and informing the count that a delegation had been dispatched from France to look into the murder of the inquisitors. Then there was last night in the great hall when she had placed a tankard of bone broth in front of him.

"You will have to do better than this tomorrow night, my little Moor," the chamberlain said with a smile.

"And why is that, Guilhem?"

He looked at her witheringly. She smiled, then shook her head slightly.

"Sorry. My lord chamberlain."

Mollified, he leaned in conspiratorially toward her. "Because we will have visitors of mark. My eyes in the countryside tell me that Queen Blanche's embassy has reached Avignonet and intends to enter our city tomorrow."

Fatima took in the information but remain unmoved. The chamberlain noticed her indifference.

"You don't understand," he said impatiently. "Our count will want to sup with the leaders of these Frenchmen. Especially with one in particular."

Her face remained impassive.

"Balian of Mallorca," Chamberlain Guilhem burst out triumphantly. "He heads the party."

"Balian of Mallorca ... " she repeated slowly. The chamberlain nodded, satisfied with getting a reaction at last. "The sorcerer?"

"Indeed, the sorcerer. If anyone can get to the bottom of this wretched business, it would be him."

The conversation lingered in her mind as she hauled the bucket to the drain and poured out its murky contents. Balian of Mallorca? What could he possibly be like? So many stories had been told of him, so many rumors spread. Fatima scarcely believed he existed. And yet tomorrow she would lay eyes on him, take his measure.

A bell tinkled from within the wing housing the kitchens. Fatima hurried to the source of the sound. The men of Count Raymond of Toulouse would soon be clamoring for their breakfast of wine, ale, and bread.

CHAPTER EIGHTEEN

The murmuration flew in from the river Garonne at dusk, as if the fishermen had cast a dark net over the waters and an updraft had seized it, sending it heavenward far above Toulouse. Pascal, his long day of work over and his beard and apron dusted with flour, tilted his head upward, in wonder, in worry, watching as the cloud of starlings swooped and swirled over the terra cotta of the rooftops, gray in their thousands, then black as night, then gray again as the great chain of flight formed and unraveled in a ceaseless palimpsest of becoming and undoing, drifting above the huddled city in reproachful majesty. What could this mean? Pascal did not believe in portents, and yet he knew this was one.

The nimbus of birds flashed past the scaffolding of the great red church the Dominicans were erecting, past the gibbet in the central square where two unfortunates dangled lifeless, twirling, spiraling up and around the towers of the Cathedral of Saint-Stephen, God's creation aloft making a mockery of the striving of earthbound men like himself, spinning round and round the still, sullen stone of the church in joyful movement, then blanketing outward over the Jewish quarter and the count's castle, the beating of tens of thousands of wings drowning out the bells tolling the monastic hours, stopping in their tracks scores of souls scurrying homeward, to look up at the airborne omen, unfurling like a flag whipped by the wind, moving off, out toward the country to find a roost for a multitude, leaving behind a city torn between delight and despair, dread and awe.

CHAPTER NINETEEN

Brother Martin of Troyes, the vinegary friar who was the queen mother's confessor, frowned as Tancred of Périgueux and his men trotted into the pebble-strewn square of Avignonet. This addition to the retinue would ensure that Balian's influence matched or even exceeded his own, the friar thought sourly. On the long trip down the Rhône, Balian and Martin had scarcely exchanged a word, having established when they were still in Île-de-France that their dispositions only came together in a feeling of mutual antipathy.

Martin took Balian to be a dangerous, unsettling fellow, perhaps a Jew. Or a Saracen. Even his horse was Arabian. The Franciscan looked upon the doctor dubiously, even if he too had heard the oft-repeated tales of the younger man's wizardry. The story of how Balian had brought back from the dead Abbot Anselm of Saint-Germain-des-Prés, of how he had saved the harvest of the Duke of Burgundy by applying magical powders to the blighted vineyards. The summer before that, the Duke of Brittany had sent the sorcerer to London to secure the release of his son, abducted by the English near Calais. Within a month, Balian of Mallorca had returned and restored the boy to his joyful father at his castle in Nantes. No one knew for certain how he had done it. Some said he had made himself invisible and had stolen into the Tower of London in broad daylight to free the prisoner. No, said others, he had removed a goiter from the neck of King Henry and received the boy in return. Nonsense, said others still, he had bewitched the entire court at Westminster. It was said that he had lain with the king's spellbound sister the night before he took ship at Folkestone and crossed the Channel. Whatever the truth, Martin noted, Balian's growing reputation did nothing to curb his eccentric behavior. The impetuous fool was forever hopping ashore to collect plants and herbs from the towpath, shouting in excitement at some sort of nonsense discovery.

Balian returned the disdain. He took Martin for a pious fraud, ostentatiously praying on every occasion, playing the pauper with his ridiculous mule, which slowed their progress whenever they left the rivers and their barges. The Franciscan might wear a coarse brown cassock cinched at the waist with a rough cord, but his soft hands and trimmed fingernails betrayed a man who had never done a day of physical labor in his life. When asked by Tancred the previous night at dinner to describe Brother Martin, Balian had replied, grimacing, "The man is a mustard poultice."

Now it was Tancred's turn to inspect the friar. The two men took the lead of the small procession as it left Avignonet by the straight stone roadway laid down by the Old Romans so many centuries ago. The men of Chantecler kept to themselves, as did the sergeants from Paris. Bringing up the rear were Matilda and Balian, at a distance. Neither of them thought it proper to refer to their strange, sweet night sharing a bed. But neither was it forgotten.

Their subterfuge had worked out remarkably well. The men from the North thought that the boy had ridden in from Chantecler, and the men from the South assumed that he had come from Paris. Even Tancred had been fooled. He gave Matilda only the most cursory of glances, as Balian dismissively identified her as an apprentice from Paris. Tancred was too distracted to recognize his sister; the smiles of the comely Judith standing on the doorstep diverted his attention entirely. Astruguetus, beside his daughter, seemed relieved to see the young lord go.

Tancred did not make much headway with Brother Martin. As Avignonet grew smaller behind them, his attempts at starting up a pleasant conversation were repeatedly rebuffed. He had asked about the fairs of Champagne held in Troyes, about the splendid new chapel that the king was said to be building in Paris, about the great success of the Franciscan friars since their founding a scarce twenty years previously. All had been met with brief demurrals that were barely audible. The sallow man on the mule was indeed a mustard poultice. The Franciscan's secretary, also a friar, frantically mimed for Tancred to give up, his jowls so aspic-like in their quivering that the young lord laughed briefly.

This drew a sharp look from Brother Martin, the only acknowledgment that he'd deigned to give since the ride had begun. Martin knew what kind of man this gallant was. A lover of feasting and music, of the amorous arts. These fellows say they are singing not to their ladies, but to the Virgin Mary. Then there must be a lot of Virgin Marys in France, one or two in every castle. The vile custom had spread from this satanic South to invade almost every kingdom and duchy in Europe. Troubadours here, trouvères north of the Loire, minnesingers beyond the Rhine. The only thing to do was let this fellow talk his fool head off, and not get drawn into conversation. Toulouse, thankfully, was not far off.

The land changed slightly in aspect. The stands of poplar became fewer, and large stretches of plowed brown loam stretched out, ready for planting, which in this clement clime came before the end of March. Balian looked with dismay at the orchards, the fruit-bearing trees spindly and barely adolescent.

"The French," Matilda said simply.

Balian knew the story; he had been a student at Montpellier at the time. Fifteen years earlier, eager to make the Languedoc finally capitulate, the French royal armies had abandoned their crusade against the heretics and gone to war with the land itself. The basin of Toulouse, a cornucopia since antiquity, became an inferno, and the hinterland of the city on the Garonne was left a charred, featureless plain of the deepest black.

That was a short time ago, yet the plucky people of Toulouse had picked themselves up and started over. Matilda pointed out market gardens, already surrounded by palisades of strong river reeds that shielded the seedlings from the wind. It was not the agricultural arcadia of Valencia, but soon the lands of Toulouse would prosper once again.

At last, the tower of the Church of Saint-Sernin pointed its finger at the sky. The pink-brick city of Toulouse was in sight.

Balian glanced over at Matilda. "You are now Mathias," he said quickly. "You are to stay by my side at all times, except when I am in the company of your brother. Then you should make yourself scarce. But if you should have occasion to speak, remember, you are French. You must not speak that language with a Southern accent."

"What do you mean?"

"Do not speak through your nose."

"What?"

"Speak from your throat. Try to pretend that you're a cow. It's easy. Here, try it: *Meuhhh. Meeuuhhh* ... Go on."

"Master Balian!"

"Go on."

Matilda weighed whether she was within earshot of anyone, then formed her lips into a pout. "*Meuhhh. Meeuuhh*," she hazarded.

"Perfect. So, remember that if you have to talk to anyone, you must always think of yourself as a well-spoken cow."

Her laugh was so unmistakably girlish that he put his forefinger to his lips.

"Mathias."

"Or is it Meuhtias?"

Balian smiled at her quickness. But Matilda did not smile back. A cloud crossed her features.

"What is it?" Balian asked.

"The world has gone red," she managed to say. "Something is amiss … something terrible … "

Balian stared at her, thunderstruck. Was she given to seizures? He had treated young women in the grip of delusion.

As if reading his thoughts, she said, "Do not think me mad, Balian. I can see things others cannot. Ever since I was a little girl."

He looked at her dubiously, then said in a low voice, "And what do you see now?"

She closed her eyes. "Red. Red everywhere. And white. And black."

Balian did not have time to respond. A rider pounded toward him from the head of the column.

"My lord Tancred requests your company. There is chaos in the town."

Balian turned to Matilda, not sure what to think. He said to her, "Follow me after a spell."

CHAPTER TWENTY

B alian, Tancred, and Martin reached the Narbonne Gate of the city fortifications and could see, not fifty feet away within the town, a street crowded with Dominicans and lay-people wailing dolefully. It was an arresting sight, like a Last Judgment being enacted.

Tancred turned to his companions. "They stand in front of the Seilhan House, on the left. The Inquisition is quartered there."

Balian spurred his horse toward the maelstrom. To his surprise, a postern door in the imposing stone building to his right swung open and a bearded man late in life emerged onto the street, followed by a few men-at-arms.

Balian and the bearded man with the soldiers arrived at the crowd at the same time.

"What the devil is going on?" the older man shouted. Several in the crowd stopped moaning and dropped to their knees. The speaker was apparently Raymond of Saint-Gilles, Count of Toulouse, Duke of Narbonne, and Marquis of Provence.

"M'lord, Brother Hildebrand of Alsace, the grand inquisitor … he has been attacked," a voice said.

"Take me to him," Balian said.

"And who the hell are you?"

"Apologies, m'lord," Balian said, dismounting quickly. "Balian of Mallorca, sent here by King Louis with Brother Martin of Troyes," he continued, indicating the approaching Franciscan. "We are here to investigate the affair of the inquisitors."

"Ah, I have received the correspondence. You come at a meet time. It seems yet another friar has been done violence. But why do you want to see him now?"

"I am a physician."

"We must pray for him," rang out Martin's stentorian voice from atop his mule. "Master Balian, you will accompany me to the Cathedral of Saint-Stephen."

"No. You go there and mutter all you want. I have a life to save."

Brother Martin took the insubordination in stride, looking murderously at Balian. Count Raymond carefully watched the two men size each other up.

Balian, seized by an impulse, turned to the count. "I'm also here as Brother Martin's personal physician. As you can see, there's an imbalance in humors; his skin has a most unfortunate piss-yellow tinge."

The magnitude of the insult was simply too great to be dignified with a rebuttal. Nose skyward, Brother Martin spurred his mule onward.

Balian saw Tancred and cried out, in Occitan, so Martin would not understand, "Go to the church with the poultice and see he doesn't get himself killed."

Count Raymond, understanding the Occitan, was beginning to like this strange newcomer. He watched as Balian was approached by a very young man with auburn hair peeking out of his cap. The youth gripped onto Balian's sleeve. "The red, the red!" came the clear, high voice. "There is no time to lose." Together they elbowed their way into the Seilhan House.

Matilda and Balian flew up a staircase, jostling the praying Dominicans on every other step. He had thought he might have to sneak the girl into Dominican precincts, but never like this. Balian said to her rapidly under his breath, "When we find him, find out where the crime took place and if anything has been moved. If so, put it back the way it was."

"Why?"

"Just do it."

Matilda started a little, unaccustomed to being addressed in this manner. So this was a man's world.

A door stood open on a landing and Balian made out a clutch of senior brothers fingering their beads and reciting prayers. He could see that they surrounded a long table. He grabbed Matilda's hand and they plunged into the group.

"I am a physician. Sent by the King of France," said Balian. "Let me see him."

The black and white cluster of cassocks and scapulars parted slightly, allowing him access to the wounded man stretched out on the table.

Balian stripped away shreds of the blood-sodden Dominican habit. Black, white, red, he thought.

Matilda spotted a trail of blood of the floor.

"Where was he found?" she said. "Where?!"

A large young fellow beside her executed a bow. "Brother Pons of Bram, at your service, sir." Matilda thought his manner odd, given the circumstances.

"Show me where, Brother Pons."

The two went to the far side of the room, where a large pool of blood lapped into a corner. Matilda noticed that the chairs were upright but arranged awkwardly.

"Is this what the room looked like when he was found?"

Pons shook his head.

"Then put it back the way it was. To the best of your recollection."

As Pons painstakingly upended some chairs, Matilda scanned the floor for anything that could tell more about what looked to have been an extremely violent altercation. She saw something glinting a few paces away.

Balian had bared Brother Hildebrand's torso under the disapproving eyes of the chanting friars who pressed in on him.

Three wounds. A gash to the arm, a stab wound under the ribs, and, worst of all, another in the neck, from which blood flowed freely. The victim's face showed a terrible pallor, and the eyes, their light fading, conveyed panic at the approaching abyss.

"Water. Fetch me a basin of water. Now." Gratefully, he heard a muffled order being given.

The water arrived almost instantly, and with cloth torn from his own cloak Balian quickly cleaned and dressed the wounds, stanching the bleeding in the arm and torso and pressing a reddening tissue futilely to the neck. He knew his Galen: the bright red flow was that of the man's vital spirits. It was hopeless.

Balian leaned in on the man and asked, "Who attacked you, Brother Hildebrand?"

The lips opened and closed, but Balian heard nothing.

"Quiet!" he shouted to the chanting Dominicans. "I can't hear him."

Another muffled command heralded a sudden silence.

"Who attacked you, Brother?"

The lips trembled as they opened, and only a horrible gurgling sound lanced the expectant silence.

Balian moved in so close that his nose almost touched that of the dying friar.

"Do you know your attacker?" he whispered.

Slowly, almost imperceptibly, the man managed the slightest of nods. Balian inclined his head for a moment, then looked searchingly into the victim's eyes. If only he could see what this poor fellow had seen…

And then he saw the pleading there. And he understood.

Addressing the friars, he said in a loud voice, "Is there a priest among you? Your brother wants the unction. There is not much time."

This statement occasioned a fresh gale of prayers, but also a determination to supplant Balian at the dying friar's side. He acquiesced—there was no more he could do. He stood up, looked back at the dying man, then instructed the nearest friar to keep the cloth pressed against the neck. It was now completely soaked in vital spirits.

Free of the crush of friars around the table, Balian glimpsed Matilda alone, at the other side of the room. She beckoned him forward.

She explained where the body was found and how it was removed to the table. Balian surveyed the scene, took in the upended chairs. The poor fellow had put up a valiant fight.

"How … how did you know, Matil—Mathias?" Balian said in a quiet voice. "The red blood, the black cassock, and the white scapular?"

"Later." She nodded to a place across the room, where Brother Pons stood, intently watching them.

The two descended the staircase and went into the open air, where a crowd was still gathered.

"The murderer must have had a concealed weapon," Balian said to her softly. "To get into the house … Two of the wounds are slight, suggesting a small dagger, but the third … " He stopped.

"What is it?" Matilda asked.

"A most unlucky placement. To the neck and the source of his spirits … His assailant was right-handed, that much we know."

"Because of the location of the wounds?"

"Precisely. Unfortunately, most men are right-handed, so that barely narrows down the number of possible suspects."

"How do you know it was a man?"

"Very good. No assumption should go unchallenged," Balian said. "But you saw the dying friar within? He's a big man. There are very few women big enough to take on such a fellow, unless she be the Queen of the Huns."

He fell silent, thinking. He turned to Matilda and said, "I think it no coincidence this occurred on the very day of our arrival. The killer is throwing down the gauntlet."

It was then that he noticed the crowd in the street was giving him a wide berth.

"You're quite a sight," Matilda said. "The blood."

"Sir, are you hurt?"

Jean-Paul, the head of the sergeants from Paris, elbowed his way toward them.

Balian shook his head and motioned for Jean-Paul to rejoin his comrades and their horses in the square adjacent to the street. He needed more time to think. Who would do this? Some devil? Or some djinn?

"Balian of Mallorca?"

The voice had come from behind them. They both turned and saw a young man in gold and red livery.

"I am in the service of the Count of Toulouse. His chamberlain."

Balian recognized the colors.

"My lord has instructed me to offer you his hospitality."

"And my men?"

The emissary looked for an overlong moment at the pretty boy.

"But of course … My lord's castle is, in fact, right behind us. It's called the Narbonne Castle, as it is situated at the start of the road to that distant city."

The fellow was a veritable font of useless information.

"Count Raymond would be honored if you broke bread with him this evening."

"We'd be delighted."

The courtier smiled at Matilda.

"Then follow me, if you will." Before setting out, he sniffed and said to Balian, "I suppose you will want to clean up a touch."

CHAPTER TWENTY-ONE

The death knell tolled from a half dozen belfries. Brother Martin lifted his eyes and intoned, "Lucky man, a martyr's death. He is already with our Savior." He crossed himself theatrically.

Tancred and his men rode behind, in single file, heads down. They had spent the afternoon behind this fellow in the cathedral, listening to his interminable droning. Where was Balian, where were the French? They were supposed to protect this Franciscan annoyance. Though he could understand why they might seize any chance to get away from him.

As if sensing what he was thinking, Brother Martin's aspic-faced secretary slowed his mount to let Tancred draw even with him, no mean feat in the narrow street.

"Brother Martin notes that his escort seems to have temporarily deserted him. As the king's representative, therefore, he deputizes you and your men to accompany him. Tonight, you will lodge in the Franciscan convent."

Tancred nodded wearily. He thought of Judith, those eyes, the dark hair, the swells shaping her garment … and now he was to spend the night in a convent with scores of grubby men. Such a cruel twist of fate. But perhaps it would inspire him to compose a song of surpassing melancholy, capable of melting the hardest of hearts. No matter how dire the circumstance, one must search for beauty and, above all else, observe and learn. Had not that been a lesson taught to him by Balian during that precious summer in Saint-Germain-des-Prés? Remembering it gave him heart. He turned and shouted to his men that they were going to accept the hospitality of the Franciscans. They looked at him askance, baffled by the broad smile on his face.

Keeping up the good spirits proved difficult. After being shown an unfurnished, whitewashed room in which all five of them were to sleep, they were instructed that speech was not permitted until mealtime. The men from Chantecler sat down dumbly on the floor, looking at their hands, wondering how they had come to this pass. Only a few days earlier they had been in the warm embrace of their wives and children, eating at the communal table, listening to the old tales. And now here they were, condemned to a sepulchral silence, surrounded by tonsured fanatics.

The evening meal promised little improvement. The newcomers were banished to a table in a far corner of the refectory, more pests than guests. They could see Brother Martin on the other side of the hall, seated at the place of honor at the high table, accepting whispered reverences from a dozen or so friars who had queued to greet him and receive his blessing. One would have thought the pope himself had stopped by for a meal. The graceless fellow with whom Tancred had ridden earlier in the day was gone without a trace, to be replaced by an affable, even genial church elder displaying a beatific smile and a serene look of solicitude. Martin was obviously a figure of some importance in the brotherhood, able to promote careers.

Tancred winced as the prior at the lectern resumed his loud reading of scripture. He had thought the ordeal at an end, but the reader had only paused for a gulp of water. The man had a peculiar voice, as if it could untie a knot at a distance. The good Franciscan friars of Toulouse must have chosen this fellow as their prior out of some collective need for penance. What terrible thing had they done to deserve this earsplitting scold every evening? These men were a mystery. Tancred understood monks—they hid themselves away in remote monasteries so that they would not be reminded of what they were missing, but these friars chose to live in towns, surrounded by the pleasures and solaces of this world yet condemned to abstain from them out of their oath of poverty and chastity. How many now regretted their youthful enthusiasm for holiness?

Tancred's musing was interrupted by a hearty round of applause. The reedy-voiced prior had seated himself, to be replaced as the center of attention by a rotund red-faced chap, a cook by the look of him, smiling through a veil of sweat. Behind him marched six friars bearing a bier-like tray on which an enormous suckling pig lay in aromatic majesty. An apple adorned its snout.

The cook bowed before the thunderous clapping and exclamations of gluttonous exhilaration, then shouted over the tumult, "For a glorious day, a glorious feast!"

Tancred saw Brother Martin laughing beside his hosts. This was poverty? And what was the glorious occasion? The arrival of Brother Martin of Troyes from Paris?

Or the death of a Dominican?

CHAPTER TWENTY-TWO

At the Narbonne Castle, the bustle in the count's kitchens had reached a fever pitch. In the great hall nearby, the lords and ladies of Toulouse had been seated at long trestles, and the high table was occupied by Count Raymond of Toulouse and Balian of Mallorca. All were awaiting their meals. Fatima raced through the noisy throng of servants, making sure to marshal them in the proper order. Mistress Esclarmonde, the head of the kitchens, had taken to her bed, ill with women's troubles. She had delegated her responsibilities to Fatima, recognizing in the girl a leadership ability far beyond her years.

Fatima surveyed the chattering servers and guided them to their places. First, the ewerers, for the handwashing, then the pantlers, to distribute the trenchers of bread. Following them, the butler and his men to pour the wine and ale. She then went to check with the cooks, to see if the first course was ready to be served. Only then would she signal for the parade of servants to get underway. Normally, the evening meal was a subdued and simple affair, unlike the richness and rowdiness of its midday counterpart, but on special occasions—such as the arrival of the sorcerer and his royal sergeants—it could become a feast to remember.

In contrast to the frenzy of the kitchen staff, the occupants of the great hall were hushed, their conversations stilled. Before the high table a youth sang spiritedly of the count's virtues, of his successes in war, in governance, and in the arts of love. Beside the performer sat the song's composer, an elderly woman, her eyes glistening. Count Raymond had explained to Balian beforehand that the woman was Garsenda of Castelnou, the greatest *trobairitz*, or female troubadour, of the day. Garsenda had come to this court some twenty-five years earlier, fleeing Carcassonne when the noble Trencavels, her former patrons, were violently dispatched by the French. She had been in Toulouse ever since, first praising Raymond's father, and gracing his bed, then extolling the virtues of his son.

The youth finished the performance. Garsenda stood up to acknowledge the clapping and whistling, then slowly made her way out of the hall. The singer took his place on the stool vacated by the *trobairitz*, placed his harp before him, and began to pluck out a well-known melody. There was a smattering of applause as the tune was recognized. The count's household was doing its best to banish the gloom inspired by the latest murder.

Fatima poked her head around the door and saw Garsenda leave. She gave the signal and the servers fanned out among the guests. The murmur of conversations resumed.

"Master Balian, I will say this," Count Raymond began. "You have been given an almost impossible task by my old friend Queen Blanche." Count Raymond recalled a memory that still smarted. A dozen years earlier he had been stripped to the waist in front of Notre-Dame de Paris, flogged like a common criminal, while that haughty bitch Blanche had looked on with her mewling boy-king, Louis. It had not been enough for Raymond to sign a punishing peace treaty with the French bastards; he had to be humiliated for their enjoyment. "You have too many suspects. There are so many people here who would want an inquisitor to drop dead."

Fatima stepped up on the dais and deposited a platter of eel in front of them. She smiled tentatively at Balian.

"This is Fatima," the count said expansively. "She is the jewel of my household. And a truth seeker, just like yourself. Fatima, this is Balian of Mallorca."

She executed a slight curtsy, then said, "What an honor, sir. Your reputation precedes you. You have performed many fine and noble deeds."

Balian acknowledged the compliment with a nod, then looked at her searchingly. "I will confess that I am surprised to find one such as you in this place. Surprised and enchanted. Where do you come from?"

She glanced at the count, then looked back at Balian.

"Toulouse."

Raymond slapped his hand on the table, delighted with the response.

"M'lords, I must return to the kitchens," Fatima said. "Esclarmonde is abed with an illness and she has charged me with ensuring the proper performance of the servers and cooks."

"Is someone ill?" Balian interjected. "I am a physician. I could look in on her."

Fatima smiled and said, "Not to worry, sir. She'll be fine in a day or two."

The count nodded, dismissing her. After she had taken her leave, Balian exclaimed, "What an extraordinary creature. Such poise in speech and bearing. Who are her parents?"

Raymond sat back, a faraway look in his eyes. "Her mother," he said at last, "was a Berber beauty of the Atlas ... One of a kind. Exquisite ... Her voice up close lay in your ear like a fairy's breath ... "

Balian said nothing in response to Raymond's intimate memory.

The two men bent toward their food. The confit of eel had been superbly prepared, with just the right touch of goose fat and pomegranate. It was good to be back in civilization, Balian thought.

He scanned the occupants of the great hall before him, looking for a familiar face. At last, Balian spotted her at a table in the rear, Matilda, head bowed, not touching her food. The girl had pluck, maintaining her disguise as Mathias while surrounded by the burly French sergeants. Their raillery would be quite unlike the gentility of her upbringing as the young lady of the castle, swathed in silks and bathed in the golden light of the South. And she was doing this, running the risk of discovery and disgrace, just to meet him and to be at his side, a companion, a partner even. Balian tried to will her to lift her head and look his way, if only to gaze again upon those luminous emeralds that were her eyes. Even dressed as a boy, she was the loveliest woman in the hall, the animation in her features that he had first beheld in the torchlight of Avignonet putting in the shade all the flowing gowns and brilliant brocades of the ladies of the court of Toulouse. But Matilda did not raise her head.

Unaware of his companion's preoccupation, the count swirled the contents of his goblet.

"We spoke of suspects," Raymond said after taking a sip. "My subjects, for one. They could be suspects. First the French put them to the sword for twenty years. When I was but a boy, the French attacked a town near Carcassonne belonging to my cousins, the Trencavels. And what did they do? They took several dozen townsmen, gouged out their eyes, cut off their noses and lips—and then had them march in single file to the stronghold of my cousin's vassal. The leader of the mutilated men had only one eye put out, so that he could guide his fellows through the fields and over the hills in the blazing-hot sun. And so the holy cause of Rome was served. Even today, any man from that village would consider it his duty to kill French Dominicans..." His voice trailed off as he sought out Balian's eyes to judge whether he could speak freely. He received a smile of encouragement.

"What was the name of that village?" Balian asked softly.

The count thought for a moment, then said, "Bram."

He took another sip of wine. "You know, Balian, as a youth I knew Dominic. A Castilian. Domingo. With a strange manner.

Anyone who met Dominic immediately recognized that he was..."

Raymond fell into silence.

"Saintly?"

"No... driven, single-minded... absolutely sure of himself."

"Would he approve of what the friars are doing now? Inflicting pain and spreading fear?"

A look of relief crossed the count's face. Clearly this fellow, this young healer, was no fool, not cowed by the priests into accepting their truth. He could see why the queen mother had chosen him.

"I think not. The only person Dominic wanted to torture was himself. Which he did every night, drawing blood and then lying on the floor in pain... and pleasure."

Balian's mind went back to Blanche's curled lip at the thought of her royal son's penchant for extravagant acts of piety.

"I think Dominic would be as horrified as I am," Raymond continued. "Think of it. I was forced by your Blanche of Castile to found a university in this city, solely for the purpose of training young Dominicans in the art of inquisition. I had to raid my treasury to teach outsiders how to torture and kill my people."

In the guttering torchlight of the hall Balian could see the sorrow in his host's eyes. His was a great family, of a lineage that reached back through time to Charlemagne. An ancestor had been on the First Crusade, and the family still ruled the county of Tripoli in Outremer. Yet Count Raymond's branch, the Saint-Gilles, was now doomed to extinction. He had had no son, and his daughter had been forced to wed the brother of the King of France. Which meant that at Raymond's death the great county of Toulouse would fall into the eager grasp of the French. Count Raymond VII would be the last of his line.

Fatima arrived to clear off the trenchers. Then she placed fresh trenchers for the second serving before them.

"May I ask a favor of you, young lady?" Balian ventured.

"Of course, Master Balian."

"You see where my French sergeants are seated, at the rear of the hall?" He discreetly pointed in their direction. "You see the young fellow farthest to the left? His name is Mathias. I should like you to refresh his trencher as well. He has a very refined palate."

Fatima curtsied again. "It would be my pleasure."

"But see to it that you do it discreetly, so the others do not expect the same."

She nodded, then hurried off.

Count Raymond looked at Balian for a long time, wondering if his playing favorites might bespeak a stronger bond between him and the boy. He recognized the youth as the fellow who had barged into the Seilhan House with Balian that afternoon.

"You too have a motive to dislike the Dominicans," Balian remarked. He considered holding his tongue, but the wine had been delicious. "What you've just said about the university and your treasury, does not that make you a murder suspect as well?"

Raymond of Toulouse chuckled in surprise. Once, he would have considered such a remark to be insolent, but he had seen too much suffering, too much death.

"Ah, there's where you're wrong, my clever friend," Raymond said. "If I were the murderer, I would not kill one or two or three Dominicans … " He smiled pleasantly. "I would kill them all."

CHAPTER TWENTY-THREE

*A*s the Dominican provincial of Narbonne, the highest-ranking friar in all of the Languedoc, ended his sojourn in Carcassonne and made his way to Toulouse to avenge the slain inquisitors, a crow in a tall poplar noted his passage, along with that of his impressive retinue. The bird leapt from its branch and soared into the blue, alive now to the prospect of food. It could hear the cawing of a murder of its fellow crows not that far away, toward the great stone city on the hill. As the bird neared the place, giving full-throated warning of its approach, it saw that the meal was not in the town but down by the river.

The crow wheeled in the sky to take in the sight. A gibbet had been erected from which were hanged three dozen men, women, and children, a dozen for each murdered inquisitor. There were already four or five crows down there, frantically hopping from one shoulder to the next, but there was still plenty of room for a newcomer. Besides, the strengthening smell was irresistible.

The bird banked, then let itself descend precipitously, pulling up at the last second to alight on the shoulder of a young girl. Her neck was broken, and her head lolled forward from the noose, her face bluish green.

The bird made a tentative step closer to the neck, then leaned over. It saw what it wanted. After straightening up for a moment to emit a loud, jubilant caw, the crow pulled its head back and then plunged its beak as far as it could into the very center of her fading but still bright blue eye.

CHAPTER TWENTY-FOUR

Matilda blinked in the morning sunlight. How those Frenchmen could snore! They did indeed speak from their throats—but they didn't forget their noses, either. The great ogive ceiling of the hall had been an echo chamber, the blackness becoming a fog of snort and grunt, like a rolling riot of rutting swine. Why had God fashioned man thus? Was he not meant to be in his likeness? Perhaps the heretics were right, that the God of Creation was an ugly, malevolent beast and that the good God had no interest in the doings of disgusting man.

It was futile to think of such things. She yawned, adjusted her cap, made sure her red hair did not peek out from under its brim. There was no use calling attention to herself. She wanted to observe, not to be observed.

The river Garonne beckoned. Matilda strode tentatively through the wakening streets, barely eliciting a sidelong glance. Shutters were being raised, stoops swept, dirty straw thrown into the street, dogs chased from befouling the stalls. For the Toulousans, there was no reason to take note of this lithe young man, a stranger, with his unusual grace of movement. Accustomed to the bowing of villeins whenever she passed through the villages of Chantecler, Matilda marveled at her anonymity. So this too was a man's world.

She heard them before she saw them. A sweet chorus of voices wafting through the spring air, like a wayward zephyr of summer reminding men and women of joys soon to be renewed. Matilda walked through the opened gate of the fortifications and looked at the river, flowing fast from the spring runoff in the mountains. A few rickety mills stood on both sides of the Garonne, deserted momentarily as the river ran too high. Months earlier, they had ground the autumn harvests into meal, which was stored inland, in granaries built on stilts in a vain attempt to deter the rodents of the town.

The crystalline chorus was punctuated with a loud slapping sound that gave the singing an odd, trancelike meter. Matilda saw the source—about a dozen washerwomen were kneeling on a large flat boulder at the river's edge beating out wet clothing on the stone. Others, skirts high and arms exposed, wrung out their laundry nearby. A few men stood perhaps twenty paces away and took in the sight, fishing poles in hand as a flimsy pretext. These servant girls were young, very young. It would take years before they would earn their place at the gossipy *lavoirs* within the walls of Toulouse, so their arduous task had to be conducted alongside the Garonne, its banks narrowed now by the swollen waters.

Their leader, Matilda realized with a start, was a very young girl, even in comparison to her companions. Her high, innocent voice beguiled the morning air with its purity. She was great with child, although she was scarcely more than a child herself. No doubt some drunken oaf in town, some red-faced burgher or soldier or friar had violated her in some squalid alleyway, or perhaps down here by the river when the leafy undergrowth of the hot months would have provided scores of secluded places in which to threaten her with a knife or a closed fist. The other girls kneeling on the rock responded to her lead, their chorus building then fading between the spaces of the rhythmic beating of wet cloth on stone. It was like a prayer. Matilda bowed her head and listened.

"*Fougasse*, sir?"

A baker's boy stood beside her, the wicker basket he held in front of him warmed by its bounty of breads taken from his master's ovens.

"What's your name, son?" Matilda asked.

"Jaume," he replied.

"Well, Jaume, you've got just what I want." Matilda fished in her leather pouch for a coin. She handed the delighted boy a denier and received two buns in return. But they were quickly forgotten. Something in her purse caught her eye, a bright glint.

How could she have forgotten? In the upstairs room of the Seilhan House, this coin had glistened sickly on the floor in its dark cloak of blood. She withdrew it, examined it more carefully. It had nothing to do with the local coinage, that much she knew. What was it doing lying on the floor of a room in which a Dominican inquisitor had been murdered? What did that mean?

She retraced her steps quickly, leaving Jaume to his transactions with the singing washerwomen. The streets were now thronged, impeding her movement. Boys carrying parcels ran before her; a horseman plodded past, to be followed by a merchant's wife in all her dusty finery. The woman gave Matilda a look that could not be mistaken for anything less than an invitation. Her hands moved to her ample bosom, as if offering wares to be sampled. Matilda hurried past, trying not to hear the woman's lewd laughter behind her. These Toulousans were not shy. Yesterday it had been the chamberlain, eyeing her as if she were a succulent stew to be swallowed.

She wished she had told Balian about the coin right away. Last night, at the banquet, he looked at home jesting with the count, their goblets of wine filled and refilled at the high table, while she sat at a lowly bench with the French sergeants. Had she, Matilda of Périgueux, felt resentful, felt denied her rightful place of honor in the hall? So much so that she had forgotten to tell the resourceful doctor of her discovery?

She had, and now a shadow of shame darkened her features. Dear Balian had agreed to her charade, to her travesty of nature, at considerable risk to himself and to his royal mission. She must not do anything to jeopardize him. She thought of the long black hair crowning his manly countenance, the mouth quick to smile and the lips to purse in thought, the strong jaw, the broad shoulders, the sound of his soft breathing that night in Avignonet.

Matilda stopped, astounded at what she was thinking.

CHAPTER TWENTY-FIVE

Despite himself, Balian was worried. When he joined his men in the courtyard, he immediately noticed the absence.

"Has anyone seen Mathias?"

"Who?"

"My boy, my assistant."

"That young fellow," a gruff voice replied. "I saw him slipping out in the early morning."

"Did he say where he was going?"

"The lad never says a word. You'd swear he'd had his tongue cut out."

There were grunts of agreement. Matilda had been a purposefully silent dinner companion.

"You men, stay here. I'll be back soon."

Balian was leaving a courtyard of murmurs behind him.

"Master Balian," Jean-Paul said, "the queen mother has charged us with protecting you."

Balian whirled about in the gateway and said heatedly, "And with protecting Brother Martin. Might I suggest you find him, Jean-Paul? I can take care of myself."

The sergeants exchanged puzzled glances but let the moody doctor leave without any further attempt to deter him.

The street leading from the Narbonne Castle and past the Dominicans' Seilhan House looked much calmer than it had been the day before, but something was amiss. Gone was the theatrical grief, replaced by a sullen silence. Balian thought he noticed resentful muttering by the stalls, as customer and guildsman traded some sinister tale. He pressed on, unsure if he were the source of displeasure—or perhaps Matilda. Had she been found out? The townspeople would not take kindly to her masquerade, especially if it emerged that she had enjoyed the hospitality of the count. Changing a charge of unnatural harlotry to witchcraft was a small step to take if tempers ran high in the cramped quarters of a city like this. Balian had seen it before, in Paris, when a poor girl had been torn limb from limb by a furious mob, all because she had had the temerity to try to escape her father's tyranny by running away from home disguised as a friar. He remembered her heartrending shrieks, the jeering of the crowd, the inhumanity. His fellow man could be moved to the cowardice of cruelty as quickly as he could snap his fingers, which is why he had kept his garden and alchemist's chamber behind high walls at Saint-Germain-des-Prés.

Dear God, where was she? Balian feared turning a corner and seeing an angry crowd gathered.

He had been to Toulouse on several occasions, so he quickly oriented himself. To the right, the streets leading toward the Cathedral of Saint-Stephen; straight ahead, the warren of alleyways stretching to the pilgrimage church of Saint-Sernin; to the left, the rue de la Dalbade leading to the white church of that name and the Jewish precinct nearby. As if obeying some homing instinct, as powerful as that of the pigeons whose use his father had learned from the Saracens of Aleppo, Balian found himself heading to the left, toward the sons and daughters of Israel. The Jewish occupants of rue Joutx-Aigues would know if trouble were brewing; their long history of endangerment had made them exquisitely sensitive to any threat of discord.

His mood darkened as messenger boys sprinted through the streets as he neared the Dalbade. Some ran past him, others plunged into darkened alleys, all spread out through the city. These flitting harbingers made Balian's heart beat faster, and he struggled to stifle feelings of dread as his footsteps quickened of their own accord over the dark cobbles. He suspected before he rounded the white façade of the Dalbade what he would see in the square before rue Joutx-Aigues.

By a central well, a large group was gathered, their wailing and shouting clear signs of heightened emotion. Balian neared them, alarmed but puzzled. This was an angry mob, yes, but they did not seem fixed on any one object. He strained to see over sobbing shoulders who stood or lay by the fountain but could make out nothing. Had his poor Matilda been thrown down the well? Yet there were no hateful shouts of triumph, no strangled cries of bloodlust.

He felt a tug on his tunic and he turned and felt the green eyes burning into him.

Instinctively, Balian took Matilda in his arms, hugged her to his breast. She could feel his heart thudding.

"Thank God," he whispered, as oblivious to the crowd as it was to him. "Thank God you're safe." He kissed her passionately on the forehead.

Matilda withdrew from his grasp, eyes wide.

"Balian…"

They looked at each other in silence, both aware of Balian's unspoken declaration.

"I'm… I'm sorry," he stammered at last. "It's just that I was so worried. A sheltered girl like yourself…"

She frowned.

"I feel responsible for you."

"Perhaps you should think of other things," Matilda said reprovingly.

Balian bowed his head, then heard her voice soften.

"Balian, it's about Astruguetus…"

He looked up at her in alarm, then at the crowd by the well. He had been so sick with worry that he hadn't even noticed their round yellow badges. They were all Jews.

"He's been murdered."

CHAPTER TWENTY-SIX

"Three dozen of them?"

Tancred looked at the young Franciscan incredulously. "How can that be?"

"That's the talk going round town. They were some of the villagers locked up in the Wall of Carcassonne. From Auriol. Hanged."

"Who the devil gave the order?"

"The Dominican provincial. He's just arrived in town now. Tempers are running high, let me tell you."

The friar mopped a droplet of sweat from his forehead. He knew that if a mob formed, there would be no distinction made between Dominican and Franciscan. A friar was a friar was a friar.

"And the Jews are up in arms, too."

"The Jews? What's this got to do with them?"

"Seems that about the same time a patriarch was killed in Avignonet."

Tancred grabbed the friar's arm.

"What did you say, man?"

The friar started in surprise. Why so much concern about a Jew?

"Yes, some merchant there."

"Astruguetus of Narbonne?"

"That was the name."

At that, Tancred released the friar and rushed back into the Franciscan convent to round up his men. He had to find Balian.

There had been far too many killings to assume he was not in danger as well.

The search did not take long. A man who had arrived the day before at the head of a retinue from France, who had tried to save the life of an inquisitor, who had shared the high table with Count Raymond—his every movement would be the subject of discussion in town. Tancred was told Balian was in the house of Rabbi Ezra near the Church of the Dalbade.

Tancred tentatively pulled the great door knocker and let it fall. Immediately, the door squeaked open a crack.

"I'm here to see Balian of Mallorca. I am his friend."

The door opened wide.

Beyond the doorman Tancred could see Balian's apprentice, Mathias. The boy flushed somewhat and wordlessly pointed to a doorway leading to an adjacent room. Without further ceremony Tancred crossed the small entrance hall and entered the reception area.

Seated around a table were Balian and a man Tancred took to be the rabbi.

And Judith.

She looked tired and drawn, but still beautiful.

Balian rose to greet him and make the introductions to the rabbi. He kept hold of Tancred's forearm as Judith's story was retold.

Early in the morning a servant had returned to Avignonet from the countryside, where he told of the terrible hangings in Carcassonne. Astruguetus, on hearing the identity of the perpetrator of the murders, ordered his steward to hide his strongbox in a concealed niche in the stone wall of the house. Judith had thought this peculiar but knew enough not to pester her father with questions.

A short time later Judith was in the stable, saddling her horse and loading it with garment bags for an extended visit to a kinswoman in the neighboring town of Bram. That's when she heard the commotion. She stood in the shadow of the stable door and looked out toward the courtyard. Her father's steward lay in a pool of his own blood before the open front door of the house. She was about to step out into the sunshine when she saw armed men drag other servants out into the courtyard. They screamed and fought but it was no use. They were run through with the sword.

Then her father was led out. His face was a bloodied mess of bruises and cuts. He had been beaten.

Before she could react, one of the armed men took out a dagger and knifed him twice in the chest. He fell to the ground. His attackers retreated into the house.

By the time Judith reached him, he was near his end. His eyes showed that he recognized her. Expiring, Astruguetus rasped, "Go, daughter, go! Go to Toulouse. To safety—"

And then he died.

Tancred looked at Judith. His brother had met a terrible end, from a peregrine falcon bite that poisoned his humors, but he had not been there to witness his suffering. Her smooth, unlined face betrayed nothing.

An obedient daughter to the end, Judith had leapt on her horse and ridden like the wind. The attacking men had heard her thunder over the pebbles of the courtyard, but they did not give chase. About a half league away, where the road of the Old Romans rises to cross a ridge, she had reined in and looked behind her. A tendril of black smoke tickled the morning blue. Her father's house had been set alight. She turned back westward and rode, unmolested, to Toulouse.

Balian released his friend from his grasp and sat down on a bench. Tancred joined him. The two men were directly across from the impassive young woman.

Balian asked gently, "Did you recognize the assailants? Did they wear any livery that might identify them?"

She shook her head slowly. The long black hair shifted on her shoulders.

"What was in the strongbox, Judith? Do you know?"

"His treasury, his ledgers, parchments … " She smiled sadly. "My jewelry."

"Then it must be retrieved," Tancred exclaimed. "It is your property and your inheritance. It is yours by law."

She looked at Tancred with sad affection. She had heard these Gentile knights could be headstrong.

"They must have found it," she said.

"No, that's not true. If they had found it, they would not have set the house on fire. They were trying to destroy something."

Balian glanced over at his friend, impressed. He was almost as clever as his sister.

"I will recover it," Tancred said, getting to his feet. "You will tell me where this hiding place is, and I shall ferret it out and return it to you, my good lady Judith."

She cocked her head slightly, unaccustomed to this form of address.

"I shall leave at once."

Judith considered for a moment. She turned to the rabbi and the two conversed for a moment in Hebrew. Balian leaned in and, in the same language, told them that his friend was very able. And very trustworthy.

Rabbi Ezra inclined his head to Balian, then stood up, leaving the floor to Judith.

"Very well, Lord Tancred, you may return it to me here. But only if you bring my father's body as well. Not one without the other."

The rabbi had moved to a wardrobe by the wall. He withdrew from it a white shroud and then handed it over to Tancred.

"It belongs to us, my son. Use it to wrap the body."

Tancred turned to Judith and saw, at last, a tear coursing down her cheek.

CHAPTER TWENTY-SEVEN

Balian and Matilda were seated at a table in his room in the Narbonne Castle. His eyes were downcast. A wan light filtered through a mullioned window.

"Astruguetus," he murmured.

Matilda looked at him sympathetically. "He led a long and rich life," she said softly.

"That he did," Balian replied, his voice gaining strength. "When my father still lived, Astruguetus came to visit us at our estate near Perpignan. When the French terror was at its height."

"Was he in danger?"

"Everyone was," Balian said, "but especially the Jews. The men from the North were charged with killing heretics, but they weren't above doing harm to the Jews. It's in their nature."

He shook his head sadly.

"One time when the danger was at its greatest, Astruguetus came with his wife and child," Balian continued. "They had ridden all night and they were exhausted. I'll never forget the infant in its mother's arms, crying out of fatigue and hunger."

"How old were you?"

"I don't know. Maybe ten, maybe twelve or thereabouts."

Matilda broke into a brilliant smile. "I thought you were a wizard," she said. "Do the sums. That crying baby must have been Judith."

Balian looked as if he had been struck in the face.

"But of course. Astruguetus had but one child."

Matilda reached into her tunic and extracted her purse. She took the strange coin from it.

"Now let's see if you can figure this out," she teased.

She handed the coin to Balian.

Intrigued, he turned it around and around in his fingers. Then he nodded to himself.

"Where did you get this?"

"At the Seilhan House."

"But the only time you've been in there was on the day of the murder."

"Precisely," she said. "I found it on the floor when I was rearranging the room with Brother Pons."

Balian paused, taking in the information. "I have heard tell of this coin," he said finally. "A friend from Granada goes to the fairs in Champagne. He told me that the Florentines have begun minting and circulating this currency. It's called a florin."

"Florence?" Matilda uttered in surprise.

"Yes, in Tuscany. What was this florin from Tuscany doing in the inquisitor's room, so far from home?"

"Could it have belonged to the dead inquisitor?" Matilda asked.

"Unlikely. He was from the North. And I've been told that the murdered man, Brother Hildebrand of Alsace, was famous in the order for his scrupulous observance of the Dominican vow of poverty. It's impossible that he would possess such a valuable coin."

"How did it get onto the floor of his study?"

"You tell me. You have the power to see things that others cannot. That's what you said to me on our way into Toulouse."

Balian was wearing a smile when Matilda looked up at him. She thought for a moment.

"Use your reason, Matilda. First, how could a coin be on the floor?"

"It was dropped, or it fell, or was shaken loose, out of an open purse?"

"Yes! And why didn't the owner of the purse pick it up?"

"Because he didn't see or hear it drop."

"Excellent! Now, why wasn't the falling coin seen or heard?"

"Really, Balian! This is getting tedious."

"My darling friend, if you are going to be my—"

He stopped, checked himself.

"Your what?"

She could not be certain, but he seemed to be blushing.

"Assistant," Balian said quickly. "As my assistant, you will have to get used to speculation. Only the playful can arrive at the truth."

Matilda took off her cap, unpinned her hair, and shook her head. The hair that had been left uncut by Alcuin and herself when preparing her disguise now flowed like molten copper to her shoulders. She smiled, just for him.

"I am playful."

Balian tried to keep his composure. The boy had been banished; before him was a radiantly beautiful young woman.

"I ... I see," he said after a pause.

"Now, what was the question you asked of me?"

There was a silence.

"Balian, it was about the coin, remember?" She could barely suppress a laugh.

"Yes ... yes ... Why didn't anyone see or hear the coin drop?"

Matilda thought for a moment.

"There was a struggle."

"Yes! There was a hell of a fight. Remember those upturned chairs? The inquisitor fought back, and hard. So, in all likelihood, the coin fell from the assailant's purse, unnoticed."

Perhaps, Matilda thought, Balian really is a wizard after all.

"And he had to have known his assassin, perhaps invited him in," Balian continued, excited. "There is only one door to that room. The murderer also had to mount the staircase of the Dominican house in the middle of the day. Everybody knew him."

The two of them paused to let this sink in. Balian put his elbow on the table, cradled his chin in his hand, lost in thought. Matilda observed him thinking.

"So ... the florin?" she said at last.

"A merchant of Toulouse?"

She shook her head.

"No, he couldn't have done the other two murders," she said. "He would have been recognized."

"Perhaps he hired someone for those two?"

Matilda looked skeptical and said, "No. How did he get in and out of the Seilhan House in broad daylight? Tell me that."

"How the devil am I supposed to know?" Balian snapped, exasperated. "You're of no use whatsoever."

Matilda straightened up, insulted. "I will not be spoken to in that tone, Master Balian," she said pointedly. "Or are you forgetting who I am?"

"Oh, for the love of God, Matilda," Balian said. "You are who you are by sheer chance, that's all. Don't put on your airs around me."

Matilda bristled. "You sound like a heretic."

"Well, then, maybe I am." Balian got to his feet and began pacing the room in frustration. A silence fell between them, chilly and unexpected. They avoided looking at each other, thinking their own thoughts about what had just occurred.

At last, Balian came back to the table and sat down.

"You know who you are, Matilda?" he said gravely.

"You tell me."

"You are Tancred's brother."

Her delighted laugh floated in the air between them and seemed to wrap itself around Balian like a warm blanket.

"I'm sorry I shouted at you, Matilda."

Their eyes met. Gingerly, she reached out and placed a soft hand on his.

"Don't let's quarrel, Balian. It distresses me."

The silence between them now was expectant, alive to a possibility that both had barely dared to think about. As if by some prior agreement, Balian and Matilda remained silent, acutely aware of their hands touching.

"So," Matilda whispered, "you said the killer had to be a big man, correct?"

"Yes."

"And did we see any big men at the friar's deathbed?"

Balian frowned, then shook his head.

"But I did."

"Now it is you who are confounding me."

"Remember? I met with a very big friar when I tried to rearrange the chairs. He had a very odd demeanor. Brother Pons."

"Who?"

"Brother Pons of Bram."

Balian looked at her, thunderstruck. "Did you say Bram?"

"Yes. What of it?"

Balian recounted to her his conversation with Count Raymond the night before, about how he had said that no man of that mutilated village would hesitate to kill inquisitors.

Matilda listened, searched her memory. Yes, the friar had seemed totally unperturbed by the chaotic death scene unfolding nearby. He had been cordial even, helping her to upend the chairs. Had there been blood on his cassock?

A knock came at the door, tentative at first, then insistent. Matilda was quickly on her feet, cap in hand, retreating to a far corner of the room to tie up her hair.

"Master Balian? It's Bertran."

Balian glanced over to look at Matilda, transformed again into Mathias. She nodded, then turned to the wall so her face could not be seen.

Balian opened the door. Bertran was one of Tancred's men from Chantecler. He would recognize Matilda at such close quarters if she turned around.

"I've just come from the Franciscan convent. Brother Martin entreats you to meet him in the cathedral square and proceed from there to meet with the Dominican provincial."

"Very well," Balian said, swiping the florin off the table. "And who is this important provincial?"

Bertran searched his memory for an instant.

"Brother Giuseppe of Fiesole. A Tuscan."

CHAPTER TWENTY-EIGHT

The cobblestone expanse in front of the Cathedral of Saint-Stephen was only faintly familiar to Balian, as it was not a precinct he had visited often. He observed the buckets at the well, saw the shops lining the square, felt the eyes peering out at him.

Pascal came out of his baker's shop for a breath of fresh air. He saw Balian waiting in silence, his colorful cloak and sweep of long black hair marking him as someone not native to Toulouse. Pascal scratched at his beard thoughtfully. Could this be Balian of Mallorca, the sorcerer everyone was talking about? The two men's eyes met briefly, before Balian turned to the façade of the church.

Brother Martin was emerging from the great doorway of the cathedral, no doubt from a fresh round of prayer. He was taller than Balian remembered now that he was off his pathetic mule. His pallid face wore a grim, tight-lipped smile.

"Good day, Master Balian." The friar bowed deeply, almost as if in mockery. "I hear you did not manage to save a life."

The Franciscan was not one to bury the hatchet.

"And did you manage to save a soul?"

The two men appraised each other, as if this opening round of unpleasantness were a necessary ritual.

"You have heard that the Dominican provincial has come to town?"

"From you, Brother Martin."

"Quite." The Franciscan set off down a main street, Balian at his side. Ever cautious around friars, Pascal retreated into his shop. Other townspeople parted to let Martin and Balian pass, a few soliciting a blessing quickly dispensed. "Brother Giuseppe is a high-ranking member of the Order of Friars Preachers. For him to have made the journey from the coast means that Rome must have asked him to come here, even before the latest murder."

"You speak of the three dozen hanged in Carcassonne, or the household of Astruguetus of Narbonne in Avignonet, or the inquisitor in Toulouse?"

The Franciscan raised an eyebrow but continued walking.

"I speak of the brutal killing of an inquisitor. No one cares about the deaths of heretics and Jews."

The chasm between the two men became wider.

"I think the queen mother might," Balian said finally. "Did she not send us here to prevent the Dominicans from causing a revolt?"

"We are here to find out who is killing the inquisitors," Martin said flatly. "I have arranged to meet Brother Giuseppe. Which is why you are here."

They were in front of the pink bricks of the Seilhan House. Unlike the previous day, there were no crowds lamenting the death of a friar in the street, only two heavily armed guards standing before the door. They were behemoths, almost feral, of the type who would do anything if ordered to by a reliable paymaster. Men such as these were the curse of the continent, making roads unsafe and journeys perilous. The lure of lucrative crusading in the Holy Land was once thought a sure way to rid Europe of this menace of lawless, landless knights, but there seemed, alas, to be an inexhaustible supply of them.

"We are here to see Brother Giuseppe of Fiesole," Brother Martin announced.

Neither man reacted.

Balian looked more closely at them. One wore a gold stud in his ear, in the manner of the Moors. The doctor smiled in recognition.

"We have been sent here by the King of the Franks," he said in Arabic. "To meet with your master, Imam Yusuf of Fiesole. Please let us pass."

The two men exchanged glances, then stood aside. Martin looked at Balian incredulously.

"And what tongue did you address them in?" he asked as they crossed the threshold.

"Magyar," Balian said airily. "I recognized them as men from Buda."

Martin nodded, entirely duped.

CHAPTER TWENTY-NINE

Giuseppe of Fiesole sat at the table where the body of the unfortunate inquisitor had been laid out the day before, riffling hurriedly through a bound leather ledger before him. The Inquisition's accounts seemed to be in order; indeed, all seemed to be in order, except for the damned nuisance of three murders.

He rose to his feet and went to the window. The glass was of an inferior kind, but he could make out the street and the square near the Narbonne Castle. That would be where the Count of Toulouse resided, the reluctant benefactor of the town's Dominican university. The sun gleamed on Giuseppe's shaved pate, as if to warm his already overheated brainpan. He would have to have a talk with the count, find out what the hell he intended to do. These outrages could not be countenanced. The people would have to be punished.

He had a mind to go over there right away. Why had he agreed to meet with Brother Martin? Sent by King Louis, yes, but still a bloody Franciscan.

The door opened and a junior friar announced that the guests were waiting. Giuseppe motioned for them to be shown in.

"What a delight to meet with you again, Brother Martin," Giuseppe exclaimed with perfectly pitched hypocrisy. "It has been too long."

"Yes, not since the synod called by the late Holy Father."

"A great man, a saint, really."

Balian looked closely at Giuseppe's fleshy face, which seemed to be held aloft by a cascade of wattles. Obviously, the man was a slave to his senses. There was no aura of piety surrounding the friar, no hint of fasting and prayer, only the suggestion of appetites to be fed and desires to be slaked. Yet the remnants of what had once been a noble Tuscan face, Balian saw, could still be discerned under the layers of fat. The usury of debauchery had not yet completed its work.

A silence ensued. The two friars seemed to be closely examining the floor. Balian sensed an opportunity.

"Brother Giuseppe, I am Balian of Mallorca. I have been deputized by the king to help Brother Martin in investigating the distressing business of the inquisitors."

Giuseppe turned to look at Balian imperiously. Despite the toll of years of dissipation, the dimensions of his pronounced Tuscan nose still seemed perfectly suited to convey condescension.

"Have you taken Holy Orders, sir?"

"No."

"Then I would suggest, Master Balian of Mallorca, that you have no business meddling in the affairs of the Dominican Order."

To Balian's astonishment, Brother Martin intervened. "Master Balian has performed many valuable services for the king and his barons. He is an able man." The Franciscan poultice, Balian thought, evidently knew of his exploits.

"That may be the case, but it has no bearing on the matter at hand. Indeed, the king has no business meddling in our affairs either. We Dominicans are answerable only to the pope. As are you Franciscans, Brother Martin."

"But we are here to help you, Brother," Balian continued, undeterred. "I have concluded, from examining the body of the murdered man yesterday, that there was a violent altercation— a fight—and that the victim knew his assailant. And"—he paused, wondering how much he should disclose about Pons of Bram—"that the assailant may well have been a Dominican like yourself."

Brother Giuseppe crossed himself in alarm. Balian recognized the expression on the Dominican's face. "I did not arrive at these opinions through necromancy," he said calmly. "I exercised my powers of reasoning."

This did not placate Brother Giuseppe. It seemed instead to incense him.

"I do not like men such as you. You crowd the universities, you fill the market squares, you squawk like chickens in the taverns. You think too much; you have forgotten how to obey."

Balian was familiar with the argument and was unimpressed. "Whatever you may think of men like me, you should also think of your Dominican brethren in the Kingdom of France. Refusing to cooperate with the king's envoys will greatly displease him. He may look less favorably upon your order."

Brother Martin looked at Balian with a growing respect. The man would not back down, and he spoke the truth. And the prospect of the king's turning a cold shoulder to the Dominicans filled his Franciscan heart with warmth.

Giuseppe's face reddened.

"How dare you. How dare you threaten us," he shouted. "King Louis is a pious man. He will take no action against us. He is not some ... some unclean sorcerer sent to cause trouble."

Balian stared directly into the friar's burning eyes. "My Tuscan friend," he said softly, "the King of France is, first and foremost, the King of France. If you want me to stop your men from getting killed, you must work with me. If you won't work with me, Paris will be informed."

He swept his cloak over a shoulder and stepped toward the door. He turned on the threshold, saying, "Now go bury your inquisitor. He's starting to stink."

CHAPTER THIRTY

Matilda waited outside in the dusty street, looking at the pink bricks of the façade. The two giants stood before the door, almost three hands taller than she was, silent and terrifying.

Why had Balian embraced her so warmly when he found her in the morning? Why did they join hands after they had quarreled? Why did those actions seem so right, so natural?

She shook her head, realizing the danger of such questions. She was Matilda of Périgueux, the sister of Tancred of Périgueux. Until he married, she was the lady of Chantecler Castle. Her grandfather had taken the Cross, gone on the Third Crusade with Richard Lionheart. Who was Balian of Mallorca?

"*Salaam*." It was Balian's voice, taking leave of the two guards. They smiled and answered in kind.

"He will not cooperate with us," Balian informed Matilda. "He's a bloody-minded, fat little puppy, standing on his hind legs."

She kept up with him as he strode down an unfamiliar street. "Where are we going now? What are we going to do?"

"Find someone who will talk to us. At the Dominican convent across town."

"Weren't we just there?"

"No. The Seilhan House is home to the Inquisition. The regular friars have a cloistered convent."

"Are those friars more humane?"

Balian smiled. "We're not supposed to say things like that. At least not out loud."

They skirted a line of beggars forming at a church door, waiting for the congregation to come outside. The spectacle was eternal, the halt and the lame debasing themselves for a measure of mercy, a scrap of humanity. Balian and Matilda hurried on.

"How is it that you speak the Saracen tongue?"

"I grew up in a land that was controlled by the Muslims. Everyone had to speak it."

"Are you … a Saracen?"

He smiled again. "Are you an inquisitor?"

"Just curious."

"Then let me be curious. How did you know that I was speaking Arabic?"

"Alcuin. Our tutor taught me well, too."

They had arrived at the door of the convent. Behind the building, in a forest of scaffolding, a giant redbrick church was being erected, a Dominican monument to themselves and to their mission.

"Can I help either of you gentlemen?"

The accent was unfamiliar, the French almost singsong. Balian and Matilda turned and beheld a tall, ruddy man of about thirty-five, his face a map of freckles and his tonsure a fiery ring of red.

"It looked to me like you were about to knock on our door, or might I be mistaken?"

Matilda smiled; the friar smiled back.

"I am Brother Brendan of Killiney. At your service."

So, this was a Gael.

"Much obliged, Brother Brendan. I am Balian of Mallorca, and this is my apprentice, Mathias. We have come from Paris."

"Ahh, haven't I heard that's a lively place? Lots of action, I wager?"

Within minutes the friendly friar had ushered them inside, past a cloister made deafening by the blows and shouts of stonemasons and woodcutters within and without. Balian was reminded of the Sainte-Chapelle building site.

"I'm afraid I'm responsible for this racket," Brendan said, his voice rising to be heard. "In its wisdom, the order has charged me with planning and overseeing the construction of its new church. Bless us, but isn't it a wonderful thing?"

He led them into a quiet room where several chairs stood around a long table.

"Here now, sit yourselves down and I'll go have one of the lads bring us some wine. It's not every day we have visitors from Paris."

Smiling, he swept out of the room.

"My goodness," Matilda said, "what a pleasant fellow."

"That's the reputation of the Gaels. Unless you get them angry."

Brendan was back very quickly, bearing a platter of fruit and cheese. "So, my friends, what brings you to Toulouse?"

Balian, instinctively feeling he was in the presence of a sensible man of science, decided to go to the heart of the matter. Besides, he needed an ally from within the Dominican Order if ever he were to pierce the mystery of the murders.

"Do you know a Brother Pons of Bram?"

"Not so well. Why do you ask?"

Balian paused before speaking. "I have it on good authority that the men and women of Bram have ample reason to detest the French, the Dominicans—and especially French Dominicans."

"Is that why you've come from Paris, my friend? To stick your learned nose in the sordid rivalries afflicting our order?"

"Three men are dead, Brother Brendan," Balian said evenly. "The queen mother fears retaliation, then revolt."

"Old Queen Blanche." Brendan laughed. "As pure as the driven snow."

Balian remained unmoved. He spoke at length about their suspicions, how he had been chosen to track down a murderer, how the provincial Giuseppe of Fiesole had hanged three dozen innocents at Carcassonne and the obstreperousness shown by him at their meeting at the Seilhan House.

Brendan's face darkened.

"At home," he said at last, "that fellow Giuseppe would be strung up before he'd had time to say a prayer."

Balian let out a grim laugh. "That's precisely our worry. That the people might not long stand for mistreatment and cruelty."

"They've been through so much," Matilda added quietly.

"That they have, that they have... Mind you, so have we. It seems every other day we hold another funeral. Terribly lugubrious, don't you know? Casts a pall over the lads, even if we're not that fond of our inquisitorial brethren. Poor devils."

Balian registered the dissension. "Then it is in both our interests to get to the bottom of this. We must find the fellow stirring up this mischief before Brother Giuseppe incites a riot."

Brendan's eyes twinkled. "Still, you have to admire their pluck."

"You might admire it less if they tear down your wonderful church brick by brick. When they're angry, the people of Toulouse are capable of anything. They won't care if you are a priest or a freemason, or both."

Brendan looked as if he'd been stabbed. His pride as a builder was wounded. Who would have the audacity to touch his masterwork?

A novice came in and served them wine. They watched him in silence.

When he had left, Brendan said tentatively, "So?"

"We need your help, Brother Brendan," Matilda said.

He looked at her in surprise. "Now, isn't that a grand voice you've got there? Sure, at home they'd be falling all over themselves to hear you sing. Pleading with you, every time you stepped outside. They'd drive you mad."

Matilda blushed slightly.

Balian cleared his throat to redirect the friar's attention. He had grown so accustomed to Matilda's presence that he had forgotten that he was smuggling a woman into a male preserve once again.

"We need information, Brother. And we need it as quickly as possible."

"It's a sticky business, this."

"That it is," Balian said, imitating the friar's singsong. "That it is. Find out about Brother Pons of Bram. Anything you can."

CHAPTER THIRTY-ONE

Tancred and two of his men rode into Avignonet at midday. Immediately they found the victims. Astruguetus of Narbonne and his servants lay in the courtyard before the house, untouched by the frightened townspeople since the attack. The three horsemen of Chantecler exchanged glances of disgust. The dogs of the village had obviously had their way with the corpses the previous night.

At Tancred's command his companions dug graves for the servants, while he unrolled the rabbi's shroud on the ground and carefully placed the body on it. Astruguetus, his face bruised from being beaten, nonetheless looked as serene in death as he had in life. Tancred wrapped the old man in the white cloth, then hefted him up and secured him to a packhorse, which he had tethered to a post outside the stable.

As his men continued their digging, Tancred turned his attention to the house. Although the roof had vanished and all the furnishings had been charred to a cinder, the sturdy stone walls still stood, lonely sentinels on a gentle hillock overlooking the valley. Tancred surveyed the doleful scene, the devastation, the ruination of a life. Why? Astruguetus had been respected throughout the Languedoc, known for probity in his dealings and kindness to strangers. Was it because he was a Jew? That was improbable, for the South was unlike the North. The sons of Abraham had been here since before the days of the Old Romans, everyone knew that. The nonsense he'd heard in the taverns of Paris, especially from students beyond the Rhine, was lurid, sensational stuff, culled from overheated imaginations. At least that was how Balian had put it, during the summer that he and Tancred had spent together at Saint-Germain. If Tancred had any lingering doubts about Judaism, Balian systematically demolished them in their conversations, describing these sons of Abraham as more like a father whose sons, the Christians and the Saracens, fought over his still-vibrant legacy.

Tancred picked his way carefully through the smoldering ruin, mindful of the detailed instructions Judith had given him. In the northeast corner, at the height of a man's knee, he grasped a block of stone, then shrank back in shock; it was still warm from the fire. He whipped off his outer cloak and wrapped it around his two hands. Again, he bent down and grasped the block. This time it became dislodged, falling to the ashes on the earthen floor with a leaden thud.

Tancred squatted down and squinted into the dimness. A large cloth bag lay at the rear of the recess. He reached in and carefully extracted it, fearful of scorching his forearms on the adjacent blocks. At last, it was out, a bit blackened by the heat but still intact.

The bag was secured on a packhorse. He would not examine its contents, obeying a code of knightly conduct drilled into him since boyhood.

By day's end, he was leading his packhorse through the throngs in the narrow streets of the Jewish quarter of Toulouse. As arranged beforehand, the body had been deposited discreetly in a synagogue down a small alleyway leading from the Rue Joutx-Aigues. Now it was time to restore the recovered property to its rightful owner. Tancred raised the knocker at the rabbi's residence.

Judith sat in the same high-backed chair she had occupied the previous day. Her eyes were downcast, her hair covered by a veil. Tancred advanced into the room.

"My lady Judith."

She glanced up. Tancred fell onto one knee before her.

"I have retrieved what you sought."

The rabbi and an elder of the community exchanged glances.

"Thank you, my lord Tancred."

She took what was proffered and loosened the drawstring. First out was a small *châsse* embossed in gold. She turned the key in the lock and opened the lid.

"My jewelry … and my mother's … "

Tears welled in her eyes, the realization that she was an orphan now upon her.

"Please, my friend. We must sit shiva … "

Tancred bowed his head, then stood up.

"I shall return."

She smiled at him through her tears.

CHAPTER THIRTY-TWO

"Thank God I've found you."

The chamberlain had caught up with Balian and Matilda in a street near the Dominican convent.

"Count Raymond wants you at his side immediately. That dreadful fat man is shouting and threatening."

"And which dreadful fat man is that?" Matilda asked, amused.

The chamberlain's demeanor changed instantly.

"Why, the Dominican provincial, my dear creature."

Balian looked at Matilda questioningly. Her color heightened; she flashed a smile.

"Should we not be going to the Narbonne Castle?" she ventured.

The chamberlain and Balian collected themselves and walked off together. Matilda took up the rear, still smiling to herself.

The chamberlain had been right. When Balian arrived in the audience hall, both the count and the friar wore thunderous looks. Brother Martin stood off to the side, his eyes averted.

"You summoned me, m'lord?"

Giuseppe whirled around, then fairly snarled at his host. "I must object, Count Raymond. This man has nothing to say here, he is—"

"My guest, Friar Giuseppe."

The Dominican could barely stifle his disgust.

"Brother Giuseppe," the count said to Balian, "has suggested that the people of Toulouse be subjected to collective punishment for the late murder of the inquisitor."

"The innocent must not be touched, m'lord," the chamber-lain said quickly. "You must ensure the safety of all your subjects. It is your sacred duty."

Balian looked at the young man with growing respect.

"All are complicit. All are guilty." The Dominican whirled round. "You are guilty. All who are not part of the Sacred Body of Christ are guilty."

"Like the Jew, Astruguetus of Narbonne?" Balian asked.

Giuseppe scowled at Balian.

"Like the Jew, like all Jews."

"His daughter survived the raid; she saw his attackers."

"That is none of my concern—"

"And the people of Auriol, hanged by the dozens? Children among them ... Were they guilty?"

Giuseppe turned back to Raymond.

"My lord, the king's seneschal in Carcassonne executed the sentence at my behest. He understood. If the people are to be brought to heel, they must fear divine justice."

Raymond thought for a moment. His lined features seemed weighted down. "Carcassonne is in the Kingdom of France," he said at last. "If the French king wants to treat his subjects that way, then that is his choice. But while I still draw breath, Toulouse stands alone, beholden to no king. And I will not treat my people in such a manner."

There was a prolonged silence.

"You risk excommunication, Count Raymond. Just like your father, you will die an excommunicate, consigned to the eternal flames," Giuseppe said in a matter-of-fact tone. "And your lands will be put under interdict. No masses, no funerals, no baptisms, no sacraments, all your subjects released from obedience to you. I have the ear of the Holy Father. He will grant my petition."

The dread words elicited no rejoinder in the hall. Brother Giuseppe looked around, satisfied. From the corner near Brother Martin a passionate voice broke the silence.

"No. No. No."

Matilda looked up, startled. It was Balian again.

"You are a man of God. Does a man of God kill innocent children? Hang them? Leave them to the crows? *Qual è la sua religione, Frate Giuseppe?*" Balian snapped in Tuscan. "*Chi è il suo Dio?*"

The Dominican drew himself up, extended his arm, and pointed a trembling finger at his accuser.

"You leprous sore on the face of Christendom—"

"I was sent here by King Louis—"

"I don't care if you were sent here by God Almighty."

The fury in the friar's voice seemed to bounce off the stone walls, intensifying, ringing. Matilda looked at Balian in alarm, afraid for him now.

"Have this man arrested at once."

The count contemplated the friar wearily.

"On what charge?"

"Heresy."

Count Raymond sighed in exasperation. "Don't be fanciful."

"I assure you, my lord, fancy has nothing to do with it. You heard him, he asked me who my God was. That's what heretics believe, that there is more than one God."

"Sheer casuistry." Brother Martin stepped forward. "Surely you must recognize that as rhetoric."

"Spare me your schoolman talk. We are not in the lecture halls of Paris; we are in the heartland of sin."

This silenced the Franciscan. Diplomacy seemed not to be a Dominican trait.

"I am no heretic, Brother Giuseppe," Balian said quietly. "My royal mistress would not have called on a heretic to do God's work."

Giuseppe looked thoughtful for a moment, as if he were having misgivings. Balian examined him, uncertain of how he would respond. This Dominican was a will-o'-the-wisp, impossible to pin down.

The friar turned to Count Raymond. "As the provincial of the Order of Friars Preachers in the Languedoc, I have, as is my prerogative, decided to show a modicum of mercy."

Surprised, his listeners awaited.

"I will not demand that a punishment be meted out to the people of Toulouse ... "

The count smiled in relief.

". . . on condition that the heretic here present, Balian of Mallorca, be arrested and brought for incarceration in the prison of the Holy Office."

The Dominican looked at his dismayed audience.

"If he is not brought to the Seilhan House by morning, I will undertake the necessary communications with the Holy Father. And rescind my decision to show clemency."

Satisfied, Giuseppe left the hall.

CHAPTER THIRTY-THREE

The first sleep was long in coming. Balian tossed on his straw, sensing that things had gone terribly awry. Had he been too headstrong, too outspoken? Who was he to speak the truth to the Dominican provincial, one of the most powerful men in the South and one of the most powerful Dominicans anywhere? He, a mere doctor and scholar, with no noble patron or protector. Queen Blanche had designated him a deputy to Brother Martin but had not placed him under royal protection. She was far too clever for that. Had she sent him as a sacrificial lamb, to be slaughtered on the altar of the Dominicans? She knew the Dominicans; she herself was a Castilian, just like Dominic had been. Had she known that Balian, as a man of science, would not be able to hold his tongue faced with the implacable certainty of the Inquisition? And what about Robert de Sorbon, with his fine flatteries and amiable compliments? Had he brought Balian into the matter only to throw him to the wolves, to the hounds of the Lord?

His father's face swam in front of him. Balian saw the lean, weathered countenance, the familiar silver stud in his earlobe. "Remember, my son, we men of learning can go from one land to the next, but we must do it soundlessly. Noise alarms the horses; shouts frighten the dogs. Speak your mind only to the like-minded." He remembered his mother, always seeming to have just arrived in from the fields she loved so much with a fresh spray of flowers to place in the enamel vases embellished with golden calligraphy. Her brown eyes smiled at him from above her veil, her perfume mixed with the scents of the blooms; she ran her olive hand through his dark locks...

A tear ran down his cheek.

He started. A soft hand wiped the tear away. Above him, in the darkness, floated the face of Matilda. She looked concerned, distraught.

"I had to come."

"But it's madness."

She ignored this and lay down on the bed beside him.

"I couldn't stay away, Balian. You will tell me what I must do."

He sighed loudly. He felt her fingers run gently over his brow.

"You should be with a man from your own station in life. Certainly not one doomed to an Inquisition prison!"

He heard a whimper. Was she crying? He turned and sought her face in the half-light. The tears glistened.

"I know, and you know, Balian," she said. "When you held me in the street...we both knew."

"I knew the first night," he said sadly. "In Avignonet."

She stroked his face. "There must be a way," she said, her voice little more than a whisper. "For us."

"Matilda, I am in grave danger. The count has been left no choice—"

"Then flee! I will go with you."

"If I flee, then the people of this city will suffer—"

"Damn you, man." Her voice was raw. "What good will you be to them if you are dead? What good will you be to me?"

A silence fell between them. Matilda placed her hands on Balian's cheeks and drew him closer to her. He could feel her breath on his lips.

The door swung open with a crash. Balian and Matilda sat up abruptly. Count Raymond stood in the threshold, backed by men-at-arms holding blazing torches. There was a look of weary resignation on his features.

"I am sorry, Master Balian, but my first responsibility is to the safety of my people. I cannot let Brother Giuseppe have his way with them."

"Of course. I understand."

Balian got to his feet and held his hands before him.

"I don't think that will be necessary. That Dominican bastard will bind you soon enough."

Matilda stifled a sob, but it was loud enough for Raymond to catch.

"Say your goodbyes here, young man. You...you won't be allowed to visit Balian in that prison. Only his family are allowed."

Raymond tactfully averted his eyes, thinking the two men would embrace. Instead, Balian awkwardly held out his right hand.

"Goodbye, Mathias."

Matilda seized his hand with both of hers and said fiercely, "This is not the end, Balian. It's the beginning."

Raymond nodded in approval. "We shall find a way, Master Balian. This is a battle lost, not a war."

The Count of Toulouse led his charge out of the room. The door closed, leaving Matilda alone in the dimness.

She sank down on the bed and wept. She had made her choice, and now he had been snatched away from her. The decision had come easily once she overcame her fear and recognized the obvious: she belonged to him, and he to her. There was no chance involved, only fate. Why else had her brother fallen ill in Paris and become Balian's friend? Why else had she traveled to meet him? Why else had wise old Alcuin gone along with her wild scheme? The hand of God had been leading her to him all along; even as a young maid she had thrilled to his name, dreamt of meeting him. She remembered those long afternoons in the tower room of Chantecler, contemplating the dovecote far below, wondering when and if he would send word from distant Paris, wondering what he was like, wondering…

And now knowing. She knew what the look in his eyes meant. The troubadours knew, as did she, a woman. He wanted her and she would let him have her. As a lover, a mistress, a wife.

Matilda thought for a moment. An idea began taking shape. She grabbed Balian's traveling bag, then opened the door and walked out toward the night air.

CHAPTER THIRTY-FOUR

Word rocketed through the city like a summer storm. Long before the morning sun had burned off the wisps of mist lingering on the river Garonne, it was known far and wide that the sorcerer sent by the French king had been charged with heresy. Heresy, indeed. More Dominican hypocrisy. That wretched Tuscan, Brother Giuseppe, had taken the good doctor hostage. Balian was a scapegoat, protecting the people of Toulouse from the vengeance of the provincial. If they, the Toulousans, dared free him, there would be hell to pay. If they dared not, then more the shame.

Tancred did not have an opportunity to hear the news. The crack of dawn had brought a messenger boy, one Isaac of Muret, to tell him that the lady Judith demanded his company immediately. She must see him now, without fail.

As he followed the boy through the streets toward the Rue Joutx-Aigues, Tancred could not help but indulge his poetic nature. Yes, the poor girl was in mourning, but she was so beautiful and so in need of consolation that he might be the only man able to ease her pain. True, he was a knight of Christ and she a daughter of Abraham, but were they not just man and woman in the sight of God? And her father was no longer here to protect her.

Isaac expertly inserted the hefty key into the lock on Rabbi Ezra's door and turned it twice widdershins until a loud click was heard. The door swung open to reveal a servant extinguishing the last of the night candles in the hall. In the main room to the left, a few tapers still flickered on a table. Sitting at it, head bent over the vellum pages of a bound leather ledger, was Judith; she had been up all night, the terrible beauty of her cobalt eyes now ringed with darkness, the long mane of black hair running wild down her white linen shift, immodestly exposed to Tancred's gaze. He caught his breath at the sight, then cleared his throat.

She looked up, untroubled by the intimacy.

"These are my father's accounts," she said, holding up the ledger. "We must avenge his murder. If you don't want to join me, I will do it myself."

She pointed to line items preceded by two initials: GF.

Tancred leaned over and looked at the recurring letters, which were always followed by a scrupulous noting of a sum of money. Sometimes two hundred, sometimes five hundred livres.

"I ... I don't understand," he stammered.

"They indicate a man," Judith explained. "GF."

"GF?" Tancred asked, completely baffled.

Judith struggled not to roll her eyes. "Yes, GF. For Giuseppe of Fiesole."

Tancred surveyed the pages with growing incredulity. The sheer frequency of the payments was astounding.

"But why?"

"Our kinsmen in Narbonne and Béziers need protection. This way my father made sure the Dominicans would not harm them."

"That's theft. Forcing somebody to make payments. Threatening them."

"Most of it was to fund Brother Giuseppe's many appetites."

Tancred look at her questioningly, afraid of what he might hear next. She held his gaze, unflinching.

"Boys, girls, whores down by the docks, sailors ... "

Tancred turned aside, as if he could not bear to behold her loveliness and hear her utter these shameful words at the same time. It seemed like a defilement.

"Lord Tancred," she said quietly. "I was not raised like your women. We must know the truth; we must see things as they are. We women of Israel cannot afford to live in a dreamworld."

He turned back to her and ventured a smile. It was so touchingly tentative that she had to smile back, through her anger.

"I understand, Judith. Truly."

She seemed reassured.

"I have done the sums," she said. "All told, Brother Giuseppe took from my father ten thousand three hundred."

"That's outrageous."

"Which is why, when he got the chance, he had my father killed. In the confusion and bloodshed, he saw his chance."

Her head sank into her hands, her eyes closed, as if in pain.

"Even when the French came down here to kill and burn, they did not treat us this way. They left my father alone. They honored their debts, as did the Good Men and the Good Women."

Tancred eyes widened at this casual, familiar mention of the heretics.

"But this ... this Dominican," she said heatedly. "He must not live a week longer."

Her eyes were open now, her head erect. Her dishevelment and state of undress no longer seemed a shared intimacy. She looked like some warrior queen of old. This girl was not what she had seemed at first, a maid who lowered her eyes while filling Tancred's goblet in her father's house. They regarded each other openly, in silence, for a long moment.

"Does Rabbi Ezra know of your intentions?"

"That mouse," Judith spat out. "He scurries between bishop and count, afraid of his own shadow."

Reflexively, Tancred drew himself up to his full height and squared his shoulders. It was as if her womanly disdain called for some response, some show of male strength. She noticed and was not displeased.

"Then we must tell Count Raymond," Tancred said. "He is a man of honor. He will bring this devil to justice, even if he himself has to go to Rome."

"The count is as weak-kneed as the rabbi," Judith said, realizing now that Tancred had not yet heard the news. "Look at what he's done to your poor friend Balian."

CHAPTER THIRTY-FIVE

Brother Giuseppe mounted the sagging stairs of an old town house, clad in a simple dark cloak and shod in sandals. He looked less a Dominican than an itinerant preacher, which was the effect he had desired.

A maidservant greeted him on the landing.

"You are a Good Man? Sent by Peire of Castres?"

Giuseppe nodded.

"My lady's in there."

The Dominican stepped into the sick chamber. Two men stood at a bedside, their felt hats clasped in their hands, their faces grim. On the bed, looking like death itself, lay an ancient woman taking her last labored breaths.

"You are good to have come," said one of the men, bowing.

Giuseppe approached the bed and addressed the green, ghastly face.

"Can you hear me, madam?"

"Yes."

"What do you want of me?"

"I want the consolamentum ... I want to join the Good God," came the whispered reply.

Giuseppe smiled slightly.

"Then you have an Understanding of the Good ... that there is a Good God, and an Evil God?"

"Yes."

Giuseppe glanced sideways to take in the puzzled looks on the two men's faces, then drew himself up to address the dying woman in a formal manner.

"Then you are a confessed heretic. And you will be punished as such."

The two men had scarcely the time to clap their hands over their mouths in horror before Giuseppe was out the door, down the stairs, and in the street.

Awaiting him was an escort of men-at-arms and Dominican friars from the Seilhan House.

He instructed the friars to build a bonfire immediately in the cathedral square, to summon the townspeople to attend. Time was of the essence. The armed men were instructed to arrest the household, the sons and the servants, and imprison them.

The old woman, however, was too ill to be moved from her bed. The bed would have to come with her.

Giuseppe pointed to the horizontal bar jutting out from the topmost gable. If the bed had been winched in, it could also be winched out, this time with the old woman lashed to the bedstead. The men must hurry, for she must not die before meeting the flames.

Pascal emerged from his uncle's bakery, his frock dusted with flour. A messenger had rushed into the shop, saying that everyone was to gather in the cathedral square. Pascal wondered what the reason for such a hasty assembly could possibly be. Although he rarely ventured out, for fear of being identified as a renegade Dominican, Pascal figured there would be safety in numbers. He adjusted his cap more firmly on his head, where the tonsure had almost, but not quite, grown out.

"Pascal. Pascal. It's terrible."

He turned and saw his young cousin Jaume running toward him, breadbasket in hand.

"What? Were you robbed of your *fougasse* money?" Pascal said on seeing the basket empty.

"No, it's Dame Marti. The friars have come for her."

He still didn't understand. Jaume tugged at his sleeve.

"Look. She'll be coming around the corner."

Pascal peered down the street, then gasped. Juddering toward them, balanced on a large barrow, came a bed, to which a groaning, barely conscious woman had been brutally bound. Each jolt of the journey elicited from her a sigh of pain. Dame Marti, the kindly old widow who had long done such good works for the poor. As she passed Pascal on her bed of torment, he crossed himself. To think that he had once willingly joined these friars, assassins all.

Pascal saw that at the head of the curious procession, now restored to his Dominican finery, strode Friar Giuseppe, pastoral staff firmly in hand, his features set in triumph. He kept a lively pace, knowing that Dame Marti's moments were numbered.

They arrived at the cathedral square, its half-timbered housefronts made lurid by a blazing bonfire. Pascal and Jaume joined hundreds of townspeople, herded there from their shops and market streets. Many were puzzled about why they had been summoned at such short notice. As Brother Giuseppe neared the fire, the grisly nature of his intentions became clear, setting off a chorus of whispers.

"It's Dame Marti."

"Has she passed?"

"She is to be burned."

"No, it can't be."

Within what seemed to be a matter of seconds, the barrow had reached the middle of the square, halted, and been relieved of its burden. Four men held the bed aloft, impromptu pallbearers in the service of the Lord.

"Good people of Toulouse. Hearken to my words." Giuseppe's voice carried over the roar of the flames, his face a rictus of malice, his arms gesticulating wildly. "This is the fate that awaits all who cling to the noxious embrace of heresy. And all who defy the Holy Office. Let this be a lesson to you. Abandon your wickedness and watch as this wretch is thrown into Hell!"

He turned and nodded to the men. With a strange and sinister sort of gentleness, they raised the bed even higher and then, on a second nod from Giuseppe, threw the woman and her bed into the flames.

Taking their cue, the Dominicans from the Seilhan House began to chant.

"*Te Deum laudamus, te Dominum confitemur…*"

But they could not drown out the loud groan from the townspeople as they saw the flames licking the bedframe and setting the linens alight. Pascal put his arms around the sobbing Jaume. Soon the acrid smell of burning flesh filled the air. She was being consumed, her cries of agony soundless.

"*Te aeternum Patrem, omnis terra veneratur…*"

The groans and lamentations grew louder. Giuseppe turned his eyes from the blaze and glared at the crowd. The intensity of his gaze could be felt, and heads swiveled in his direction. His malevolence was palpable, his anger real. He brought a forefinger to his lips.

Gradually, the groans and protests petered out into silence. Only the voices of the Dominicans remained, and the whoosh of the fire, belching a pall of black smoke into the noonday air.

CHAPTER THIRTY-SIX

"Matilda! What in God's name ... ?"

The girl stood in the threshold, radiant, looking at her brother in amusement. She had spent the night in Judith's care, first taking a long luxurious sleep in a comfortable bed, then bathing and beautifying in the morning hours and selecting a garment from Judith's wardrobe, a green tunic dress, slit up the front to reveal a richly embroidered bodice. Her hair was concealed by a loose shoulder cape in a different shade of green. She had erased all traces of Mathias and now stood in resplendent beauty.

Tancred glanced from one smiling woman to the other, thunderstruck. They had been spared the summons to the cathedral square for the burning, as the household was Jewish and therefore, in the view of the church, beyond any hope of salvation. Instead, Tancred had listened, aghast, as Judith told him how Balian had been hauled off by Count Raymond and delivered to Friar Giuseppe of Fiesole. The young knight had barely had time to react when, like a homing pigeon from Chantecler, his sister had alighted in the room, embracing him in a mist of sandalwood and rose water. Her green eyes had flashed in triumphant mischief as she disclosed to him that she had been at his side repeatedly, that she had even welcomed him into this house not three days past, disguised as Mathias.

"Then it must have been sorcery, sister, for I would know you anywhere."

"Not," Matilda said gently, "if your eyes were fixed elsewhere."

The color rose in Judith's cheeks at this intimation of the obvious. Tancred opened his mouth as if to speak but said nothing.

"Come, come," Matilda continued, delighted at the effect of her pointing out the truth, "we have other matters to attend to, brother."

"What do you mean?"

"Tancred, you are to accompany me to the Seilhan House of the Inquisition."

"To what end?" he said, surprised yet again.

"To visit my husband."

CHAPTER THIRTY-SEVEN

"Chac-chac-chac-chac." A pause, then: "Chac-chac-chac-chac."

Fatima smiled and went to the window. The magpies had returned.

High up in the great oak tree of the count's gardens, a bird could be seen rearing back its dark head and letting out its raucous cry. Its black tail feather, as long as its body, lifted stiffly in the spring air. The magpie's white breast swelled, its black wing feathers trembling into movement.

"Chac-chac-chac-chac."

Fatima retreated inside for a moment and opened her sewing basket. She took out a shiny bronze button and then placed it on the windowsill. The bird would find it soon enough.

The sun bathed the gardens in a brilliant light. Sparrows bounced around in the dust of the pathways, chirping and pecking at whatever looked edible.

The gleaming button did not escape notice for long. The magpie drew itself to its full height, then launched itself in the air, first hurtling earthward before easing up and ascending at speed to alight on the stone sill. It poked at the button with its black bill, then looked through the open window at Fatima.

"Good day, Mr. Magpie," she said with a smile. "A present for your lady friend."

The bird cocked its head to one side and looked at the girl intently.

"Go on," she continued. "'Tis the season for courtship."

In a flash, the bird had secured the shiny object in its bill and flown to the oak, disappearing behind its green foliage to deliver this gift to his partner in an unseen nest.

Satisfied, Fatima closed the window. Courtship. Mating. This sad city, she thought, could use more of it.

From outside came the cry, "Chac-chac-chac-chac."

CHAPTER THIRTY-EIGHT

The door to the Seilhan House swung open on its hinges, creaking in protest. Within awaited a familiar presence, the red tonsure, the sparkling eyes, the smile of welcome.

"Brother Brendan. What are you doing—"

Red eyebrows shot up.

"I... I mean..." Matilda stopped, defeated.

Brendan gave her an appraising glance, then grinned. "Now, wouldn't I know that voice anywhere. I believe I've met your twin brother. He must be your twin... A fine lad... if a bit... feminine... don't you know?"

Matilda couldn't help laughing. The friar's smile widened.

"And who might this strapping young fellow be?" Brendan asked. "He's a far sight more manly than that Mathias boy."

Matilda looked down to recover herself. "He is my brother. Tancred of Périgueux."

"Now, isn't that grand? Pleasure to meet you Tancred of Périgueux. I'm Brendan of Killiney."

Tancred nodded, less to acknowledge the introduction than to hide his confusion over his sister's familiarity with this strange Dominican.

"And to what do I owe the honor of such distinguished visitors?"

"We are here to see Balian of Mallorca. My husband. I believe immediate family have the right to visit a prisoner."

Brendan clapped his hands together. "So you're his wife today. Bless us and save us. And what might your name be now?"

"Matilda. Of Périgueux."

"Pleased to renew our acquaintance, Matilda of Périgueux," the Dominican said, eyes twinkling. "And pleased to offer you the hospitality of the Holy Office."

With an exaggerated gesture, he motioned for the two to step through the threshold. They walked together down a long stone hallway and out into an inner courtyard, Brendan affably explaining all the while his reason for being there.

"They've all gone to the convent for a great feast, the whole lot of them. To celebrate that fierce business in the square this morning. There'll be no work done on the church today, none at all. You know, I fear they've all lost their heads, or if not their heads, then their hearts. The whole thing is a right scandal ... I'm sure our sainted Dominic must be turning in his grave, or tearing out his hair at his place in Heaven ... Watch your step ... Who'd have believed it, men of God acting like heathens? The brother provincial travels nowhere without his Saracen guards, as if he were the caliph of Christendom. I can't stomach it, I tell you, the fine food from the kitchens would have gone rancid in my mouth. I couldn't bear the thought of staying there and watching their antics, the stench of that poor old soul still hanging in the air and three of our brothers still warm in the ground. I saw my chance, so I said to him, 'Why don't I look after your prisoners while you and the lads enjoy your reward at the table?' And says he, 'Why, that's very generous of you, Brother Brendan.' And so here I am, jailkeeper for the day. And besides, I wanted to look in on"— Brendan paused, holding Matilda in his gaze—"your husband."

Satisfied on seeing her blush, he turned away and unhooked a large set of keys from the rough cord cinching his cassock. As he inserted one into a rusty lock, Tancred and Matilda surveyed the façade of the Inquisition jail. Two cold stories of stone, with a few slits for windows, placed there almost grudgingly.

Once inside the gloom, Brendan grabbed a sputtering torch from a wall sconce and motioned them to follow him. They

STEPHEN O'SHEA

padded down a seemingly endless flight of stairs, their shadowy figures in the flickering light a danse macabre against the chiseled blocks. The prison had been built to last, for God's work would take generations.

They reached a flat surface. Directly ahead of them stood a heavy wooden door surmounted by a formidable array of ironwork.

"Take this."

Brendan thrust the torch into Tancred's hand and then fumbled with his keys. The lock clicked, and he depressed an iron handle.

The door swung open to reveal a windowless, black space, the only sound the scurrying of frightened rats. Matilda gasped in dismay.

Slowly, a bedraggled figure took shape in front of them, shuffling hesitantly, the heavy shackles on his feet clanking.

With surprising swiftness, Brother Brendan squatted down, small mallet in hand, and freed the prisoner from his restraints.

"You have visitors, Master Balian."

Balian squinted into the torchlight, his eyes unaccustomed to the brightness.

"It is your lady wife and her brother."

When Balian's eyes widened in confusion, Brother Brendan let out a whoop.

"Now, isn't the groom always the last to know."

Balian turned to Brendan, perplexed.

"Come forward, my lady," the friar said in explanation.

Matilda stepped through the threshold, her dress rustling on the straw of the floor. Balian's mouth opened in astonishment.

"Is it you?"

"Now, really, Master Balian," Brendan chided. "When a man sees his wife for the first time, does he make a speech?"

142

Balian looked into her eyes. They glistened, said yes. She nodded.

He took a step forward and they kissed. For a long moment.

In the dim light, Brother Brendan beamed while Tancred lowered the torch, amazed at what he was seeing.

CHAPTER THIRTY-NINE

The tankards of beer stood on the table before them. They had emerged from the depths of the dungeon and taken their places in the front chamber of the house, the same room where Balian and Matilda had watched helplessly as Brother Hildebrand of Alsace expired in a torrent of blood. Matilda noticed a dull brown stain on the floorboards in the corner, where she had found the glittering florin.

"Aren't you taking a chance bringing Balian into the light?" Tancred asked of Brendan as he reentered the room bearing a small cask.

"Why, I am putting him to the question, am I not? The way we do at home."

He lifted the mug.

"Your health!"

Smiling, they accepted the toast and drank. Matilda made a face.

"Come, come, my lady," Brendan reproved. "It may not be sweet mother's milk, but it will nourish you through a long night…especially if your husband is languishing far from the comfort of your arms."

Tancred looked pleased, judging their host a boon companion. "Well said, my good friar." He raised his tankard again, as did the Dominican. The two drained their cups in one long draft.

"Pardon me, sirs," Matilda interrupted. "Is this to be a drinking party?"

But Brendan was already refilling their mugs from his cask. "Not to worry, m'lady," he said as he occupied himself. "They'll all be in their cups at the convent before long. Mark my words. Lauds will be a lonely vigil at dawn. They'll all be snoring and grunting like lords... Begging your pardon, my lord Tancred..."

Balian ignored the banter, taking a careful sip, then placing the cup back down.

"Brother Brendan, what have you found out about Pons of Bram? Have there been any unusual visitors among you?"

"That there has, that there has."

The three waited in expectant silence.

"You lot."

Balian shook his head as the friar laughed.

"Anyone who might have been able to go in and out of this house undetected?" Balian continued. "Who could have gone to Auriol and Carcassonne? Someone with freedom of movement? A friar from Lombardy? Or Pons. Does he have brothers?"

Brendan's face became grave. "Why do you suspect someone from within the order?"

"Who else?"

"Could be anyone. Lord knows the inquisitors are roundly hated by the people. I'm not too fond of them myself."

Brendan took another deep draft.

"Will you let Balian go free?" Matilda's voice was pleading.

"Now, you know I can't do that, miss. I mean madam. There'd be hell to pay. With Balian gone, Giuseppe's tonsure would spin like a top. He'd go after anyone in reach. The merchants, the peasants, the Jews, anyone."

"The Jews would not go down without a fight," Tancred said. He related what he had seen in Astruguetus' ledgers, what he had learned from Judith of Giuseppe's depravity. Both Balian and Brendan listened thoughtfully.

"So the girl has got it in for Brother Giuseppe?" Brendan mused.

Tancred realized his indiscretion. "That she hates him is true. But Judith is a strong woman, like many of her Israelite sisters... and she is intelligent. She would not do anything to put her community in danger."

"In further danger," Matilda corrected.

"Do you think she's contemplating violence?" Balian asked, incredulous.

Tancred searched his friend's eyes, beseeching him not to ask such things. Balian saw the look, understood.

"Of course she can't be," Balian said, answering his own question. "I knew her father well, as did my father. He was a man of peace."

Brother Brendan placidly took in this exchange, satisfied that his new friends kept nothing from him.

"I'm afraid, Master Balian, that it is time for me to put you back in the hole," he said gently.

"But you can't," Matilda said. "That's sending him to his death. We all know that Brother Giuseppe is a murderer. He's already murdered poor Astruguetus. And the dozens in Carcassonne. What's to stop him from killing our Balian?"

"All of Toulouse is watching, Matilda," Tancred said.

"Brother, don't be such a fool. These men, these Dominicans, they have no decency. Are they not drinking themselves silly at this moment, all because they burned some poor old woman on her deathbed? They fear nothing. They know nothing. Nothing but fear and fire and death."

"I'm assuming," Brendan said, "that you mean present company excepted, my dear—"

A loud knock sounded from the door downstairs.

"Sweet Mother of Jesus!" Brendan exclaimed. "You stay here, you three, and not a peep out of you."

He rushed out of the room and could be heard pounding down the stairs.

CHAPTER FORTY

The three looked at one another complicitly.

"Do we overpower him?" Tancred said quietly.

Balian's face clouded. "He's a good man."

"But he's a Dominican," came the reply.

"We have no need of your brawn, Tancred," Matilda said in a matter-of-fact tone, unlacing the top of her bodice. "Balian, I took the liberty of going through your things last night. Brought them to the house where Judith is staying."

She extracted a small vial from her bosom and slipped off the leather cord from which it had been suspended around her neck.

"Valerian?" Balian asked.

"With two drops of essence of hemlock."

"How long?"

"He'll be out till matins."

"Alcuin did teach you well," Balian said.

Tancred watched in wonder as his sister emptied the contents of the vial into Brendan's tankard. She grasped it, swirled around the liquid in the ale, and had just placed it back on the table when the friar appeared in the threshold.

"We have a visitor of mark," he said, visibly shaken.

Count Raymond of Toulouse strode into the room. The three sprang to their feet.

Raymond looked at the trio, puzzled. He had not expected to burst in on a party.

"Tancred of Périgueux, m'lord. At your service."

STEPHEN O'SHEA

Raymond acknowledged the reverence, then paused to search his memory. "Of Périgueux?... Périgueux... Yes, a fine old family... Your seat is at Chantecler, no?... I knew your grandmother Sibilia... Now, there was a beauty in her day..."

The count caught himself. The implication had been unmissable. As if to prolong his embarrassment, he then turned toward Matilda, whose curtsying afforded him a generous view of her half-opened bodice. He couldn't help looking.

"This is Matilda, my sister," Tancred explained.

"And my wife," Balian added.

Raymond turned to Balian, then saw that he was serious. The count exploded with a laugh. "Your wife, Master Balian. Your wife? Why, man, not three nights past when you supped at my table, you told me that you had no wife. Will you have me doubt your word?"

"We have just been wed," Matilda said quickly. "By... by Brother Brendan."

All eyes turned to the Dominican, who seemed to relish the attention. He met Matilda's gaze of supplication with a certain amusement.

"Wed them?" he said at last, as if to himself, "So I did... Yes, indeed... Man and wife..."

Matilda let out her breath. The news was met with silent skepticism. Raymond looked back at Matilda with studied admiration, as if remembering her grandmother.

He then addressed Tancred. "Your sister is of a great family. Yet she has been wed to someone far beneath her station."

"With my blessing," Tancred said. "I am the head of the family."

"I see, I see," the count mused. "Then you are a very lucky man, Master Balian."

"I grant you that, my lord," Balian replied.

"Promised a fair bedmate and"—the count appraised the swell of Matilda's hips brazenly—"a brace of strong sons, I daresay."

148

Matilda held his gaze, eyes flashing.

"Sons? What sons? My Balian will die here. Betrayed by his betters." She let her words of accusation hang in the air. "But if he is to die here, sent to this hell by the cowardice of others, then at least let him die in the knowledge that he has a lady wife who loves him, and will always love him." Matilda grasped Balian's hand and laid an ardent kiss on it.

No one spoke. All skepticism had evaporated.

"My lady," Raymond said, chastened. "This is not a time for despair." He bowed deeply to her, which Matilda acknowledged, serene now in her rights as a noblewoman. "No, dear Matilda of Périgueux, it is a time for celebration."

The count drew himself up to his full height and turned to Brendan. "My good friar, fetch me a tankard so that we may drink to these nuptials. A man of great wisdom united to"—Raymond inclined his leonine head toward Matilda—"a woman of great spirit. I know not the customs of your country, friar, but a union such as this cries out for merriment."

"In my country," Brendan said, leaving the room, "we have no need of an excuse."

Raymond motioned for the three to regain their seats. They obeyed, sensing that something had changed in his demeanor.

He looked at Balian thoughtfully. "My son, I sent the friar out because I wanted a moment with you," he began. "I take it your lady wife and your friend, or rather your kinsman now, are privy to your counsel."

"They are," Balian replied, sharing a complicit smile with Tancred.

Raymond paused, went over to the window to look out at the day's failing light. He rubbed his chin with a hand, then collected himself and returned to them.

"I came here to beg your forgiveness for my actions."

Tancred, Matilda, and Balian exchanged glances of astonishment. This was not how the mighty addressed the mean.

"It was unworthy of my lineage, of my forebears, of my father. It was … as you have so rightly said, Lady Matilda, cowardly … I know that I have but few seasons left on this earth, but I will not sully my remaining days—"

Brother Brendan returned, a tankard for the count in hand. As the others fell silent, he unstopped the small wooden cask and set about filling the cups to the brim.

"There, now," he said.

He grasped the handle of his tankard and raised it in the air.

"My God, but you're terribly slow. By the time you've raised your cups we'll be drinking to the memory of the newlyweds."

Raymond smiled broadly and seized his cup, as did the others.

"To Master Balian and Mistress Matilda. To the power of love," he said ceremoniously.

"And in my country," Tancred added, "we drain the cup to the dregs. All in one go."

"All in one go," Balian repeated pointedly.

A curious scene unfolded, Count Raymond standing, his head inclined backward, draining his cup, with Brendan and the others, seated at the long table, doing likewise.

The tankards were banged back down on the table, making a hollow sound. Matilda wiped her lips.

"And now, my good friar," Raymond said, "my men-at-arms and Balian's French sergeants are in the street. It is my intention to bring the newlyweds to the castle for a wedding banquet, whether you like it or not."

"The use of force, my lord," Matilda said sweetly, "will not be necessary."

Brendan looked at her, suddenly feeling a bit woozy.

CHAPTER FORTY-ONE

The Languedoc spread out before them in the sunlight, a rumpled blanket of hillocks stitched with stands of cypress trees separating squares of brown loam. Balian spurred his horse north, toward the dark outline of the Black Mountain. Beside him rode Matilda, her pale blue riding outfit snapping in the warm spring breeze. She paused, then said, "I don't know why, Balian, but I see you now as a boy."

He looked back at her, puzzled. "I can assure you, I am a man now."

She smiled. "I'll be the judge of that."

They rode on in silence.

Balian turned to her. "What else do you see, Matilda? What does your gift tell you about our murderer?"

After a moment, she said, "I see red."

"No white and black this time?"

"It's not the same. Not the same red." She paused, searching for a word. "More like terra cotta."

Balian snorted. "Well, that would suggest every town in the Languedoc. Perhaps Brother Pons' town, Bram, is the reddest of the lot."

He received a shrug in reply.

A peasant digging in a distant field looked up and observed them crest the ridge, a lord and his lady moving smartly over the land, followed by an armed escort. No banner flew, so there was no telling who they were or whence they came.

Slipping out of Toulouse had not been difficult, especially as Count Raymond had been their accomplice. While the Dominicans slept soundly in their convent and Brother Brendan lay drugged at the Seilhan House, Balian and Matilda had packed their provisions and saddled their mounts, rested after a few idle days in the stables of the Narbonne Castle. It had been decided that six of the French sergeants would accompany them and that the other six would remain behind to protect Brother Martin— and that Tancred and the men of Chantecler would also stay in the city to deal with Brother Giuseppe's reaction to Balian's escape. They, and the count's men, would have to ensure that the Dominican provincial, who would no doubt be furious, did not overstep the bounds of the reasonable, if such a thing were possible when dealing with a zealot. Tancred had willingly volunteered for the delicate job, citing his concern for the Jews, who often were the first to feel the anger of the great and the powerful. Matilda had grinned when her brother said this, knowing that he was concerned most with one particularly lovely Jew.

They reached Auriol-Cabardès in the late afternoon. A few songbirds greeted them, signs of the spring that had emblazoned the mountain with wildflowers. Balian dismounted and made his way down the sole street of the hamlet, a muddy affair barely wide enough for two men abreast. The doors to the thatched huts swung listlessly on their wooden hinges, neglected and unused. Balian peered through one threshold, seeing the cold ashes of a long-dead fire and a crude straw crib with no squalling occupant. A few wooden utensils hung silently on their hooks.

He left the stillness of the street to thread his way between two houses and head down the slope to the fence enclosing a pasture. He hopped up on a stile for a better view, then, alarmed at what he saw, jumped down into the field and emitted a loud yell and clapped his hands together. The dozen or so vultures at work on carrion looked up at him, appraising the danger. With a sullen flapping of wings, they took to the sky and floated far above the field, circling covetously.

Not ten yards away from Balian lay a ewe, bleating miserably, its fleece soaked red. Balian knelt beside it, took a dirk from his waistband, and slit the poor creature's throat. There was a slight hissing sound, then silence.

Balian stood up and surveyed the pasture. With the shepherds gone, the wolves of the mountain had had a feast, not bothering even to finish off their prey, so great was the bounty. Lambs to the slaughter, just like their caretakers, hanged by the dozens before the ramparts of Carcassonne. Balian could make out more animals in the middle distance, in varying stages of distress and mutilation. He stepped forward, dirk in hand, ready to continue the dread business of mercy killing. It occurred to him that he had been trained to save life, to heal, yet here in this land blighted by hatred and suspicion, he was now forced to mete out death. He would have to tell the men to be careful because the wolves would be back. Though they would not be ravenous, they would be numerous, and therein lay the danger.

"Balian!"

Matilda's voice. He turned and saw her standing atop the stile.

"Balian, we've found someone."

His look must have been uncomprehending, for she began to gesture for him to come quickly.

"Someone from the village. In the chapel."

CHAPTER FORTY-TWO

The old man had a kindly look, his eyes sparkling even in the gloom of the small nave. The garment hanging from his gaunt frame had once been white, but wind and sun had weathered it to a dull gray. His grizzled skull was of the same color.

Balian studied the lined face and came to a conclusion.

"*Salaam alaikum,*" he said.

The man's face widened into a grin of delight.

"You're saying he's a Saracen?" Matilda said to Balian.

The stranger turned to Matilda, executed a swift bow, and replied, "I know not the meaning of that word, my lady. But, yes, I first saw life in al-Andalus."

His accent in Occitan was thick, almost impenetrable.

"But what are you doing here?"

He tilted his head, as if surprised at the young woman's forwardness.

"This is my home. It is where I have lived for many long years."

"But how? What is your trade?"

He looked at Matilda thoughtfully, then made a decision.

"I am a seer, madam. I help the villagers. If a woman is barren she comes to me. If she is with child she comes to me. If a child is ill, or ill formed, it is brought to me. I tell husbands when is the best time to plant their seed in their wives, if they want children, or if they do not. I can see by the sun if the rains are coming, if the wind carries snow, if it is time to harvest the grapes or shear the sheep." He stopped, satisfied that he had explained himself fully.

Matilda appraised him with newfound respect.

"And the people of Auriol support you?"

"I ask for little. And there are many other villages I serve. Everyone on the mountain knows me."

"Even the priests?"

He smiled serenely. "I help them too. Many priests do not want their womenfolk to bear the children they carry in their womb. For fear of scandal. I can help there too," he concluded.

"You are ... an angel maker?" Matilda asked softly.

The old man nodded, serene as ever. "At your service."

Matilda flinched and drew away. Instinctively, she took Balian's arm. "I have no need of your services."

Maddeningly, the old man nodded, as if he understood everything about her. Balian could feel her stiffen beside him.

"And how is it that you speak the language of the Prophet, blessed be his name?" the old man asked in Arabic.

Balian responded in kind. "I grew up in a land of Islam. Mallorca. I am Balian of Mallorca."

The man clapped his hands together. "Mallorca," he said in Arabic. "The Green Jewel of the White Sea! I knew it well as a young man. My wife, God give her peace, was from Mallorca. We spent a few brief years, too brief, on the islands. Then she was gone." His look was far off, as he remembered a happy past.

"Who controlled the island when you were there? The emir, or the King of Aragon?"

"Good God, man. The emir, of course. I knew him too. A wise old man and a good ruler of men."

"My father served him," Balian said. "As physician. Arnaud of Mallorca. Perhaps you knew him?"

The old man stopped, as if thunderstruck.

"Your name again?"

"Balian."

"Blessed be the Lord. But I knew you when you were a little boy. Do you remember? I am Ibrahim ibn Abdullah, of Sevilla."

Balian searched his memory. "Yes! You always had almond candy for me. You were ... you were a trader."

"Come here, my boy." The old man opened his arms, and Balian stepped forward and accepted the embrace.

Matilda looked on in bemusement, having no idea what had just transpired. Sensing this, Balian turned to her and said, "This is Ibrahim. He was a friend of my father's. I knew him when I was a child."

Matilda's eyes flashed triumphantly. "You mean you knew him when you were a *boy*."

Balian nodded in admiration. "Now we need only find out about the terra cotta you see."

"And this is your wife?" Ibrahim said in Occitan.

"Yes," Balian said. Saying this was becoming very easy.

Matilda smiled. "I am Matilda of Périgueux," she said simply, performing a small curtsy. Ibrahim bowed his head as if to protect his eyes from the incandescence of her beauty.

"I am honored, my lady," he said in a voice thick with emotion. "And I am pleased to see our boy has been so lucky."

CHAPTER FORTY-THREE

They sat in the main room of the biggest of the vacated houses, a fire blazing in the central hearth. The sergeants had butchered a few of the sheep, and now large slabs of mutton swam in a bubbling cauldron hanging just above the flames. Balian had added herbs so that the stew would not be blandly French.

Their faces flickered in the firelight, earnest and convivial. Balian and Matilda pressed together on a low bench; Ibrahim sat comfortably on the straw-strewn floor, legs crossed.

"What do you know about the murder?" Balian asked at last.

"Very little."

"Did you see anything?"

"Only the victim. And the murderer."

The couple laughed out loud together.

"That is 'very little'? You said you were a seer," Matilda exclaimed, "not a jester."

Ibrahim directed an avuncular look at her.

"One may see many things, lady, but not see much. There are Franks who have gone beyond the sea to Palestine and returned as if they had seen nothing."

"Come, come, my friend," Balian said with a trace of impatience. "We are not in al-Andalus now. We are in the land of the infidel, where we do not speak in riddles."

The old man's face creased into a smile.

"You have been here too many years, my Balian."

"As have you, Ibrahim."

Matilda sensed the deadlock. She leaned forward, her face just a few inches from the old man's, and whispered, "So what did you see?"

Few could resist such an entreaty from a lady of Matilda's charm, and the old man was not among them. He straightened up slightly and began his story.

"On that day I was staying in a small cave near here. I have many such places scattered about the mountain, and people leave their offerings there; sometimes they wait for days until I come to a certain place so that they can make a request of me."

Balian thought of his residence at Saint-Germain-des-Prés. There, patients came to him; he did not travel, as Ibrahim did, to find those in need of care.

"From that place, there is a fine perspective of the slope of the mountain. I can see which fields are blooming, where the birds are gathering, and who is coming and going to the villages."

Matilda smiled encouragingly.

"I like this particular place. The view is commanding, spiritual even. I have heard said that the Good Men and Good Women claim that Creation is evil, that a bad God is responsible for all that we can see and touch. I cannot disagree more. There is such beauty around us; we need only stop for a moment and let the worries of the world float away. It is then that we see how beautiful our world is. It can only be the Creation of a loving God."

"Ibrahim?" Matilda said gently.

"Yes, my dear?"

"The murder?"

The old man laughed briefly. "I realize that a hermit's existence can make one talkative. I implore your indulgence."

The two on the bench looked at him expectantly.

"Well then. I saw the poor fellow on his way up to the village. An imam—"

"An inquisitor," Balian interjected.

"Yes, an inquisitor. From the looks of him he seemed not to have eaten well in at least twelve months. There was a pallor to his face; his movements were leaden for one so young. I felt sorry for him, as if the tenor of his thoughts must weigh him down. Or perhaps he'd had a premonition of what awaited him here, in Auriol. It is not uncommon, you know, for the holy among us to foretell the future. I myself—"

Matilda cleared her throat.

"Yes, yes… In any case, I had a clear view of him and his men. They were not fifty paces away, on the track leading from Montolieu up toward the village. My shelter is well concealed, for those who do not know its location. I can see but not be seen, if I so choose. You understand?"

Matilda nodded out of politeness.

"I did not then know the nature of his errand, but I thought it odd such an important retinue should be visiting my humble friends in Auriol. We do not usually see lowland people up here. It's as if they are afraid of us."

Ibrahim stopped, as if to collect his thoughts. But no, his face showed no sign of further reflection, just its customary serenity, as if he were ready to drift off to sleep. A long silence descended upon them, the only sounds the spitting of the fire and the bubbling of the pot. Matilda got to her feet and grabbed a ladle hanging from its hook to dole out the stew into small earthenware bowls. Spoons were soon found and the men took out their knives to cut the large cubes of meat. Ibrahim ate his portion with animated pleasure, slurping from his bowl like a famished dog finally given its due.

Matilda looked over to Balian as if to say that it was a pity that the old man did not put as much effort into his storytelling.

"Ibrahim," Balian began gently. "I have told you why I have been sent here from Paris. To find out who is killing the inquisitors, and to put a stop to it before there is rebellion."

The old man's spoon paused on its way to his mouth.

STEPHEN O'SHEA

"It is vitally important that I find this out. And, as far as I know, you are the only witness. You said earlier that you saw both the victim and the murderer. You have told us about the poor friar but not about his assailant. We believe it to be another Dominican, From the town of Bram. When and where did you see him?"

Ibrahim placed his bowl on the floor. He rubbed his chin with a gnarled hand.

"It was very late. The time of the second sleep. The time when none but the owls keep watch. But then came the sound of hooves close by, pounding the dry earth, echoing in the darkness. I rose and saw in the moonlight a rider racing down the slope as if pursued by the devil himself. It had to be the murderer—with all the brigands abroad, no one else would chance a night ride alone."

"Could you make it out who it was? A knight? A friar?"

"He wore a hooded cape, so I could not tell."

Balian frowned.

"But he was not from here. A Frank, perhaps, or even a Teuton."

Balian frowned again. Brother Pons of Bram was a man of the South. But he was not ready to give up his suspicions. "Was he tall?"

"Yes, but his horse was not of the type used by the men of Languedoc. It was smallish … "

"A hobby?"

"Yes, not the usual mount at all. Small and swift."

"The men of al-Andalus have small mounts, too."

"But they ride them differently. There is no telling where the rider ends and the horse begins, so fluid is their horsemanship. You know that, Balian. The Franks sit atop their mounts; they command their horses; they do not ride with them as we do."

Balian nodded thoughtfully.

"It is true what you say … But is there anything else you can tell us about the rider?"

160

Ibrahim paused.

"I am not certain of this ... but not far from my place of concealment is the point where the riding path divides into a fork. To the left is the way to Carcassonne; to the right, the way to Toulouse. I'd say from the sound of the hoofbeats that horse and rider took the direction toward Toulouse."

That would square with the actions of Pons. He had been in Toulouse for the third murder.

Ibrahim took his bowl from the floor and began to eat once more. He was no longer with them.

"That is not much to go on," Matilda said quietly.

"It is something," Balian said, wiping his mouth with a cloth. "And that is better than nothing."

"Master Balian?"

Jean-Paul, the leader of the French sergeants, hovered above them.

"We have found lodging suitable for you and your lady wife. I have personally seen to its arrangements."

"Thank you, Jean-Paul. That is most kind of you."

Balian avoided looking at Matilda.

"The hour grows late, sir. If you were to retire now, the guards outside could take their place at the repast."

"Of course, of course. You must be off," Ibrahim cried out. "The men must be fed, the fire must be tended. And you, dear Balian, have another sort of fire to tend."

Jean-Paul cleared his throat to stifle a laugh.

Balian and Matilda rose. He felt her hand take his.

"Good night, Ibrahim."

The two left the house and went out into the darkness of the village street, Jean-Paul leading them under a vault of blameless stars toward their wedding bed.

CHAPTER FORTY-FOUR

A humble but comfortable dwelling. A low fire burned in the hearth carved into a wall. Opposite the fireplace, across the room, stood a hollowed-out rock that served as a sink. The French had thoughtfully filled it with fresh well water so that the two might wash off some of the dust from the day's long journey.

Balian poked at the fire nervously as Matilda splashed at the makeshift sink. He had his back to her.

"So, the culprit may have been a man of the North," Balian said absently. "But then how do we explain the florin?"

"Perhaps it was obtained at a fair in Champagne. The Tuscans go there every year. And perhaps there is more than one killer."

"And what about the hobby?" he continued as if not hearing her. "A rouncy or a palfrey is more common north of the Loire. That's what Jean-Paul and his men ride."

Over his right shoulder he heard the rustle of fabric, of clothes being removed, then a further rustle of a blanket on the straw of the bed.

"Balian?"

"I think I'll have a wash."

Without looking at the bed, he crossed the room and plunged his hands in the water. He moistened the stubble on his chin, loosened his doublet, and scrubbed the matted hair on his chest. To his left, on a wicker stool, lay Matilda's riding outfit, carefully folded. He closed his eyes for a long moment.

"Balian?"

He leaned on the sink, perfectly still. A vine cutting in the hearth crackled as it was tickled by the flames.

"Come to me now."

He caught his breath.

"You ... you said on that very first night that you had not come here for me to take your maidenhead."

"That was before we were wed."

He bowed his head, stared into the clouded water. "But we are not wed, Matilda."

"Tell that to the world, to Brother Brendan, to Count Raymond, to Jean-Paul, to my brother ... "

"But that does not change the fact that we have not been wed."

"I need no priest to bless us, no ceremony. All their sacraments are frauds. There is no God meddling in our business here on earth."

"Now you're the one who sounds like a heretic."

"I don't care."

He trembled slightly in the ensuing silence. He heard another rustling, then from behind him the sound of soft footfalls on the earthen floor.

"Turn around, Balian. Behold what is yours."

He turned slowly in the dimness. The first thing he saw were her eyes, glowing, her lips, half-opened, in a slight smile of invitation. She took his hands and placed them on the bare swell of her hips, cool and smooth to the touch. He looked down, saw a small hemp pouch hanging between her snow-white breasts.

"Herbs," she whispered. "So that I will not be with child."

"Alcuin?"

She nodded, then stepped back. Her form stood illumined in the flickering light, her pale skin flowing like a wave on the surface of the sea. Matilda felt his gaze devouring her and smiled.

"Now, man," she said evenly.

Balian could feel the blood pounding in his temples. He stepped forward and kissed her. He could hear the catch in her breathing as her hand gripped his head to press his lips harder onto hers. Against him, writhing, was her soft nakedness, pushing forward, impressing itself against him, insistent, probing.

A low moan escaped her.

Clang. Clang. Clang. From outside came the sound of a stick striking metal.

Balian and Matilda stopped, looked at each other in surprise.

"May you live long and may your children be many. *Inshallah*." The accent was unmistakable.

A burst of low, lewd laughter, then more banging of pots. If this was their wedding night, then they deserved a charivari.

"May you live long." A deep, disordered chorus of male voices and laughter, this time in French.

The racket subsided as the men outside gradually filed away.

But then one final voice, Jean-Paul's, faint in the distance, "May you live long, Master Balian … and Lady Mathias!"

Another gale of laughter, then, at last, stillness.

Balian looked into Matilda's eyes, bright with laughter. She took her place on the bed and said, "Now, Balian, come to your Lady Mathias."

CHAPTER FORTY-FIVE

For several days Brother Giuseppe failed to reappear, leaving the city seething with rumor. He had been seen down by the Garonne, leering at the washerwomen. No, the provincial was still in the convent, disporting himself with his favorite novice. Nonsense, he had left the city to find reinforcements in Narbonne and Carcassonne. Or, best yet, the hated Giuseppe was stone-cold dead, felled by a pestilence visited upon him by a wrathful God.

It was a disappointment of sorts when the summons to the cathedral square was issued. All were to assemble to hear the friar preach a sermon. Each household was to send one member to listen to what the great Dominican had to say, with no exceptions—not even the Jews this time.

Tancred escorted Judith to the expanse in front of Saint-Stephen's. A makeshift stage had been erected in front of the old Romanesque porch of the cathedral, mercifully free of nooses and other instruments of torment.

"You will know him when you see him," Tancred whispered to Judith. She nodded grimly, her coal-black mourning veil covering her even darker mane of raven hair.

He looked about the crowd, tense with anticipation, chattering excitedly, as if about to witness a bearbaiting or a cockfight. Standing aloof toward the rear, wearing his customary dour expression, loomed the tall figure of Brother Martin, surrounded by a sea of brown Franciscan habits. A contingent of French sergeants stood behind them, elbowing one another whenever a pretty woman came into view. Above them, in the upper window of a town house, Tancred could make out the figure of Count Raymond pensively looking down at his subjects, his eyes narrowed. The dwelling was no doubt the house of one of his many mistresses, thoughtfully lent to him by the cuckold who owned it. Behind him stood an older woman in colorful clothing. Tancred knew that she had to be Garsenda of Castelnou, the count's famed *trobairitz*. She would listen carefully to what Brother Giuseppe had to say, perhaps turn it into a *sirvente*, a satire for Raymond's amusement.

To the other side stood a contingent of Dominicans, their black-and-white clothing standing out from the motley colors of the townspeople. He spotted the red hair of one of them, then recognized Brother Brendan. Their eyes met, and to Tancred's dismay, the Dominican moved toward him, the crowd respectfully parting to ease his passage. In no time the two stood face-to-face. The Gael's pale blue eyes bored into Tancred with a wholly unnerving ferocity, but the rest of his demeanor suggested nothing other than geniality.

"You know, Tancred of Périgueux, I think we are due for another round or two. Let no man say that Brendan of Killiney cannot hold his drink."

He smiled, but his eyes remained fiery.

"Nothing would give me more pleasure, my brother."

"I received quite a tongue-lashing from Brother Giuseppe, as you might imagine. Oh, the fellow is something of a hothead, don't you know, never one to miss an opportunity to pour out some venom. I'm still smarting at the memory of it. He's a fierce one, our friend."

"He is not our friend."

A woman's voice, low and adamantine.

"But I'm forgetting my manners. My apologies, dear lady. And who might your companion be, Lord Tancred?"

"Judith. Judith of Narbonne."

"Ah, I see ... My respects ... But, my fair creature, why all the black? Surely you can't be already widowed at such a tender age?"

"Orphaned," Judith said flatly.

"She is the daughter of Astruguetus of Narbonne."

"A fine man. I knew him well. I'm sorry for your loss. He helped underwrite the costs of constructing our new church."

Tancred could feel Judith stiffen beside him.

"He was murdered," she continued in her curious flat tone. "By the Dominicans."

"You don't say."

"Yes, I do." Her voice had lost its neutrality. "You're all murderers. Every last one of you."

Tancred turned in alarm to see if anyone had heard. Both Brendan and he had felt the passion in her accusation. He saw one young man nodding vigorously nearby, a baker by the look of his whitened apron.

"They are all murderers," Pascal said loudly to them. Judith nodded.

Brendan appraised the young woman in black, noticed her unconquerable cobalt eyes directed at him.

"My dear lady," he said, the beginnings of a smile forming on his lips. "Be careful what you wish for."

Raising his hand to bless them, then thinking the better of it, he walked off through the crowd to rejoin his fellow friars.

"Judith," Tancred said once the friar was out of earshot, "you must be more temperate. These men are dangerous. They are loyal to no one but themselves and their order."

"I don't care," she replied calmly.

CHAPTER FORTY-SIX

Judith and Tancred stood in silence, for the first time awkward together. In an uncanny echo of their private contretemps, a hush fell over the men of Chantecler behind them, who hitherto had been loudly enjoying the hustle and bustle of the townspeople, trading japes with the merchants and their wives and fending off teases about being country bumpkins.

A figure mounted the steps to the stage, a young cleric bearing, with difficulty, a heavy wooden armchair. Amid muffled merriment from the onlookers, he struggled to heave the chair into place. That being done, sweating, he climbed back down the steps.

Within moments, an aged form, weighed down by the regalia of his office, mounted the steps, one arm unsteadily bearing the crozier, the other supported by the same young cleric. Bishop Ivo of Reims, tottering from his four-score years, executed a half-hearted blessing of the crowd, then sank down into the chair, exhausted. Many in the assembly crossed themselves; many did not. A stony silence ensued.

"I thought he was dead," a voice shouted out. A wave of tittering rippled through the crowd. Bishop Ivo, from faraway Reims in the North, had been appointed to the see during the days of the French terror and, as a result, was almost universally hated. The animus was mutual, for the old prelate had never bothered to learn the language or customs of his parishioners.

Brother Giuseppe, sure of step and with surprising vigor for a man carrying extra pounds, followed the bishop onto the stage.

He stood, hands on hips, surveying the crowd malevolently. No blessing was proffered, and none was expected. There was a collective intake of breath.

"People of Toulouse!" the friar shouted. "Men, women, children. Sinners all. Wretched sinners. Fallen Christians. Leprous heretics. Filthy Jews. Heed my words. Heed my words."

He fell silent. Judith's hand found Tancred's and squeezed it tightly.

"As of late there has been a shameful return to the old ways in this city. Not thirty years ago, the Christian King Philip of France and the sainted Holy Father Innocent sent an army here to teach you a lesson, to show you the error of your ways. But you have returned to them."

Giuseppe began pacing the stage, as if to make sure that everyone assembled felt the sting of his address.

"But there can be no returning, do you understand? There is but one way, the way and the truth and the life. So quoth our Savior, yet why is it that you will not listen?"

Tancred looked down and dug at a cobble absently with his left foot. Must it always be like this? Reproaches? Threats? Anger? He thought fondly of his harp, lying unused in his baggage at the Franciscan convent, an instrument of love and of praise deployed to bring forth in the breast of man and woman the noblest of sentiments. Yet beside him stood the fairest maiden of Creation, forced to endure this injury of the basest kind.

He could sense similar distress among his neighbors. A few cowed souls crossed themselves repeatedly, desperately, intoning half-whispered prayers and abjectly begging forgiveness. But a great many faces had darkened, as Giuseppe's harangue reached new depths of vituperation. They did not feel so sullied, so diabolical. They had been living their lives in peace, until these black crows descended on their city with their Holy Office and their insistence on fear and obedience. Tancred noticed the baker nearby, his fists now clenched in anger.

Giuseppe had reached his peroration, and none among the educated few expected it to inspire enthusiasm.

"The Holy Father, in his wisdom, has anathematized Count Raymond Saint-Gilles of Toulouse. From this moment on he is an excommunicate. He is to be denied the embrace of our Holy Mother the Church, and all of his subjects are henceforth released from any allegiance to him. He is a pariah, cast out from Christendom."

Raymond frowned from his window. His father had endured the same indignity for many years.

"And you, sinners of Toulouse, until you have delivered up all the heretics among you, including the wretched Balian of Mallorca, late of this city and escaped from our custody through your active complicity … your city is now under interdict. You are all, as of now, expelled from the Mystical Body of Christ. You are hereby deprived of the comforts of the Confession, the Holy Eucharist, and all the sacraments. You are now at risk of eternal damnation and the fires of Hell."

Giuseppe paused to gauge the effect of his terrible words. He smiled, as if enjoying the deathly silence.

"And as for those of you outside the church through your obstinacy and your perverse attachment to the vomitus of Judaism, you are to settle your affairs within the next three days and then report to the prison of the Holy Office, where you will be held until your fellow townsmen come to their senses. This you will do on pain of death."

An angry muttering spread through the crowd, as if this were the final straw. Tancred felt Judith's hand slip from his own. She drew back her veil.

"You lie!"

Her voice carried through the square, echoing clear and true off the half-timbered façades and down upon the multitude of caps and bonnets filling the enclosure.

Giuseppe froze, thunderstruck, his eyes desperately searching the hundreds of faces for his interlocutor.

"You lie. Your pope has said no such thing."

The muttering became a tumult of voices and exclamations.

"That's right," Pascal shouted. "You lie. What did you do? Fly to Rome and back in three days?"

Tancred couldn't help smiling in the ensuing gale of laughter, knowing Balian to be the only man in Christendom practiced in the Saracen science of homing pigeons.

"Yes, can you fly, Dominican crow?"

More laughter.

Judith cupped her hands around her mouth and shouted the familiar taunt, "Caw! Caw!"

Tancred took her by the shoulders and shook her roughly, but it was too late; the crowd had found its rallying cry, the call usually muttered under one's breath when a Dominican passed in the street.

"Caw. Caw. Caw."

The refrain grew in volume, cacophonous, triumphant, mocking.

Giuseppe shouted out something, his face livid, but he could not be heard over the tumult. Bishop Ivo, roused from his ancient torpor, straightened up in his seat as if he had just noticed, now, that something was amiss.

It was then that a rock struck him full in the shoulder. The old man sagged back in his chair.

The melee was on. Missiles flew through the air, rocks, bricks, cobbles; the crowd surged forward, to the stage, to the clutch of Dominicans to the side, toward the Franciscans in the rear.

Pandemonium.

"Caw. Caw."

"French bastards."

"Death to the crows."

Tancred whirled about and saw his men reaching for their swords.

"Don't attack unless attacked!" he shouted. Seeing them stand down, he turned once again and wrapped his broad arms around Judith, anchoring them both in a sea of furious townspeople. He could make out over the sea of bobbing heads the figure of Brother Brendan, standing his ground, landing punch after punch, smiling, shouting, enjoying himself. Behind him cowered the other friars, fending off the blows of the baker in his apron.

"Bastards!" Pascal was shouting. "Murderous bastards!"

One Dominican, struck squarely in the jaw by Pascal, crumpled to the ground, senseless.

Giuseppe, the old bishop's right arm slung over his shoulder, retreated from the stage under a rain of rock that pelted his broad back and almost buckled his legs. He stumbled down the steps, then raced into the cathedral, the door shutting behind him smartly with a leaden boom.

CHAPTER FORTY-SEVEN

Some resourceful soul within the church rang its great bell once. The sound was sobering, its resounding toll causing heads to turn and fists to pause. Brother Brendan, panting but still smiling, wiped a trickle of blood from the corner of his mouth. The square fell silent. Pascal stood mutely over his unconscious victim on the cobblestones.

"Toulousans. Toulousans. Our beloved Toulousans!"

From above, as if from God himself, came the voice of centuries of authority. The crowd turned as one to its source. Count Raymond stood in the window of the town house.

"We understand your anger. We share your anger. We have been wronged. We have been maligned."

"Long live the count!" a voice cried out. The sentiment was taken up en masse. "Long live the count. Long live Count Raymond."

The count raised his hands, acknowledging the acclaim and then requesting silence. The crowd obeyed.

"You have legitimate grievances. We have legitimate grievances. But this is not the way to seek their redress. We shall take it upon ourselves to plead our cause with the Holy Office, the bishops, and the Curia, and with the Holy Father himself. Of this you can be sure. I give you my word."

He paused, looked out over his subjects sternly.

"But civic disorder must cease. As of sunset there will be a curfew in our city. No one must venture out of his home once night falls. And there shall be no public gatherings until further notice."

Tempers had cooled by now, and few grumbles greeted the announcement of these restrictions. But the people of Toulouse had made their point.

"Now we entreat you all, we who love you dearly, to regain your homes and occupations, to regain the embrace of your families, and to quit this place peaceably and without further disorder. At once. Long live Toulouse!"

"Long live Toulouse!" the crowd responded enthusiastically.

The count shut the mullioned window and disappeared from view.

The assembly began to disperse, silently, its appetites sated. Aside from a few shoulders lowered to take parting shots at the Dominicans as they filed from the square behind Brother Brendan, it was as if there had been no commotion whatsoever.

Tancred, his arms still around Judith, ordered his men back to the Franciscan convent. Homeward bound, people streamed around the couple, lost in their own concerns. Pascal rubbed his sore knuckles and made his way back to the bakery. He realized with a start that he had seldom been so happy.

Judith quivered slightly in Tancred's embrace, birdlike, comforting herself against the hard contours of his chest and arms. He looked down at her features, unveiled and turned upward in the spring sunlight.

"I'll escort you home, Judith."

Her face wore an expression he could not decipher.

"Not that you need protection."

For the only time since Tancred had first laid eyes upon her, Judith laughed.

CHAPTER FORTY-EIGHT

The river meandered lazily through the valley, its banks caressed by the long tendrils of willow branches swaying slowly in a warm wind from the south. The day had dawned bright, and an Arcadian promise of the plenty to come was being held out to man and beast alike. Two swans floated along the green water, followed by their three gray cygnets, half the size of their parents now but still wary of striking out on their own. The mother sensed the rich, new vegetation under the surface of the water and submerged her long, graceful neck deep into the green. Her body righted itself vertically as she fed unseen, looking like a wayward white pillow stranded in midstream. The larger, adult male drifted with the current, leaving his young in a quandary about which parent to rejoin. At last, he turned upstream to meet his mate, who had finished her feeding and now headed toward the opposite bank with the younger birds following. The five swans, beautiful in the water, waddled onto the land, suddenly ungainly, and found their nest in the reeds near the shore. They settled themselves down there, heads on one another's backs, like a white snowdrift that the sun had forgotten to melt.

CHAPTER FORTY-NINE

"Lady Matilda? Is it you?"

Matilda threw her head back in a laugh. "Yes, it is, my dear Bertran."

"But ... but ... how?"

"You shall have to ask my brother when next you see him."

The man of Chantecler looked in bewilderment at Matilda, then at Balian, then back at Matilda. Bertran had been ordered by Tancred to catch up with Balian before he reached Carcassonne, yet now, having overtaken him and his party not ten leagues from that city, he was faced, entirely unexpectedly, by the chatelaine of Chantecler. Struggling to contain his curiosity, he informed Balian of the events in Toulouse and of Tancred's suggestion that he return there immediately.

"Tempers are running high, Master Balian. Very high," he concluded.

Awaiting a decision, Bertran led his horse down to the river-bank to drink, for he had set a fast pace on the ride from Toulouse and the animal was still panting from the effort.

Balian and Matilda wandered off from the French sergeants and stood looking at the river.

"Look at the swans, Balian. On the other bank."

"Beautiful but dangerous. Just like this country. It's a wonder they haven't been put in a pie yet."

Matilda threaded her arm through Balian's and encouraged him to walk on.

"If you go back, the count may be compelled to give you up again."

"I know."

"And we'll be no closer to finding out who Ibrahim saw the night of that first murder."

"True."

"And we … you and I … could be separated. I don't know if I could bear that now."

"Dearest Matilda … "

Balian stopped and kissed her. From his place down by the river, Bertran saw the two embrace and shook his head at the sight. What in God's name was going on?

The couple disengaged.

"May I ask you something, Matilda?"

"Anything."

"Before I lay with you last night, you were a maiden. I know, I felt it … and then there was the blood."

The color rose in her cheeks.

"How is it then that you, a maiden, were so schooled in the art of love?"

Matilda looked at him teasingly.

"You're not jealous, are you? I've been yours but one night!"

Balian grinned. "Of course not. I'm delighted … but a bit curious, that's all. I hope it wasn't Alcuin."

"Oh, dear God, what an idea."

He sought out her eyes. Seeing his perplexity, she relented.

"I had a nurse. A countrywoman from the Poitou. She took it upon herself to teach me that not all love was courtly. She told me things that I should know and the things that I could do when I came of age. She always said that if God made us for pleasure, then we should please him by giving pleasure to each other."

Balian paused for a moment.

"God bless her," he said with a broad smile. Balian kissed her again, this time more vigorously.

Bertran's voice came to them, slightly exasperated.

"Master Balian. Am I to return to Toulouse alone? What is your pleasure?"

The couple shared an amused look.

"Tell your Lord Tancred that I will not be long gone," Balian shouted back. "Tell him my pleasure is here."

CHAPTER FIFTY

The town of Bram stretched out sullen in the sunlight, its two concentric circles of red-roofed housing surrounding a grand church. There was but one entrance to the town, a gate in the east side of the fortifications. Tentatively at first, Balian and Matilda clopped into the town, followed by their retinue. Shutters closed on them, but a curious white cat approached the party, as if relieved to see visitors in the midday heat.

"*Minou*," Matilda said softly as they proceeded through the curving empty street, "Are there any people living here?"

An answer was not long in coming. A young man in a leather apron emerged from a doorway and held up his hand. Balian did likewise, signaling to his escort that they were to rein in.

"There is no inn here," the man said. "There is nowhere for you to stay. You'll have to ride on to Carcassonne. It's not far."

Balian and Matilda exchanged a glance. Not exactly the welcome the South was famous for.

"We come not to stay," Balian explained. "We have been sent here from Paris by King Louis of France."

The young man's eyes widened.

"We should like to speak to the family of a certain Brother Pons, a Dominican friar from this place. We have met him in Toulouse."

"Pons Bélibaste!" the fellow exclaimed. "A traitor to his race."

A woman emerged from the doorway, evidently the man's wife.

"You'll want the Bélibaste family," she said. "They lodge in the first circle, opposite the main door of the church." She gestured for her husband to come back inside their house. Speaking to strangers could only spell trouble.

Ignoring his wife's warning, the man set off down the street, waving to the newcomers to follow him. Dismounted, Balian and Matilda walked a few paces behind, careful to keep up with their guide's brisk pace.

Balian glanced up at the ubiquitous terra-cotta roof tiles. "Is this the red you saw in your vision?" Balian inquired. "When you see things others cannot?"

Matilda remained silent for a moment, searching her memory. "No, I don't think so … I'm not sure, Balian."

"If it is the same red, then Brother Pons must be our murderer," he said softly. "His place of birth betrays him."

"There is a lot of terra cotta in the South," Matilda countered.

They reached the façade of the church. Balian handed over the reins of their two mounts to Jean-Paul in silence. He and Matilda readied themselves to meet the family of Brother Pons Bélibaste of Bram.

Their guide was deep in conversation in the doorway of the house directly opposite the church. A young man in the threshold cocked his head to appraise them, apparently prey to curiosity. He bade them approach.

"We do not often have royal visitors," the young man said in faltering French. "Paris leaves us well alone. Even the French seneschal in Carcassonne does not come calling."

"We have been sent by the French," Balian responded in rapid Occitan, "but we are not French ourselves. We are here to find out what we can about Friar Pons of Bram."

"My half-brother?"

Balian nodded. Their eyes met.

THE SORCERER AND THE ASSASSIN

"Then you must come in," the man said. "I do not remember Pons. I was very young when he left. Our mother can answer your questions."

Madame Bélibaste was seated at a spinning wheel in the main room of the house. Stooped with age, she raised her head when her son introduced the two visitors. She smiled in approval on seeing Matilda's beauty.

"I was young once, my dear. You mustn't let it go to waste."

Matilda lowered her gaze, flushing, as Balian outlined the nature of their errand.

"Pons! The firstborn of my first husband." the old woman exclaimed. "My husband was a fine man. And then he was taken by the French. Mutilated. Killed ... So long ago ... "

"Which is why we are here," Balian ventured in a low voice. "How is it that a boy from this town, with such a terrible past, how is it that he could have joined the Dominican Order of Friars? His father was killed by the French. How is it that someone orphaned in such a horrible way could have made common cause with those responsible?"

Madame Bélibaste looked at Balian questioningly, then came to a decision.

"Pons was misled, bewitched by a devil," she announced sadly. She pointed to a window through which the church loomed large. "The curé poured poison into his head. All of their Roman hocus-pocus, their lies, their cruelties."

Matilda blinked in the ensuing silence. Clearly, she thought, heresy or no, there was no love for the church in this town. The younger son advanced toward the spinning wheel and said under his breath, "Mother, you must be careful of what you say. Especially in front of strangers."

"But why," the old lady resumed, ignoring him, "why are you interested in my Pons? Why has the King of France sent you to see me?"

Her eyes twinkled, displaying a mix of mischief and malice.

"I have not spoken to my son since he left for Toulouse. He is dead to me."

Balian cleared his throat. "There has been some tumult in the Dominican Order. My mistress the queen mother has charged me with finding its cause. I come not as an inquisitor, but as one seeking to bring peace back to this troubled place."

A broad smile crossed the old woman's face. "You speak of the murder of the inquisitor in Carcassonne. That dog who had his head cut off, and rightly so!"

"Other friars in the order have met similar fates."

She clapped her hands together in delight. "Truly a happy day: The crows deserve to die. They are a leprosy on our lands."

Balian stifled a smile at the sentiment. "But you must tell us about Pons. About a man who comes from this town, where everyone hates the church and the Dominicans as much as you do."

The woman took a deep breath. "You are saying that Pons, as a son of Bram, might somehow be involved in these murders. That he is just pretending to be a lackey of the church."

Balian reluctantly nodded.

The old woman's hands came together again. Her eyes clouded with tears. "Oh, would that it were so. I would die a happy woman knowing that my boy had a hand in ridding us of these Catholic maggots."

Balian rose to his feet from his place on a bench. Matilda joined him.

"Thank you, madame," Balian said with a flourish. "Thank you for speaking your mind. Fear not any action by the church against you for your outspokenness. You have my word."

She closed her eyes, then whispered, "If you find Pons is the one, please tell him he has all his mother's love."

CHAPTER FIFTY-ONE

"**C**ut them down!"

Balian's voice rang out imperiously, directed at Jean-Paul, head of the French sergeants.

"But, Master Balian—"

"Now."

The swollen bodies swung in a slight breeze that carried a foul stench across the river Aude and into the Lower Town of Carcassonne. The two wooden beams from which the nooses hung groaned in unison from the collective weight of martyred humanity.

"Balian," Matilda gasped, "on the left…"

Three children, none older than ten years, dangled above the platform of the gibbet like limp rag dolls. Their feet hung at the level of the adults' waists, out of reach of the ravenous dogs who had gnawed off the lower extremities of some of the taller men.

"Giuseppe of Fiesole will burn in Hell for this," Balian said solemnly as his French soldiers set about their grisly task. One by one, the innocent of Auriol began returning from the sky.

"We will bury them here, right away," he ordered, his voice rising. "We'll have a priest consecrate the ground. Now some of you men go into the town and fetch some spades. And a pickaxe or two."

A small crowd of onlookers had gathered on the stone bridge spanning the Aude, relieved that this festering eyesore was now being taken down. The smell of death had for too long permeated their homes.

"What do you think you're doing?"

The shout came from a stout, broad-shouldered man emerging from the Aude Gate of the fortified Upper Town. Clad in the finery of a lord and possessed of a face reddened by too many years of good drink, he led a retinue of men-at-arms and two Dominican friars. Balian ordered his startled sergeants to continue what they were doing. He did not deign to shout back an answer at the man approaching.

The lord came up to him, furious.

"Who the devil are you?"

"You are Sir Robert of Amiens, the Seneschal of Carcassonne?"

"I asked you a question."

"I am Balian of Mallorca, the king's special envoy to the Languedoc. Along with Brother Martin of Troyes. You were informed of our mission, yet when we came here on our way to Toulouse to pay our respects, you had gone on the hunt. I trust you bagged some hart ... the king will be most pleased with you."

Robert stroked his beard, measuring the implication of the insult.

"You have no authority to do this," he said at last.

"I am also a physician. It has been my privilege to minister to the health of the queen mother ... "

A look of alarm crossed Robert's face at the mention of Blanche of Castile.

". . . and as a physician, I know that the presence of so many cadavers constitutes a threat to the health of the good people of Carcassonne. In his wisdom, good King Louis cares for the health of his subjects, especially those who have so recently been embraced by the realm, as have the people of this country."

Robert looked at Balian, now sensing this strange man to be a danger to his sinecure.

"But the Holy Office has instructed the bodies to remain in place for a month."

Balian gave him a withering look. "Do you serve the Kingdom of France or the Dominican Order?"

In the ensuing silence, only the exertions of the sergeants at work cutting down the bodies could be heard.

"My good friars," Balian cried out to the two Dominicans behind Robert. "Please come forward."

Two disconcerted young friars took their place alongside the seneschal.

"Is either of you connected to the holy work of the Holy Office?"

Matilda smiled at Balian's irony.

"I am," answered one.

"In what capacity?"

"I was the assistant to the late Inquisitor Pierre of Tours."

"And you are?"

"Brother Philippe."

"Well, my dear Brother Philippe, I should like to visit the Wall. I need to talk to the suspects from Auriol. As part of a royal investigation."

Philippe clearly wanted to voice an objection, but Balian raised his hand and turned back to Sir Robert.

"You, of all people, are aware that the king had the Wall constructed at royal expense. And as Seneschal of Carcassonne you disburse monies from your treasury for its upkeep. Or am I wrong?"

Sir Robert frowned.

"The only reason I asked to speak to a Dominican was to get the key to the place. With your permission, of course."

Although he had not played chess since his boyhood, Robert instantly recognized a checkmate.

"Granted," he said gruffly before turning to face his men. He gestured toward the gibbet. "Help your fellow sergeants at the task they have undertaken." As he began to make his way back up to the fortifications, he said loudly, without turning around,

"You and your charming companion will dine with us this evening, Master Balian."

Balian nodded affably, more to himself than to Sir Robert's retreating figure, then turned his attention to Brother Philippe.

"Shall we visit the Wall now?"

CHAPTER FIFTY-TWO

The Wall of Carcassonne stood by the right bank of the Aude, directly across the river from the Lower Town, its stone silhouette visible from most of the upper-story windows in the maze of half-timbered houses. Unlike the great administrative and ecclesiastical Upper Town on a height behind it, which bristled with fortifications and armed sentries, the prison had neither a wall walk for guards on its upper floor nor slitted *meurtrières* on its façade from which archers and crossbowmen could safely loose their bolts at a besieging army. There was no moat. The Wall had been built not to keep people out but to keep people in.

Brother Philippe reluctantly led Balian and Matilda into the courtyard filled with the villagers of Auriol. Sunlight streamed into the enclosure, exposing a dusty swirl of misery, men lying listlessly in dirty straw strewn on the ground, babies crying, women tending a small fire to cook whatever food was given to them, which wasn't much, given their emaciation. Balian and Matilda beheld the haggard, huddled mass of humanity, hungry, despairing, exposed to the elements in the open courtyard, treated with less care than a sack of grain. Life seemed to have drained out of the prisoners, and even the little boys and girls, who could normally be expected to dart about with the vigor of childhood, squatted disconsolately in small groups, their improvised games with pebbles and coins no longer of any interest. The smell of excrement from a makeshift latrine in one corner and of unwashed bodies everywhere was overpowering.

Balian looked at Brother Philippe accusingly. "These are your people, for God's sake. How can you do this to them?"

"They murdered Brother Humbert."

"All of them? Even the children?"

"You wanted to speak with them? So speak with them."

Brother Philippe turned and left the courtyard through the archway by which they had entered. Balian, seething, sought out Matilda, whose hand had covered her mouth in dismay at the tableau of squalor before them.

"Take care of the women and children. Distribute the food we have brought. I'll see to the men; many of them seem to be suffering."

Matilda nodded dumbly and picked her way carefully past the recumbent figures on the ground toward the largest clutch of women at the central fire. No one was bestirred to take an interest in the visitors.

Slowly, methodically, his bag of medicines and tinctures in hand, Balian made the rounds of the prisoners, gently explaining who he was and what he was doing there, asking them of their ailments and trying to offer some relief. One man had an arm that had been broken on the rack. Balian recruited other villagers to restrain him as he set the withered arm in a splint. The cries of pain were piteously weak. Another took off his shirt to display a back made raw by the sting of a cat-o'-nine-tails. Balian surveyed the crosshatching of angry scabs and gingerly applied aloe balm. Yet another held up a fingerless hand, the knuckles where the cleaver had met flesh now riotous and revolting in a gangrenous green and black. Fighting nausea, Balian dripped a yarrow tincture on the wound, covered it in honey, then wrapped it tightly in a linen cloth. Others now gravitated toward him, their litany of complaint due not to the attentions of the torturer but to the conditions of their confinement. Gradually, he was winning the men's confidence, and a look of hope, however frail and fleeting, suffused their weary faces. They gladly answered Balian's questions.

At the fire, the mutton Matilda had salted from the previous evening's butchering in Auriol spat and sizzled on a discarded breastplate that served as a griddle. Children of the village had gathered around her, mesmerized by her fine clothing and by the mouthwatering aroma of the meat she was cooking.

"My lady?"

The young woman had a face lined with worry.

"Yes, my sister?"

"You're from the outside ... You see ... they took my husband and my little boy ... Do you know where they are?"

Matilda shuddered at the memory of the ghastly gibbet, with its rag dolls. She paused. If the dead deserved the truth, so too did the living.

"They are with their Maker now," she said in a low voice.

The woman's hands went to her face and her shoulders heaved with sobbing. Matilda took her in her arms, cooing softly and stroking her hair.

"They are happy," she said. "They are happy in Heaven, my sister."

The two remained in a silent embrace for a long moment. At last, the woman broke free and regained her place on the ground, cradling a toddler on her knees. Tears streamed down her face.

As Matilda went to squat down to turn the meat, the heat of the fire made her uncomfortable. She untied her riding cape, pushed back the hood, then folded the garment and laid it on the ground. One of the little girls ran her hand over the soft fabric, marveling.

Head bared, Matilda tended to the meal, aware of the telltale whispering that now greeted her presence.

"They say only the devil has red hair," one of the women finally ventured.

"I am no devil," Matilda replied, smiling.

"Then you are his servant. Just like the man who caused all our suffering."

There was a murmur of agreement, of a secret shared. Matilda tensed, a presentiment of dread gripping her.

"What man?" she asked, slowly. "Of whom do you speak?"

The women exchanged glances, unsure of what to do or say next. Finally, an older woman nudged the elbow of her neighbor, who held a baby in her arms.

"That night…" the young mother said hesitantly, "a man knocked at our door, a man with his head on fire, just like yours… Beggin' your pardon, ma'am… He asked me where the big crow was lodged… I mean—"

A titter of laughter, the first in a long time, rippled through the courtyard.

"I mean… the preacher from Carcassonne. The visitor asked me where he was, and I told him. In the chapel."

Matilda tried to banish a thought that was forming but could not.

"Did you tell this to… to the crows?"

At the sound of this epithet coming from a grand lady, the hesitancy in the young face disappeared, to be replaced by peasant resignation.

"The crows? They've left us alone ever since they took so many of us out. God knows what happened to them. But I swear the crows are not interested in us anymore. They just want us to rot in here forever."

The woman's outburst occasioned a chattering of assent, the others cursing the Dominicans and their cruelty.

But Matilda paid them no heed. She searched the courtyard for his familiar face, saw him deep in conversation with a graybeard.

"Balian!" she shouted. "Balian. Over here."

CHAPTER FIFTY-THREE

The night was cool. The hoot of an owl came through the open window of their chamber and resonated under the coffered vault. A fire glowed dimly through the grate of a metal stove. Matilda and Balian embraced under the covers of a fine bed, honored guests of the Seneschal of Carcassonne. They lay side by side, silent, still, each remembering the awful certainty that had descended on them earlier in the evening.

"We must ride to Toulouse at daybreak," Balian said. "He must be apprehended before he does more harm."

Matilda nodded, still recalling the damning conversation they had just had with the seneschal's groom. It had occurred after they unceremoniously left Sir Robert's table. Their host, true to form, had slumped in his chair, dead drunk, unable to give them any information that might be of use, or any information at all. Clearly the poor fellow, appointed to his post by virtue of being the natural son of the king's late father, was not up to the task of his office. Even before swooning into a stupor, he had proved singularly uninformed of the doings in his county, preferring the pleasures of the hunt and the vine above all else.

When they stepped into the evening air, Balian said to Matilda, "If you want to know anything about what goes on in a city, you must talk to the grooms. They know who comes and who goes."

It had not been difficult to find the seneschal's man. The stables occupied a fine, capacious stone structure to one side of the castle courtyard. The second floor of the stables had dwellings for the hostler and his hands.

A knock at the door and a boy appeared, chewing a duck leg. When told of the nature of the visit, he called inside and another man came to the threshold, older and far more affable.

"Master Balian of Mallorca?" he said warmly. "Now, that's a fine mount you have there. Arabian. We don't see many like that here. A bit skittish, but a beautiful beast."

"Thank you. I am very fond of her."

"What did you do? Steal her from the Saracens? They must not be very pleased with you, that accursed lot."

The man paused, smiled at his own joke. Balian saw which approach he must take.

"I assure you I am no horse thief. But I cannot say the same of my lady wife."

The groom bowed toward her.

"Matilda is forever taking my Arabian out without my permission."

"Ahh, the ladies these days. I swear, what is the world coming to?

"And I assure you, good sir," Matilda retorted, "that you would have no world without us ladies. Or was your mother a man?"

The stablemaster slapped his thigh in delight. "Oh, you've got a spirited one there, Master Balian," he exclaimed. "A real filly. So you must be careful how you ride her."

They burst out laughing, Matilda the loudest, causing the two men to look at each other in surprise and laugh even more. Matilda blushed.

"Well now," Balian said once he had recovered himself, "I came not to speak of my fair helpmeet, but of horses. Can we have a look around?"

The groom had no need of encouragement. He bounded round the corner and in no time had unlocked the stable doors and invited them in to look at the occupants of the stalls. A pleasant, earthy smell enveloped them. Intelligent eyes looked out at them.

"I have some real beauties here. The seneschal loves his sport."

"And his wine," Matilda said.

"Aye, too true. Did he make it through dinner?"

She shook her head.

"But Sir Robert's a fine fellow, all the same. Very good to his animals, which I say is the true measure of a man's character."

"Does he stable a hobby?" Matilda asked with feigned innocence. Balian looked at her in admiration.

"Lord no. No self-respecting French noble would sit atop a mount like that."

"Who would?"

The groom searched his memory.

"The Gaels. It's said they're mad for them, though I don't know why, they're such puny little things."

"Have you ever had a hobby here?"

"Funny you should say that. I stabled one here not long ago. And it was a Gael in the saddle, just like I said. He came and went the evening of that dreadful business with the inquisitor in the church."

"What did the Gael look like?" Balian asked sharply.

"When I came to lock the stable doors later in the night, the hobby was gone and its rider with it."

Matilda held her breath as Balian asked the question once more. "What did he look like?"

"Biggish fellow. With red hair. A friar."

CHAPTER FIFTY-FOUR

A wraith slipped through the darkness of a side street. Faint candlelight illumined but a few windows, laughter floated through the air, fading before the slap and sigh of lovemaking, the wail of an infant, the singing of a drunk, the careless sound of the city before the first sleep. The figure hugged the walls, careful not to form a silhouette that could be distinguished by the count's men on patrol. The curfew was being strictly enforced, for Raymond was said to have been angered by the uncouth spectacle of the previous day.

The shape paused, peered around a corner, then set off again, its footfalls soundless on the cobbles dampened by a shower at dusk. It was a warm spring evening.

The door of the Seilhan House confronted the veiled figure. Its hand emerged from its cloak and turned the knob. As promised, the door had been left unlocked and the Saracen bodyguards called away somewhere.

Upstairs, at the long table, Friar Giuseppe idly flipped through leather-bound Inquisition registers, the painstakingly kept records of who had been interrogated when, and what they had said under torture or admitted out of terror. He refilled his cup with wine, then drained it before refilling it again. Perhaps he had been too rash to threaten excommunication of the count and interdict for the town. His bluff had been called by some damnable wench in the crowd, and he had been lucky to escape the square alive. These heathens of Toulouse may have won this round, but he would ultimately prevail. A letter had been dispatched to the Holy Father immediately after the riot. Now he had only to wait.

A sound in the doorway distracted him from his reading. He looked up and saw a veiled figure enter.

Placing his hands on his stomach, he said, "So you have come for the Jews?"

The figure removed its hood to reveal a cascade of raven hair and coal-blue eyes that pierced the Dominican to his core. He had never seen such a ravishing creature as the one who now stood before him.

"Good friar, I am Sarah of Moissac. I have been sent here by my elders."

"Why did not they not come themselves?"

She removed her cape to reveal a voluptuous form encased in a linen shift bleached a blinding white.

"They thought I might be more persuasive."

Giuseppe grabbed for his cup and drank deeply, as if to save his life. He wiped his lips with the sleeve of his cassock, recovered.

"Yours are a very wise people. Always have been. And you, my dear Jewess, are indeed very persuasive."

A bag of coins landed with a clank on the table.

"We want no trouble with the Holy Office. We know that you will have your way. We want you to spare us the pain of imprisonment. You do not need us to win."

Giuseppe was barely listening.

"Come here, my child."

She took a step closer.

"Come round the table."

She obeyed. She now stood before him, close enough to touch.

"No need to be afraid, Sarah. I will not hurt you."

Giuseppe's hand, trembling from the strength of his desire, reached up and cupped the young woman's breast. He could feel her youth, her softness, through the fabric. He lingered there, caressing slowly, circling her nipple, feeling it stiffen, watching her impassive face as his hand rose and fell with her uneven breathing.

"I want you to be more persuasive. In fact, if you want to save your people, you have no choice."

"Yes. I have prepared for that."

She took his hand from her bosom, then stepped back.

"I have brought an ointment. It will ... it will help me receive your manhood into me."

Giuseppe's eyebrows shot up as she returned to the other side of the table and with her back to him reached down for her cape on the floor to retrieve something. He surveyed her round buttocks as she did so and determined what he would do to her. He'd have her lean facedown on the table, right now, and take her as he did his boys, his delightful little minnows, in Narbonne. It would be a pleasure to hear the bitch cry out as loudly as they did. Only he would keep her around for a few days, for she looked in good health, this Jewess.

The woman returned to his side.

"Take that off, whore," Giuseppe snapped, fingering her garment.

"No. First there is something I want to do."

Giuseppe watched uncomprehending as her hand whipped from behind her back and plunged a dagger into his chest. The blade came out and stabbed in again and again as the woman cried, "Astruguetus was my father! Now, die, crow." She stabbed a final time, right up to the hilt. "They say you have no heart, but I have found yours."

Giuseppe shrieked, eyes wide, as he watched the blood spurting rhythmically out of him onto the woman's white linen. She stood before him in triumph. Then he slumped to the floor with a groan, dead.

From without came the pounding of feet on the stairs. Judith whirled around just in time to see Brother Brendan burst into the room followed by soldiers.

"Bloody murder!" he cried.

Standing luridly in her blood-soaked dress, she could see over the friar's shoulder the pale face of Tancred.

CHAPTER FIFTY-FIVE

Balian and Matilda had learned the astonishing news on their journey westward back to Toulouse. A strange, serene old man had been waiting for them on the road of the Old Romans. He bade them rein in and dismount; impressed by his authority, they did as he asked.

"Balian of Mallorca," the man said, "we who have an Understanding of the Good would like to express our gratitude for the solicitude you have shown to our followers from Auriol."

Balian looked at the man's simple attire, his lean features, his air of serenity, then understood. "You are a Good Man?"

The heretic nodded. "We know of your mission. It is good to stop the killing, even if those being killed are evil. But you should know that we are not responsible. We are not killers."

Matilda, fascinated, took a step forward. Alcuin had taught her that these Cathars made no distinction between man and woman, felt that neither was superior to the other, because all human beings were hapless creatures of matter and changed gender and station in life with every reincarnation.

"We know who the killer is," said Matilda.

"You are to be congratulated, sister."

"And what of the man who killed the three dozen people of Auriol?" she ventured. "Do you Good Men and Women not want to exact revenge?"

The man smiled tolerantly. "Those who perished at the gibbet of Carcassonne have already been reborn, to live another life in this vale of tears. As for the man responsible, he too is dead. Such was his evil that he will return to his next life as a dog."

The news took a moment to sink in.

"Wait," Matilda said. "Are you saying Brother Giuseppe of Fiesole is dead?"

The man nodded. "Murdered. By a daughter of Abraham."

"Who?" Matilda asked, dreading the answer.

"Judith, daughter of Astruguetus."

"That can't be," Balian said. "How can you know such things?"

The Good Man allowed himself a little smile. "We are from this country. Our eyes and ears are everywhere. We are not like the inquisitors, foreigners who know nothing, see nothing. That is why they torture and maim. But they fight blackness with blackness."

He stepped off the Old Roman road, paused, and looked at the couple. "You have chosen the way of the flesh. So be it, you will return to this world. In the meantime, be good to each other, love each other; that is all there is."

He smiled and soon his figure disappeared behind a row of cypress trees.

CHAPTER FIFTY-SIX

Fatima picked her way through the quiet streets of a chastened city. Soon it would be sundown, a time to shrink farther indoors and wait in obedient silence in the darkness. Her master, Count Raymond, had let it be known that merriment and feasting were in no way to be tolerated in these tense times. He had ordered Mistress Esclarmonde to send most of the kitchen staff home to their dwellings in town. He had no use for butlers, ewerers, and pantlers now; he would take his meals only with his closest advisers. Together they had to find a way to untangle Toulouse from the grip of a murderer.

Fatima heard the news of the count's wishes and immediately had a thought: he and his personal household would still have to eat. With the castle's bread ovens cold, there would be no fire to bake the trenchers, no heat in which savory treats could rise and be delivered piping hot to her grateful betters. She would not let the count down.

Mistress Esclarmonde had gladly given Fatima a few coins from the household strongbox. She knew the girl to be of uncommon ability and level-headedness. Fatima would not be hoodwinked into overpaying by the sharp merchants of the town.

On the street leading from the cathedral square, she reached her destination. Out of the city's most frequented bakery stretched a line into the street. Fatima took her place at the end of the queue, ignoring the looks of those unaccustomed to seeing a daughter of Ishmael in their midst. She rarely ventured out of the precincts of the castle.

When her turn finally came, the young baker smiled broadly, his straight white teeth gleaming through a bushy beard and mustache.

"Now, what have we here, young lady?"

Wordlessly, Fatima plopped a large empty basket on the counter.

"That's a rather capacious basket you've brought. Surely you don't want me to fill it up?"

Fatima finally returned his smile. "My master has a large household. And our ovens are cold.

"Your master? Who might that be?"

Fatima grasped her change purse and let its contents jingle. "Count Raymond of Toulouse."

The baker's aspect changed immediately. "The count? A fine man. I saw him only yesterday in the square. Yes, a fine man." He executed a mock bow, causing some flour to be dislodged from his beard. "I am the baker Pascal, at your service." He straightened up. "And you?"

Laughing, Fatima waved away the flour dust in the air. "I am Fatima," she said. "Ward of the count."

Pascal thrust his peel in the oven and extracted several loaves. He loaded the basket with the steaming bread. Unhesitatingly, Fatima fished out two coins and handed them to him. He smiled, then said, "That basket will be heavy. Let me help you."

As if not hearing, Fatima hefted the load on her arm and strode toward the door. Pascal dashed to the back room.

"Uncle Tomas," he exclaimed. "You must finish with the customers. I have a delivery to make."

Tomas sourly got to his feet, unused to working ever since the arrival of Pascal.

"Delivery? What delivery?" He scowled.

"To Count Raymond. To the Narbonne Castle."

His uncle's eyes lit up at the mention of such a wealthy customer.

"Then off with you, Pascal. I'll finish up here."

But by then Pascal was already sprinting down the street, catching up with Fatima as she rounded a corner. He snatched the basket from her grasp and placed it on his shoulder.

"I can assure you, baker Pascal," Fatima sniffed, "I have no need of your brawn."

"I should like to see the Narbonne Castle. I have never been invited within," Pascal said. Seeing her skeptical look, he continued, "And I could make this delivery whenever you needed more of my bread. Just send word and I can take the goods to you. No need for you to brave the dust and noise of the city. Or to wait in line."

Fatima walked ahead in silence. This bearded giant was not as guileless as he looked. She stopped and reached into her pouch of coins.

"That sounds like a reasonable arrangement." She handed him two more coins. "An advance for the next delivery."

He smiled. "And I shall include a written receipt with each basket. To avoid any misunderstanding."

Fatima looked up at him quizzically. "A baker who can read and write? How is that possible?"

Pascal cleared his throat. In no way was he going to reveal his past life as a Dominican scribe.

"My father schooled me," he lied.

Not fully convinced, Fatima placed her hands on her hips. "So, do we have an agreement, Pascal the baker?"

"We do, Mistress Fatima. We do. From here on in, we can be partners."

The two set off for the castle, a spring in their steps.

CHAPTER FIFTY-SEVEN

Balian and Matilda spurred their mounts as the pink city walls of Toulouse came into view. Before long, the same messenger of the previous day, Bertran, came galloping toward them, with an urgent request from Tancred to make the utmost haste. Their already smart pace quickened as horses and riders pounded toward the great city on the Garonne.

Now here they were, in a ghost town. In the street between the Seilhan House and the Narbonne Castle no vendors cried and no passersby shared gossip. Most of the townspeople seemed to have stayed inside, cowering behind locked doors, as if bracing for a coming storm.

Entrusting their mounts to the sergeants, they entered the Narbonne Castle to seek out Count Raymond. A page walked them through the empty great hall and ushered them into a small adjoining chamber where the count was seated at a table. Also present were Brother Martin, the chamberlain, and the witnesses to the crime, Tancred and Brother Brendan.

Ashen-faced, Tancred rose and embraced the two in turn.

"Where is she?" Balian asked in a whisper.

"In the dungeon here. I didn't speak to her, but I've been told she's well. Rabbi Ezra has expelled her from the community."

"Welcome, Master Balian, Lady Matilda," Count Raymond said in a pointed manner to put an end to their private parley. "Fetch chairs for these two," he instructed the page.

As Matilda waited for the boy to return, she could feel the eyes of chamberlain on her; he was thinking that he had seen this woman before but could not remember where or when. He did not make the connection between Mathilda and Mathias.

Balian's eyes were trained on Brother Brendan and noticed his tonsure was the color of terra cotta. Matilda had a gift, he had to admit.

Balian searched Brendan's countenance for any sign of underlying villainy. In vain, for there was none. Perhaps their suspicions were unfounded—or perhaps the Gael possessed astounding audacity.

"Must the woman be included?" Brother Martin asked.

"I know the accused," Matilda said tartly as she took her seat.

"The accused?" Martin snorted. "I think the only question to be settled is the manner of her execution. Burning as a Jew who has murdered a Christian, drawing and quartering then beheading her as an enemy of the country, or hanging her as a common criminal. Or tying weights to her feet and drowning her in the Garonne."

In the ensuing silence, Tancred put his head in his hands.

"Do I have to remind you, Brother Martin," Count Raymond said, "that as long as I draw breath, this county is independent of the kingdom of France? I seek counsel, not commands."

The Franciscan bowed his head deferentially.

"I think she should be set free," said Brother Brendan.

Surprise dawned on all faces, except that of the speaker.

"The law of talion. Lord Tancred here has told me that our late provincial had the girl's father murdered. Are we forgetting our Deuteronomy?" Brendan continued, clearly pleased by his listeners' bafflement. *"Non misereberis eius sed animam pro anima oculum pro oculo dentem pro dente manum pro manu pedem pro pedes exiges."*

Brendan noticed a few blank looks. "The Good Book says 'Show no pity: life for life, eye for eye, tooth for tooth, hand for hand, foot for foot.' The law of talion. By killing the provincial, the girl was taking perfectly legal revenge."

"You can't be serious," the count exploded. "You. A Dominican."

"I am serious," Brendan replied. "Is this county not governed by law, my lord?"

The conference broke up into shouts of disbelief.

"Friar Brendan of Killiney!" Balian's voice rang out loudly, silencing the others. "That's all very fine and well for the murder of Brother Giuseppe. Perhaps she should go free."

A brief murmur of wonderment greeted this concession.

"But what of the other three inquisitors murdered? Or do you know something about those murders that we don't?"

Brendan looked sharply at Balian. A hush descended, a sense of unease pervading the room.

"Furthermore, how did the girl get into the Seilhan House? Did someone give her a key? And where were the Saracen bodyguards?"

The gathering gave Balian its full attention. No one had speculated on how the murder had been carried out.

"Are you insinuating that one of our order colluded with the girl? How dare you impugn the followers of Saint Dominic."

"Did you not just say now that Brother Giuseppe murdered Astruguetus of Narbonne? Was Giuseppe not a follower of Saint Dominic?"

"The man's infamy was known far and wide. He was not a true follower," said Brendan.

Balian paused, almost in admiration. Brendan was a hard fox to corner.

"Very well then, the girl goes free. The Holy Office takes its revenge. The people rise up in revolt. And yet another inquisitor is murdered. Then the circle starts up again. Is that why you are invoking the law of talion? So there will be constant turmoil?"

"Balian, you speak in riddles," the count interrupted testily. "You were brought up with the Saracens, we all know, but you are in Christendom now, where we speak our minds clearly."

"I shall be direct and to the point then, my lord," Balian said evenly. "The murderer at Auriol-Cabardès, at Carcassonne, at Toulouse, is in this room."

The count stared at him, thunderstruck.

"Why did you stable your hobby at Carcassonne, Brother Brendan? And why were you seen in Auriol the night of the murder? And how was the third inquisitor murdered in the safety of the Seilhan House, to which you possess the key? And who was it that left the door unlocked there last night for that poor orphaned woman? Perhaps some friar who can go anywhere, as he is their master builder."

Brendan rose to his feet.

"Nonsense. This is all nonsense. You are severely deceived, my friend."

"He is not your friend," Matilda said.

"Balian, have I not shown you anything but kindness? Even when you were imprisoned by Brother Giuseppe? It was I who volunteered to go to the Seilhan House, even though I hate the place and what it stands for."

"So you hate the Holy Office," Matilda said quickly. "That is motive enough."

"Dear lady, did I not marry you?" Brendan said with a complicit smile that Matilda could not help returning. "At your request?"

She nodded, and the tension in the room eased.

"My lord," Brendan addressed Count Raymond. "These suspicions are baseless. I have given you my opinion of what to do with the girl. As you said to Brother Martin, you seek counsel and that is all. Now that my counsel has been heard, I beg permission to return to my convent. My brothers await me at the vigil."

Balian noticed that the friar's customary singsong accent had disappeared. Count Raymond dismissed him with a wave of a hand. Brendan walked quickly from the room, without a sideways glance at Balian. He shut the great wooden door behind him.

The count looked at Balian as if demanding an explanation. After a moment, Balian said, "I must talk with Judith." Then he turned to Tancred. "Follow Brendan. He must not leave Toulouse."

"I must talk to Judith too."

"Then I will go!"

The men looked in astonishment at Matilda.

"Very well," Raymond said at last. "My men will accompany you. Though I find Balian's accusations difficult to credit."

"No," Matilda said. "If Brendan sees me with soldiers, then he will know that he was not believed. If he sees that I'm alone, he is more likely to think that nothing is amiss."

The count nodded wearily, as if these visitors to his city were becoming tiresome.

CHAPTER FIFTY-EIGHT

The story was quickly told. Not only had Brendan unlocked the door to the Seilhan House and lured the Saracen bodyguards away on some fool's errand, but he had also served as an intermediary between Judith and Giuseppe, telling the provincial to expect a visitor from the Jews. He had even given Judith the murder weapon when he surreptitiously visited her a few hours after the riot.

"Brother Brendan was getting you to do his dirty work," Balian concluded after hearing Judith out. "Very clever. He does not have to do the deed. He has someone with a legitimate and lethal grievance against Giuseppe do it for him. And, in the process, he draws suspicion away from himself."

Judith sat on a crude bench in the cell, her bloodstained shift in tatters, comforted by a solicitous Tancred.

"But how did he know about Judith?"

"You told him, Tancred. You told Brendan about the grievances of the Jews, the day you freed me from the Seilhan House."

"Nonsense," Judith protested, surprising them both. "The whole county knew about my father's murder, and that I had survived to avenge him. You know how the townspeople gossip."

Balian nodded, taking her point.

"But why?" Tancred said. "Why does Brother Brendan want to kill inquisitors? Dominicans? He is one of them."

"I don't know," Balian replied. "But I am convinced Brendan is a good man at heart. Which is all the more puzzling. There must be a reason."

The leave-taking had been difficult. Tancred had held Judith in his arms, assuring her that he would do all in his power to win her release. Judith had looked up at him, her eyes clouded, not believing this kind Gentile knight. They left the cell and began the climb up the stone steps to the ground floor.

"I must speak with Count Raymond immediately," Balian said once they reached the castle courtyard. "I must tell him what I found out in Auriol and Carcassonne. I have to convince him... At the very least, he must be made aware that Brendan was an accomplice in the murder of Giuseppe."

"And will you convince him to set Judith free?"

Balian looked into his friend's troubled eyes. They had known each other for ten years now, and never had Balian seen Tancred so distraught. The faint lines on his brow had deepened; the great golden sheen of his hair had dimmed.

"The law of talion, Deuteronomy..." Tancred ventured feebly.

Balian put his arm around Tancred's shoulders.

"I will do what I can. If he cannot be persuaded to set her free, then perhaps he will let others do that for him."

A flash of hope glimmered in eyes made tired from a sleepless night.

"Balian... that girl means so much to me."

"Tancred, she is a daughter of Israel."

"She is my lady. To the devil with everyone else. I am the head of my family. I do what I will. I am decided."

"I know, I know. It has been evident to all of us. Matilda said you were much changed."

The two men paused, as if the mention of Tancred's sister had conjured her presence in their midst.

"Matilda..." Tancred said. "I was quite surprised. I never thought..." He held the thought to himself. "Are you happy with her?"

"I am, my friend. She is wiser than her years."

"She always has been."

"And I ... I thank you for approving our union."

"If I hadn't, do you think she would have listened to me? Now that you know Matilda, you'll know what I say is true."

The friends smiled, then disengaged.

"Now, go join her at the convent and I shall seek out Count Raymond."

They went their separate ways.

CHAPTER FIFTY-NINE

Gradually, as Tancred left the deserted precincts of the Seilhan House, the city began displaying its usual bustle. Out of wisdom won by years of unpleasant experience, the townspeople of Toulouse had decided to give the locale of the Inquisition a wide berth, perceiving it as an animal licking its wounds, ready to lash out at anyone who approached. When Tancred arrived at the square closest to the banks of the Garonne, he saw the burghers going about their business normally—presumably, they were far enough away from the dread presence at the other end of the city. And even though the Dominican convent stood in redbrick majesty to one side of the square, he realized that the people made a distinction between the crows of the Inquisition and the ordinary friars of the order. Rightly or wrongly, they felt that they had nothing to fear from the black-robed men of the convent—unless the Inquisition made life difficult in the town.

Tancred's impressive bearing attracted the attention of passing servant girls and merchant wives. Ignoring their admiring glances, he scanned the busy square for any sign of his sister. Nothing.

Impatient, he moved into a side street, dodging a passel of small boys running and kicking up dust. But once they had gone, the alleyway returned to its silent emptiness. Around the other side of the convent, he was met by a similar scene—no sign of Matilda, only a few stray dogs yelping at one another in the sunlight. Thorough to the last, Tancred then walked the entire circuit of the convent and around the adjoining church under construction. There were no workmen there today, and access to the building site was made impossible by a high wooden palisade that surrounded the structure. A large door had been fashioned in this fence, the only way to get men and materials into and out of the site. It was locked.

He began to feel disquieted. He returned to the main square, looked at the door of the convent. As far as he could tell, this was its sole egress, so this is where he would have positioned himself to see whether Brendan attempted to leave the convent. Where the devil was she?

"*Fougasse*, sir?"

Jaume, with a wicker basket suspended at his waist, was smiling up at him. He gave the boy a denier and was about to take a bite of the warm bun when a thought occurred to him.

"Boy, do you go all over town with that bread?"

"Yes, sir, every day. Even Sunday."

"Then tell me, have you seen a beautiful lady with red hair today? Wearing a riding cape?"

The boy paused, thinking.

"I would remember the hair ... "

"And?"

"No, sir, I've seen no one like that."

Tancred handed the boy another denier.

"If you do see her, will you come back here and tell me? And if I'm not here, I can usually be found at the convent of the Franciscans. My name is Tancred."

Jaume set off on his mission, shoulders squared at his new responsibilities.

Tancred surveyed the people passing in the street, stopping at the market stalls. Matilda was the needle, Toulouse the haystack.

He approached the door of the convent and lifted the knocker. It landed with a thud. Within a few seconds, the door creaked open to reveal a lean, swarthy figure gazing out malevolently.

"Go away. We are in mourning," the friar said. "One of our own has been murdered. By a Jewess."

"I'm looking for my sister."

"A woman," the friar hissed. "Such filth is not allowed within these walls."

"Is Brother Bren—"

The door closed in his face.

Chastened and a little unsettled by the dark young friar's fierceness, Tancred turned once again to the bustle in the square. The sun was lower now, shining brightly in his eyes. He squinted into the glare, his worry growing. What had happened to her? He'd been a fool to let her go alone.

Then he saw her. Dressed as Mathias. She was squatting against a wall, grinning at him.

CHAPTER SIXTY

Tancred strode over to her. "Have you been there the whole time, watching me wander around like a nervous chicken?"

"Yes, Tancred."

She stood up and embraced him.

"You are such a big fool, my brother."

Her green eyes danced before him. At times like these, she reminded him of their mother, the most beautiful woman to have graced Chantecler. Only their mother had not gone around travestied as a boy.

"I assume you've put your disguise back on for a reason?"

"It's a man's world. If I am to do a man's job, then I must put away my maiden's weeds."

"Maiden? I think not," Tancred said with a laugh. "Try matron."

Matilda pouted. "I do not think I like that. Two nights do not a matron make."

"My apologies. Married or not, you are still the fairest flower in the field."

"The fairest? I daresay that you might think that of another."

Tancred's face darkened, and Matilda immediately regretted bringing up Judith.

He looked at her mournfully and said, "What is to become of her, Matilda? What is to become of her?"

A thoughtful silence fell between them for a moment, soon to be replaced by a shared curiosity, for both sensed a sudden ripple of expectation coursing through the crowd. They turned toward its source, at the far end of the square. Two soldiers were wading into the throng, motioning people to get out of the way.

"Make way. Make way. Make way for the count."

Count Raymond, flanked by Balian and Brother Martin, advanced briskly into the square, paying no heed to the shouted acclamations greeting his arrival. His features were set in a grim, determined expression, as were those of the men-at-arms following him.

Tancred let out a low whistle. Balian must have been supremely convincing in laying out his case against Brother Brendan.

As the procession neared the convent door, Balian broke into a smile. He had spotted Tancred and Matilda, seen his beloved wife's transformation. He whispered into the ear of the count, who turned and, with a quick flick of his hand, bade the two to join them.

Under the watchful gaze of scores of pairs of eyes, brother and sister hurried across the square, arriving just as the door knocker landed with a boom.

From its perch high atop a chimney pot, a crow responded by giving voice to a piercing cry.

CHAPTER SIXTY-ONE

"What do you mean, I have no right to be here?" Count Raymond exploded at the Dominican abbot. "Who paid to have this structure built? Whose treasury bleeds to keep your damn inquisitor mill in business?"

Abbot Jean of Béthune was not a man to be intimidated. Heavyset and of immense girth, he stood in the central garden of the cloister, arms folded across his chest, glaring at the count.

"This is a sacred precinct. You are violating it," he replied.

"Sacred? Ha," the count sneered. "From the looks of you, the only place sacred here is the kitchen."

He turned to his men, who were standing about in the ambulatory of the cloister. It had been established that Friar Brendan was in the convent, as he was charged with preparing Giuseppe's burial place. "Fan out," Raymond instructed. "Search every nook and cranny. And you," he said, pointing to a muscular sergeant, "take the door. No one must leave, on any pretext."

The soldiers obeyed, and soon shouts of outrage could be heard throughout the convent, as indignant friars confronted the intruders.

"You will pay for this, Count Raymond. Rome will be informed."

"To the devil with you. I will tell Rome that it is the Dominicans who are the source of all our discord. Dominican victims, Dominican murderers, Dominican inquisitors, I'm sick of the whole lot of you."

The abbot lumbered off, muttering to himself about the impudence of princelings.

"Where is his cell?" Balian said loudly. "Brother Brendan's?"

The large man stopped, then turned around slowly, like some great Crusader galley maneuvering in a harbor of Outremer.

"Why do you want to know?"

"I want to search it."

"That is not permitted."

"It will happen anyway. Better it be his friend who does it than one of the soldiers. I know Brendan well."

The abbot paused, considered. Brendan was the mastermind of the great church taking shape beside the convent. It would be a pity if some lout destroyed the plans. "Very well, then. On the uppermost floor, facing the new church. You'll know it by the architectural drawings on his desk."

Balian and Matilda found the cell with no difficulty. Sunlight flowed in through a large hinged window, illuminating a desk strewn with parchments, scrolls, and the rulers and straight-edges needed for the minutiae of architectural plans. Otherwise, the room was spartan; aside from the bed and a lone wicker chair near the casement window, the only item of interest they found was a small wooden chest, discreetly lodged in a low cavity in the whitewashed wall beside the desk, invisible unless you crouched down, as Matilda had, to have a look around.

She triumphantly placed the chest on the desk. Balian lifted the latch, then sighed in dismay at the sight of a keyhole.

"We'll have to pick it," he said, extracting a dirk from his sleeve. He bent over and tried to insert the knife into the lock, but its blade was too broad to fit into the narrow aperture. He felt a tap at his shoulder and turned to see Matilda holding out a much smaller dagger, almost like a knitting needle.

"A lady's aid," she explained, smiling.

Balian set to work, inserting the needle into the lock, feeling around for the mechanism. Matilda stepped over to the window and looked out at the great church rising nearby. A forest of scaffolding and platforms obscured much of the view, but she could see the great piers and the wooden stays that would support the flying buttresses under construction. The clerestory around the apse was complete, its delicate window tracery awaiting colorful glass. The panes would be blown outside of the city near a forest, for the appetites of the glassmakers' ovens were ravenous. Even without its painted statuary and kaleidoscopic glass, Brendan's half-finished church looked ready to float into the sky. It was as if the friar were a sorcerer, conjuring a great edifice out of air. The redbrick building would tower over the humble terra-cotta roof tiles huddled round its lower reaches, including those of the convent itself. How could a man capable of creating such a wonder be capable of cold-blooded murder?

Balian swore an oath. Surprised, Matilda crossed the room and ran her hand through his dark hair.

"Trouble?"

"It is … it is diabolically made," Balian said as he strained with the lock. "It must be of Lombard origin."

"How do you know?"

He paused to look at her.

"Because the richest bankers commission the best locks."

He turned back to his task, his imprecations now a stream of Arabic. Matilda looked at him, knowing he was sparing her the indignity of understanding what he was saying.

"You know, my friend," Matilda said softly, "I heard that Balian of Mallorca can do anything."

Balian snorted in frustration.

CHAPTER SIXTY-TWO

At last, the lock clicked. The trove was ready to yield its secrets. Balian mopped his brow, then he and Matilda leaned over the chest. He nodded.

Matilda lifted the latch and opened the lid.

They both gasped. Scores of florins sparkled in the sunbeam streaming into the room, their metallic glow mixing with the golden motes floating in the air.

"So much for his vow of poverty," Balian remarked.

Matilda dug down into the coins and found a rectangular cloth purse beneath them. She opened it and found within a carefully folded parchment and a stack of letters bound with a string. She set them both down on the desk and first opened the parchment. A decorous hand had written in Latin: *To the bearer of this letter all assistance must be afforded. He is of the Assembly.*

Below that, a signature, consisting solely of the letter *R*.

"Who or what is R?" Matilda asked, more to herself than to Balian.

"And what's the Assembly?"

Balian picked up the strange letter and examined it carefully. Whoever composed it had access to exceptionally fine vellum, and the writing appeared to have been executed by an accomplished scribe. The lettering was remarkably florid, not of the kind churned out by monastic drudges in a scriptorium. Clearly, R was a wealthy individual, if, indeed, that letter signified a person.

"Perhaps the answer's in the other letters."

Matilda nodded and carefully untied the string holding the small packet. It became immediately clear that these parchments were of an inferior quality.

The first read: *We are in good health. The mother of Eamonn is Maeve. K.*

"More riddles." Matilda sighed.

"Open another one."

We are in good health. Ciaran drowned at Dun Laoghaire. K.

"How odd!" Balian exclaimed. "Both open with the same phrase, then conclude with an obscure detail."

"It's only obscure because we don't know the people named."

Balian thought for a moment.

"That's it! A type of code, meant to show Brendan that the author of the letter is not an impostor. He knows the author. The others will probably be the same."

They were.

We are in good health. Siobhan is a good cook. K.

We are in good health. Oisin had a dog named Carraig. K.

We are in good health. Liam is our best archer. K.

"Let's see what we have here," Balian said, laying the last of the letters atop the pile. "Inferior vellum, inferior calligraphy, inferior Latin. And all of the people bear the names of Gaels, as do the place and the dog. R and K must be two different people entirely."

"Do you think there's a connection?"

"I don't see one."

Balian sat down on the bed, Matilda on the chair by the window, stumped.

"Why the constant mention of health?" she asked with trepidation, after a moment.

She had never seen him look so frustrated, even when they had quarreled. He turned his eyes from hers and gazed absently at the sunlight pouring into the room through the window.

"I don't know," he replied, "I don't know."

CHAPTER SIXTY-THREE

The hunt for Brendan was not going well. Reports from Raymond's soldiers had been discouraging. Brendan was not in any of the cells, or the kitchens, or the refectory, or the chapel, or the prison, or the infirmary, or the cellars. And no mount was absent from the stables, not even the hobby.

Count Raymond paced one side of the cloister, lost in thought. The man must be hiding somewhere in the convent. To think that Brendan had had the gall to sit before him in the Narbonne Castle just hours ago, giving advice about what to do with Judith of Narbonne. The fellow must be mad.

From their vantage point on either side of the yew tree in the center of the cloister, Tancred and Brother Martin watched the count as he paced back and forth, hands clasped behind his back. Neither exchanged a word; indeed, the last time they had spoken was long ago, when riding from Avignonet to Toulouse together and discovering that they detested each other. And although Tancred stayed at the Franciscan convent, their paths seldom crossed.

The young lord's thoughts wandered to Balian and Matilda. Perhaps they were finding something in Brendan's cell that would yield a clue to his whereabouts. If anyone could make sense of the matter, it would be Balian, even if Brendan was a slippery character who had demonstrably proved himself a genius of deception. Balian might have met his match in the Gael.

A sound brought Tancred to his senses, the scuffing of feet across the granite flags of the cloister walk. Without knowing why, possessed of some vague presentiment, he raced toward the count in the far corner. Tancred had almost reached him when he saw the strange friar who had shut the door on his face earlier in the day. The man was flying across the stone walkway toward Raymond, dagger drawn and lifted high above his head. Tancred lunged over the low wall surrounding the ambulatory and tackled the count just as the dagger came down. He felt a sharp pain in his right shoulder but had no time to think about it as he now wrestled desperately with the man on the stone floor, who shouted, "Heretics! Violators of the temple!"

The count scrambled to his feet, yelling, "Guards! Guards!"

Within an instant the man was overpowered and brought before the count, whose face was white with rage. Raymond slapped the man so hard that two teeth could be heard bouncing off the flagstones.

"So what say you, good friar? Holy man? Servant of Christ?" he hissed.

"You defame the house of Dominic," the man snapped back. "You are unholy filth. The scum of the earth. The inmates of Hell."

Raymond punched the friar in the stomach. He doubled over from the blow, despite the soldiers holding his arms fast.

A low groan was heard. Raymond looked down and saw Tancred lying in a pool of his own blood, his head lolling back and forth in pain.

"Balian," Tancred croaked, "Get Balian."

A man was dispatched at once. The count knelt beside the recumbent figure, cradling Tancred's head in his right arm.

"It will be all right," he whispered, "my most loyal and brave friend. It will be all right." He grimaced on seeing the reddened dagger on the floor some distance away.

By the time Balian and Matilda arrived, a crowd of Dominicans had gathered, including the abbot, aghast at the sight of the Count of Toulouse holding a gravely injured man and of a friar in custody, all within the holy precincts of the cloister. Balian pushed his way through the friars, ignoring their protests. When Matilda arrived, she let out a shriek, unmistakably the cry of a woman. A murmur of disbelief rippled through the brothers.

"Where, Tancred?" Balian asked.

"My shoulder ... Back ... "

Balian turned him over and ripped off the bloodied tunic. An ugly wound oozed blood from near the right shoulder. He noted that the color of the blood was dark, indicating venous blood, originating in the liver, as Galen had taught. Matilda took off her cap and pressed it to the wound to staunch the flow. Her hair fell, revealing her for what she was.

Raymond exclaimed, astonished, "Lady Matilda?"

Scandalized shouts were heard from the friars.

"A woman!"

"Sacrilege."

The would-be assassin cried out, "A vile daughter of Eve in our house." The count got smartly to his feet and walked over to the man, then delivered a tremendous blow to his face with the back of his hand. The man lost consciousness. Raymond turned, fists clenched, and stared murderously at the others. They fell silent.

Balian's voice broke the stillness, addressing the abbot. "Do you have an infirmarer? An herbalist?"

"Here," two voices replied hesitantly.

"Then, infirmarer, have Cook mix me some egg whites with vinegar. Now. Herbalist, some mint, myrrh, and yarrow, ground separately. Hurry."

The two friars scurried off.

"No mustard poultice?" Tancred said weakly.

Balian smiled. "No mustard poultice, my friend."

He turned back to the abbot. "Now some hot water and clean linen strips. In a trice—he is losing blood."

When he faced his friend again, Tancred's eyes fluttered closed. Matilda, on her knees in her brother's blood, sobbed wordlessly.

CHAPTER SIXTY-FOUR

"A pretty picture here," said the count. "Wouldn't you say so, my good abbot?"

The fat man remained silent, chastened.

"We look for the Dominican murderer of Dominican inquisitors in the Dominican convent, and then this Dominican friar tries to kill us. There is a common thread here, wouldn't you say?" The count moved closer to the abbot. "This is actionable. This is treasonous. By any standard, even Rome's." Raymond paused, then said evenly, "You have one day to leave this city. All of you."

"My lord, we must put one of ours to rest," the abbot said tremulously. "The provincial, Giuseppe."

"Very well. Do it tomorrow. Put the bastard away. Put him in a deep, deep hole and cover him up with rocks."

Abbot Jean of Béthune gaped at the count.

"Spare me your Dominican hypocrisy," Raymond snapped. "When the lecher Giuseppe's in the ground, all of you, out of here, do you understand?"

"But you ... you cannot ... you do not have the authority."

"Very well, then stay here. But if you stay, you die," Raymond said simply. "I will protect you no longer. My people hate you, and they are right to hate you. If they revolt against you, which they will once they know that I will not interfere, expect none of my men to come to your rescue. The mob will tear you limb from limb."

The abbot crossed himself ostentatiously. Raymond snorted. "Pack your bags, wineskin. Rome will side with me."

CHAPTER SIXTY-FIVE

Balian returned to Brendan's cell to collect the letters and the chest filled with florins. Moments earlier he had managed to stop the bleeding and spread herbs over Tancred's wound to prevent infection. Once the bandages had been set, his friend was strapped onto a stretcher for the journey back through the streets to the Narbonne Castle. Matilda walked alongside holding her brother's limp hand, oblivious first to the glares of the Dominicans within the convent, then to the townspeople crossing themselves in dismay as the lugubrious procession passed. The urge to hail the count, who walked on the other side of the stretcher, died in many a throat, once his bloodstained tunic and the condition of his stricken companion became clear.

But Balian was not too worried and had told Matilda as much in parting. "We got to him in time; he will live," he had said to her as they embraced in the cloister, not giving a damn about the friars' sensibilities. "Unless some fool bleeds him. Stay by his side at all times, make sure that that doesn't happen. When he wakes, give him cold water." She had kissed him on the cheek in reply and returned to see the stretcher hoisted in the air by four strong sergeants.

Balian surveyed the cell in the dying sunlight. Was he missing something? He put the chest on the bed, then walked slowly about the room. There was no place to hide here, yet Brendan had not been found anywhere in the convent. Normally Balian enjoyed puzzles, but only if he could solve them.

Where could he have gone? The door was the only way out. Balian stopped in the middle of the room and looked carefully around him. The doorway, the wall beside the bed, the wall beside the desk, the window, and the chair.

The window and the chair?

Balian moved to the window, a realization dawning. The glass was encased in an iron frame and could be opened inward on its hinges. All one had to do was lift the latch.

But that had already been done. The latch hung vertically down the iron frame. As it was made of the same iron as the frame, it was difficult to distinguish at first.

Balian stood on the chair and drew the window back. The opening was large enough for a man to squeeze through. That was it—Brendan must be hiding in the church. He had got up on the chair, opened the window wider, stepped out onto the convent roof, then carefully closed the window behind him. As he was on the outside then, he had not been able to put the latch in place or move the chair away from its telltale location under the window. Brendan must have left in a hurry, with no time to collect his florins.

Balian gingerly emerged onto the roof. The terra-cotta tiles were covered with a thin film of dust, kicked up from the building site adjacent to them. Descending the slope of the roof, even though it was gentle, would require uncommon agility, as the dust made for treacherous footing. He immediately distinguished the footprints of Brendan, who had apparently sidestepped his way down the roof to the sure footing of the scaffold ringing the half-constructed church. Balian did likewise in the dying light of the day, slowly heading downward, checking to see if each of his steps had found purchase in the concave area between the half-barrel-shaped tiles. Legs shaking from the effort, he at last reached the edge of the roof and surveyed the void separating the convent roof from the scaffold. It was about five or six paces in width; he would have to leap that distance or fall to an almost certain death three stories below.

Balian caught his breath and willed his legs to be still. He would have to make the leap from a standing start. Not looking earthward but rather concentrating on the platform of woven twigs at the triforium level of the church, he squatted down, then launched himself in the air. Time seemed to stop—until he thudded chest-down on the platform, his legs dangling over the abyss. A clatter came from below; the dagger had fallen from his sleeve.

Panting, he swung his legs up, then slowly rose to his feet. The open window from which he had started this journey looked very small and far away. From where he stood, on a rickety hurdle between the outer buttress and an interior pier of the nave, Balian had a commanding view of the construction site. The maze of platforms at different elevations would normally be manned with a master mason and his bricklayers and mortar makers, but today was deserted, as the site had been closed until Brother Giuseppe's remains were properly buried. Which meant that Balian and Brendan had the church to themselves.

CHAPTER SIXTY-SIX

The master builder could be hiding anywhere, in a place almost impossible to find, as every detail of this vertical labyrinth had sprung from his imagination. Balian advanced along the platform toward the apse, where the building process was at its most advanced. Perhaps Brendan was lodged in a radiating chapel behind where the altar would eventually rise.

Balian inched his way cautiously along the platform, which ran from one end of the church to the other. Brendan's brainchild was to have no transept, just one vast chamber roughly in the shape of an elongated lozenge. When the woven-twig platform came to the choir, it was replaced by the solid stone floor of a completed triforium gallery. Through the fluted columns Balian peered down at the floor far below, littered with ropes and masonry, awaiting the return of the workmen. Above, toward the rear of the apse, he could see a tall platform at the level of the clerestory on which a large windlass was placed, its cranking device used to hoist large loads skyward now standing unused.

He stopped, straining to hear any sound. The silence was sepulchral. His noisy landing on the platform must have been heard, so that Brendan would be taking care not to give himself away.

When Balian reached the final stage of the choir, before its straight wall gave way to the curvature of the apse, he saw that the last buttress had been constructed to allow for a spiral staircase within it, providing access to the ground floor. Something told him that Brendan must be below; the shadows were deepening, and the protective blackness of night would not be long in coming, the time when the hunted friar would have to make his move.

Without the benefit of torchlight, the descent down the staircase was akin to wearing a blindfold. Balian stepped down slowly, his hands sliding along the great stone blocks of the buttress on either side to give him some sense of balance. At last, he took the final step and came out, blinking, onto the cold floor of the choir. To his immediate right were the radiating chapels of the apse. With his dagger gone, he would have to improvise his own protection. He surveyed the floor for some makeshift weapon, some tool that the workmen might have left behind, an adze, a mallet, a chisel, even an auger. But there was nothing lying about, as each skilled craftsman would have taken the means of his livelihood back to the house in which he was billeted. Balian saw only a few boards on the floor of the apse and a large straw mat in its center.

Soundlessly, on tiptoe, he went forward to inspect the first of the chapels, peering round its corner before stepping into it. There was no one within, just construction materials neatly piled up against its walls to spare those working on the main floor of the church the clutter of timbers and stone to be used much later in the building process. The second chapel served as a storehouse as well, leading Balian to conclude that all five were similarly employed. Once consecrated they would be alive with riotous decoration, gilded candelabras, glorious statuary, stately tombs, but for now they were just places to house the humble materials that would come together and make a stupendous structure. In the last of the chapels he saw a great oak beam with a splinter the length of a man running parallel to it. Without too much difficulty he prized the splinter from the beam and surveyed it. It was like a long walking staff, with a murderous point at one end: in short, a fine weapon.

He proceeded down the aisle on the north side of the sanctuary between the piers and the buttressed outer walls. Brendan was too clever to play peekaboo behind the pillars. About midway down the nave Balian reached an opening—a future doorway—that led out into the work area on the exterior of the building. As the space between the convent and the church on the other side was too cramped, this area was perforce the place where all the workshops were located. He surveyed the humble buildings with their thatched roofs, the sheds of the masons, the carpenters, the bricklayers. No one was within, only the ghosts of the bustling activity of the day before.

Balian picked his way through the piles of red bricks and solid stone masonry, at a loss. He checked the door to the palisade surrounding the worksite to keep out vandals and thieves—it was locked securely, so Brendan had not slipped out into the darkened streets. No tall ladder was leaned up against the palisade, or lying nearby, again showing the architect had to be still within the enclosure or the church. What could he possibly be thinking? By the light of day, the site would be crawling with the count's soldiers, the French sergeants, the men of Chantecler—unless he had a means of escape, he would be found before the cock crowed.

By the light of day, by the light of day... Balian squinted in the darkness. Night had fallen, moonless. Only the faint light of the stars struggled to create the looming silhouette behind him. His quarry had to be in the church.

CHAPTER SIXTY-SEVEN

Balian reentered the sanctuary and took his place at what he estimated was the midpoint of the nave. His voice would thus be heard in every corner in the church. He made up his mind. He threw his pointed oaken staff into the darkness, its clattering on a board echoing off brick and stone.

"Brendan!" he shouted. "Brother Brendan."

As the last of the echoes died down, the familiar singsong rang out.

"Master Balian of Mallorca. 'Tis a bit dark to be admiring my handiwork."

Balian strained to determine from which direction the voice came. It was as if the blackness had swallowed up sound, as well as light.

"What handiwork might that be?" Balian countered. "Three men dead and a fourth slain at the hand of a young girl goaded on by you?"

"You've got me there. I feel terrible about the poor thing, I do."

Still having no clue as to where the voice came from, Balian jerked his head back and forth, hoping to hear some movement, discern some shadow darker against the dark walls.

"And the three others? Have you no remorse? Are you not afraid?"

"That God might strike me down? Damn me to Hell? I don't believe that drivel and neither do you," Brendan said loudly. "God doesn't build my church; I do. And God doesn't cure your sick; you do."

Balian felt buffeted by the echoes coming from all direc-
tions. It was as if the church itself were uttering the blasphemies,
as if it were laughing at its own existence, as if it had taken on the
innermost thoughts of its creator.

Starlight tickled the piers of the sanctuary, filtered through
the fluting of the triforium. Balian, the lone figure in the center
of the nave, turned around and around in the darkness like a
dervish disembarked from distant Antioch. Where was the voice
coming from? It seemed to well up from the ground and grow
and spread until finally filling the entire enclosure.

"Brendan," Balian ventured at last. "I know you are a good
man. I know you. Who put you up to this? I am your friend—you
owe me an explanation."

A long silence ensued. Balian held his breath, lest he might
miss a sound, a shifting in the dark.

"Brendan?"

A throat cleared. Balian started—it came from somewhere in
the rear, not the front, of the church. He took a few silent footfalls
forward.

"Very well, my friend," Brendan said, his voice much lower.
"My two brothers, they are in captivity. They made the pilgrimage to Rome."

"I hear they are in good health."

"You have read Kevin's letters."

That explained the odd missives from K, Kevin, with the same
salutation and then a personal detail that would be known only to
Brendan and his kinsmen. Poor Brendan would have recognized
his brother's hand. So this is how the blackmail worked. Brendan's
brothers would be kept alive, kept in good health, only if he followed the orders of their malevolent captor. A captor who wanted
to foment chaos in Languedoc by murdering the inquisitors.

"But who imprisons them? Who wants the inquisitors dead?"

Balian felt that he could almost hear Brendan struggling to
decide somewhere out there in the blackness. The shuffling of

what must have been a very large rat punctuated the stillness, its noisy passage growing fainter as it reached the front of the church.

"The Assembly?"

"Hush," Brendan exclaimed, his panic palpable. "They are not to be named."

"Tell me, Brendan. So that I will know. You must help me; you owe me that."

Balian took four more hesitant steps toward the back of the choir, certain now that the unseen speaker stood in front of him.

"This will be adieu, my brother," Brendan said shakily. "The Assembly ... They ... they are everywhere. You must take care, Balian; you must be on the watch for them, for they span the length and breadth of Christendom, everywhere, all in the service of one great lord ... Goodbye, my friend."

"The lord is R," Balian cried out. "Who is R?"

He knew there would be no response. He had heard the fear, naked and raw, in Brendan's voice, as if what he had admitted had been heard by every member of the nebulous Assembly.

Another rat trundled through the apse, its passage muffled but insistent. No, perhaps not. It didn't sound at all like its predecessor—this was no rat.

Curious, Balian got down on all fours and pressed his ear to the ground. The sound was unmistakable. Someone was digging, he could hear the faint ring of a spade striking a surface and the rain-like pattering of dirt being tossed aside. He got to his feet, looked for the digger ahead of him. But it was no use; what little starlight there was to guide him was now snuffed out by an errant cloud. The digging sound ceased.

Balian stared into the blackness, vainly willing his eyes to become those of an owl. But the blackness remained impenetrable, enveloping him like a shroud. Uncertain of what to do, he stretched his arms out in front of him, like a blind man fearing a wall, and took a few more steps toward the rear of the church.

Suddenly he saw a small glow, directly ahead, at ground level, in the center of the apse, then a much brighter light accompanied by a sibilant whoosh. An oil-soaked torch had been lit, not thirty paces in front of him, yet he had seen no flame. Balian broke into a run as the light dimmed, then disappeared. He had almost arrived at the apse when a stray coil of rope caught his foot and sent him sprawling to the ground, face-first. He rose to his feet, feeling the blood pouring down over his lips, and put a hand to his face. His nose was broken.

Cursing under his breath, Balian pressed on to where he thought the light had originated. It had to have come from here, right in the center of the curved enclosure, where the altar would stand. He felt his footing change, from earth to woven straw mat—and then to nothing.

He was in free fall.

In an instant, he landed with a jolt, then fell on his back. He shook his head, stars of his own making dancing in front of his eyes, then rose, once again, to his feet. He winced—his left ankle could not support much of his weight.

Where was Brendan? Balian reached out, felt an earthen wall on one side and the same on the other. He reached up, found that the hole he had fallen into was too deep for him to climb out of. Searching, feeling with his hands, Balian soon realized that his prison was a rectangle, deeper than a man standing with his arms stretched out over his head.

A grave. He was standing in a freshly dug grave.

CHAPTER SIXTY-EIGHT

Balian's mind raced. Perhaps the grave had been dug to receive the body of Brother Giuseppe, the first burial in what was to be the crypt of the new church, below the altar. In time, it would be made grander, decorated with marble, with an underground room for the friars to pray before the remains of their illustrious predecessors, but for now it was a simple hole in the ground.

And it was a hole in the ground traced out by Brother Brendan. There had to be a reason for its emplacement in this spot. The center of the apse could be reckoned in several different ways, give or take a few paces, yet Brendan had chosen this place and had somehow escaped from it undetected. Balian, his ankle aching, leaned against the earthen wall. He started—it was as hard as rock. This was not freshly dug; Brendan had had this grave dug six or seven months ago, judging by the solidity of the unyielding earth. It was not intended for Giuseppe.

But where had Brendan gone?

Balian attempted to squat down, to see if he was missing something that was not at eye level, but the pain was too great. Instead, he got down on his right knee, like a squire paying obeisance to his knight. His instinct paid off, for ahead of him, on one of the smaller sides of the rectangle, he could make out an indistinct glow, as if somewhere deep in the ground some subterranean creature had lit a taper.

He advanced toward the light. His hand crept its way down the wall until suddenly it felt nothing. There was a hole, a small tunnel, carved out at ground level, this one freshly dug. That had been the digging sound Balian had heard.

Getting down on all fours, he crawled through the confined space, his back scraping against the top of the tunnel. It was unnerving, leaving a grave for an even murkier place, but the wan light ahead urged him on. After a few seconds, he felt solid stone blocks under his hands and knees. Disbelieving, he carefully got up; this tunnel was tall enough for him to stand. To his right, he could make out a mound of rubble and broken brick—no doubt a collapsed section of the tunnel—but to his left, several hundred paces away, he could see the light of a torch, and, if he squinted, the silhouette of a figure performing some strange repetitive motion.

Brother Brendan.

Balian limped slowly a few paces toward him, his hands on both sides of the tunnel to maintain his balance. Surely Brendan had not had the time to have such a splendid escape route built— the workers would have talked among themselves and the whole town would have known within the week. Balian remarked the cool smoothness of the stone, as planed and polished as porphyry, alternating with bands of brick and pebbled mortar. Then it struck him. This was the work of the old ones, the Old Romans; it had to be—its perfection was its proof. It was an underground aqueduct leading from the river Garonne. The sturdy roadways of the ancients still crisscrossed the Languedoc, the fields of France, the valleys of Italy, traveled and admired generation after generation. He remembered his father telling him about the days of the caliphs, some three hundred years earlier, when Sevilla and Toledo had still used the stone watercourses of the Old Romans to feed their plashing fountains and dripping clepsydras and to wash away the waste from their kitchens and privies. The foolish local despots who succeeded the caliphs in the great cities of al-Andalus had neglected these practical treasures and let them fall into disuse and disrepair, perhaps hoping that their courtesans, or maybe even God, would supply the needed water to their parched subjects. Brendan must have come across the old waterway during the excavation for a foundation, perhaps a pier of the choir; he might have found the central cistern and followed this feeder out until he reached the pile of rubble Balian had seen when first entering the aqueduct. It would have been child's play for a man of Brendan's science to determine where the tunnel resumed. The canny Gael had planned his escape long ago.

The far-off figure continued its curious movements, back and forth, back and forth. Even at a great distance Balian could hear the chink of metal on mortar and stone, a chisel at work, or perhaps a pickaxe, reverberating down the stone passage. Brendan must have blocked up the egress of the tunnel so that no foolhardy boy venturing into the long grasses by the river's edge would discover the Old Roman marvel. Doubtless scores of youngsters had passed the masonry without a second thought, intent instead on finding tadpoles and sharp sticks.

Balian's right foot became moist, then wet. He looked down, puzzled, wondering if he was imagining a rivulet of some sort snaking between his feet and then going behind him, down the gentle slope of the aqueduct. The sound of the chisel came to an abrupt halt.

"Sweet Jesus!" Brendan's voice bounced off the smooth walls and echoed—but now not in any silence. Balian heard a mounting roar, a ferocious animal bestirring itself, then suddenly an ear-splitting explosion of brick and mortar and stone. Brendan's guttering torch was instantly extinguished, plunging Balian into the blackest of darkness.

He strained, his ears not believing what they heard, a deafening sound like the charge of war-horses at full gallop, growing louder and louder, thundering down an incline toward him.

Then it hit. A wall of water, furious and roiling, filling the tunnel, striking him square in the chest, hurling him up and throwing him down, like a twig tormented in the rapids. Balian flailed, gasping for breath as the raging torrent thrust him backward and then downward into its deadly embrace. The force of the current threw him up against the rubble of the collapsed part of the structure, then mercilessly forced him through the small dirt tunnel he had just crawled through. Its walls were caving in; he could feel the dirt against his closed eyelids, until suddenly he felt himself being forced upward, buoyed by the sheer force of the raging flow, and his head broke the surface. Gasping for breath, he reached out and touched a wall—he had been given life by returning to the grave. As the water rose, bringing Balian with it, he felt the floor of the church under his outstretched hands and he hoisted himself upward, panting and sodden. He rolled away from the frothing gravesite, rolling and rolling and rolling until he felt at a safe distance.

He lay on his back, eyes open now, breathing heavily. The moon had at last come out, a shaving of a sickle, but casting enough light to leaven the darkness. He watched the water gush out of the grave, spread quietly throughout the church, then, as if summoned home, reverse flow and head back to the hole in the ground, from which the gurgling sound of retreating water was now clearly audible. The torrent subsided, seeking its own level.

Balian closed his eyes. Brendan's plan had been foolproof—almost. He had chosen the wrong time to make his escape. The snows of the Pyrenees were melting, their gorges filled with the thunder of icy cascades, spilling into the watercourses winding down the slopes and into minor brooks, streams, and rivers, swelling them, hastening their flow, until at last they joined the mighty Garonne. The river of Toulouse was in flood, its spring gift to be harnessed by tillers of the soil downstream. Brendan had chipped away at his masonry when the river was at its highwater mark—and the entrance to his tunnel lay well beneath its surface. At any other season, when the Garonne resumed its low, lazy flow, his plan would have worked, and he would have emerged onto a dry riverbank. But at high water, his escape hatch was underwater.

A curious slapping sound roused Balian from his reverie. He quickly located its source, a marooned carp in the middle of the choir, fighting for dear life in a shallow puddle. Moved by an instinct he did not know he possessed, he got to his feet, then hobbled over and picked up the struggling fish. It squirmed furiously in his hands, but he managed to make it to the grave site and toss the fish into the receding water with a splash. The grave had saved him; perhaps now it would save another of God's creatures.

But not all his creatures. Balian spied a large dark form on the ground a few paces toward the rear of the apse. He dreaded what he would find, but he knew already. Brendan. Lifeless. The face that had worn laughter so lightly was now almost unrecognizable, a battered and pulped surface already blue and black. His limbs were splayed at unnatural angles, as if some mocking animal had destroyed a scarecrow. And his crow's cassock lay in tatters around him, exposing his still-pink skin to the elements. Balian leaned in for a closer look—on Brendan's upper right arm there was a tattoo, or rather a brand. The florid script of the brand read only one letter: *R*.

Balian bowed his head, exhausted. He adjusted the cassock on the corpse so that it would not be immodest when they were discovered. And together they would be found. Balian lay down beside the body of his friend, stretched out his hand, and laid it on the dead man's shoulder.

Sleep came at once.

CHAPTER SIXTY-NINE

The black kites had arrived from Africa, carried by a steady sirocco that had deposited a fine layer of sand on the blooming garrigue of the Languedoc. Ibrahim ibn Abdullah stood on a hillside purple with lavender quivering in the slight breeze. With him were three little boys, squinting up at the birds cavorting in the blue.

Auriol was alive once again. Outraged by the news of Brother Brendan's infamy, the king's seneschal in Carcassonne had ordered the release of the villagers from the Wall. The friars had objected, but not too vociferously, as details of Dominican mischief had spread throughout the Languedoc. The crows had been silenced.

But not the raptors, whose cries could be heard echoing across the countryside. Harriers wheeled in the sun, their wings outstretched to catch the updrafts rising from the warm earth in an elaborate aerial dance enacted every spring.

"They're mating," Ibrahim explained. "When they fly in circles, they are telling each other it is time."

The boys said nothing. One pointed to a spot far off, toward Carcassonne. From a great height, a gray goshawk dived in what seemed to be a death spiral, nearing the scrubby ground at great speed. A stand of holm oaks blocked the view of its talons closing on its quarry, but the spectacle of the bird hurtling downward had been enough to inspire awe.

The birds seemed to be everywhere, calling to one another, engaging in lethal frolics, culling the young of the groundlings; only the fleetest and the canniest of these would survive to mate the *following spring and to restart the great cycle. The birds of prey would arrive from Africa, from al-Andalus, from the Pyrenees, to nest, to mate—and to hunt.*

Ibrahim looked down at his three young charges from Auriol, their faces upturned in the sunlight. They too were groundlings, subject to the vagaries of their times, the sudden accesses of misfortune, the slow workings of an uneventful and thus happy life, members of the nameless legions of humanity whose passage on this land would one day fade, then disappear altogether, to be recalled only by the whisper of the wind in the cypress, the cry of the eagle, the toll of the church bell. But they were young now, not fully fledged, like the chicks who squealed in concealment somewhere in the canopy of trees farther up the slope.

The birds in the Languedoc were not all benign.

CHAPTER SEVENTY

"I owe you my life," Count Raymond had said. "And I pay my debts. I have not long to live, and I do not want to leave any creditors."

Tancred, raised up on his sickbed, looked at Matilda and Judith, sitting, as they had for the last week, on chairs on either side of him. Despite the dark circles under their eyes, the two women could not help but smile.

Fatima arrived bearing a platter with several goblets and two ewers of wine and water. She set about distributing them.

Count Raymond looked at her fixedly.

Feeling his gaze, she raised her eyes and said, "M'lord?"

Raymond turned to the others. "I will pay all my debts."

"I do not think that your debt to Tancred will be difficult to pay!" Balian, on crutches, came into the room, smiling broadly, his face a lurid collection of bruises and welts. His nose, which he had set back himself with a pair of pliers borrowed from the count's carpenter, an operation that had required the unflappable Matilda to immobilize his head in a firm grip, now rose in some semblance of its former self, long and prominent, noble even.

The friars had found Balian and Brendan on the floor of the cathedral at dawn. A quick-witted novice had spotted the open window in Brendan's cell and alerted the abbot. Showing surprising agility for a man of his girth, Abbot Jean had rushed around to the back of the worksite, unlocked the door to the palisade, and discovered the two, lying in the apse, their blood commingled with water.

Jean had been surprisingly candid with Balian in the infirmary where both he and the body of Brother Brendan had been taken. He admitted that the Dominicans had brought these miseries upon themselves, but that the punishment Count Raymond had decreed was far too harsh.

"Toulouse is where Saint Dominic began his ministry," Jean said. "We must continue his holy work here."

Balian recognized the plaintive note in the big man's voice. What he was not saying came across plainly: if the Dominicans were expelled from Toulouse, then he, Jean of Béthune, would be the scapegoat. The Dominican hierarchy would show no mercy to such high-profile failure. The Order of the Friars Preachers, no longer in the place of its founding. Unthinkable. Jean would doubtless end his days on some dark shore of the Baltic, surrounded by hostile people wearing hides and furs, suspicious of the men preaching this strange new gospel, ready to draw their broadswords at a moment's provocation. Martyrdom held no appeal for the abbot.

"Tell me, Brother Jean," Balian said. "What do you know of the Assembly, and of a certain lord who goes only by the letter *R*?"

He pulled up Brendan's tunic to display the brand on his arm.

The abbot moved forward, looked at the mark, then turned to Balian.

"What are you talking about?"

His puzzlement seemed genuine.

"I take it you are innocent of any involvement with them?"

Jean spluttered. "You speak in riddles, sir, I know not the custom of the Gaels," he said, referring to the dead man.

"So let us not speak in riddles anymore," Balian said. "If you wish to remain in Toulouse, what is the price you will pay?"

"But this is intolerable."

"Tsk, tsk, silly fellow. I speak not of money, but of price."

"Riddles again!"

Balian waved away the infirmarer and sat in his chair.

"You have two bodies in this convent. Giuseppe of Fiesole and Brendan of Killiney. What links these two men?"

Jean scowled, beginning to understand.

"You are the abbot, are you not? Now that Giuseppe is no longer with us, your authority over *all* Dominican friars in the city is paramount... Or am I wrong?"

"You are not."

"Now then," Balian continued, like a magister in one of the Paris schools, "if there is an irritant, it should be removed, should it not? For the welfare of all concerned. For the people of Toulouse and for the friars of Dominic. A wound must be treated, an illness attended to, a source of contention and strife eliminated. Would you not agree, Abbot?"

"You... you speak of the Holy Office," Jean said quietly.

"Precisely. That is the price. I knew you would come around to it eventually. You are to be congratulated."

"For how long?"

"For as long as Count Raymond shall live," Balian stated, irony now absent from his voice. "No more inquisitors in Toulouse. You friars may stay, but there will be no Inquisition, no arrests, no tortures, no sentences, no executions... Do I make myself clear?"

Jean considered the proposal. The Baltic nightmare began to recede in his mind.

"How do I know you can make the count change his mind?"

"You don't! That's the beauty of life, isn't it? Uncertainty. Surprise. The unexpected."

The abbot had not one jot of fondness for this doctor from Paris, or from wherever he came. His speech was disturbing, unsettling; he spoke against everything Jean had ever learned. This devil spoke as if there were no absolutes.

"Now, now, my dear abbot," Balian said soothingly. "I have the ear of Count Raymond. He is an eminently sensible ruler. He wants no quarrel with Rome or with your order. I am certain that you two can come to some arrangement."

Jean of Béthune hitched his cassock over the great globe of his stomach. There would be hell to pay for suppressing the Holy Office, but far worse would be the reaction were the Dominicans to disappear entirely from this wretched city on the Garonne.

"Very well," he said at last. "You speak to the count. Tell him I am willing to do as you suggest."

Balian got to his feet.

"Good! Now with your permission, I will go." He grabbed the crutches supplied by the infirmarer and placed them under his arms.

"I won't detain you any longer." He placed his hand on Brother Brendan's shoulder for one last time. "Be good to my friend Brendan, Abbot. He had no choice."

CHAPTER SEVENTY-ONE

It had taken some getting used to, accustomed as he was to his solitary pursuits, but Balian now welcomed Matilda into his home, or rather *their* home, for it felt as if she had always been there. When a few of the older monks at Saint-Germain had protested the presence of a woman on the grounds of the monastery, Abbot Anselm silenced them with a stern warning. Whatever we must do to keep the learned Balian of Mallorca as our tenant, we will do—the man of science is too valuable to the well-being of our community.

Balian had not heard from the queen mother since his return to the North in early June. Brother Martin of Tours had preceded him by several weeks—Balian stayed in the South until his ankle mended—and no doubt the Franciscan's report to Blanche gave the friar the leading role in what had been accomplished. The murderer had been unmasked, the Holy Office shuttered, and the sulfur of revolt dissipated. In short, a job well done, exactly what the queen mother had asked. When Count Raymond died, the French Crown would take possession of a quiescent, prosperous county. The only acknowledgment from Blanche to Balian was the delivery of a felt bag laden with his payment. The second half due on successful completion of his task. No note, no receipt slip, just the currency of her dealings with men like him.

Matilda emerged from the doorway, a slip of vellum in her hand. "It is ready," she said with a smile.

Balian led her through his Saracen garden, which his man had carefully tended in his absence. When he first showed Matilda the carefully shielded patch, she had gasped in amazement at the variety of vegetables and fruit she had never before seen. Alcuin had not taught her about this abundance and variety.

They approached the dovecote. Balian instructed Matilda how to hold her forearm level, parallel to the ground; then he extracted the pigeon from its cubby and placed it on her wrist. He tied the vellum securely to the pigeon's right leg, twisting the twine several times around to make sure it would not come loose in flight. The pigeon cocked its head at Balian, as if unconnected to the proceedings.

"Now, lower your arm once, twice, thrice, and then throw it up in the air," Balian instructed.

Matilda pursed her lips, concentrating. Her arm went down three times and then she slung it far above her shoulder. The pigeon took flight, heading straight into the blue like a bolt loosed from a longbow. Within minutes, it was a mere dot, and then it was gone.

"Oh, Balian," she said, "why do we deserve such contentment?"

He placed his arm around her waist and kissed her.

A day later, the pigeon master at Chantecler noticed the green tab showing on the lowest tier of the dovecote. He grasped the bird, undid the twine, then proceeded to the gate of the castle. As he knew his lord was out visiting his far-flung holdings, he would deliver the message to the lady of the castle.

Judith thanked the man for the message. She strode through the sunshine pouring through the windows of the solar and unfolded the note. She read it and smiled:

To the recipients of this letter all happiness must be afforded. They are of the Beloved.

It was true, they were all the Beloved. Judith loved Matilda and Balian almost as much as she loved Tancred. What an odd fate was hers! Orphaned, thrown out of the community, imprisoned awaiting certain death, and a scarce two months later, the lady of Chantecler, the first quickening of life in her womb. She would tell Tancred when he returned.

Count Raymond had indeed paid his debts. When Tancred requested Judith's release, he had promptly complied. "She should be rewarded, not punished, for finishing off that loathsome Tuscan," he had remarked. And she had been rewarded. Raymond, mindful that the girl had been outcast from her kin and dispossessed, ordered Rabbi Ezra to restore her confiscated property, on pain of incurring his displeasure. Ezra, ever cautious in the face of Gentile authority, quickly complied. Then Raymond had married them in the great hall, his entire court in attendance.

Alongside him stood little Fatima, whom the count, to much stupefaction, had declared the day before to be his natural daughter. Henceforth, there would be no scullery chores for her, only tutors to prepare her for a match suitable for one of her station in life. On announcing the news, the count had said that the time had come to pay all his debts. Foremost among these was his debt to the truth. For too long the girl had been left in ignorance of her parentage; now it was time to redress the wrong he had done her. He had begged her forgiveness and kissed her brow. Fatima remembered the gesture as her father performed the wedding, standing stock-still in her unaccustomed finery and her newfound place of honor.

There were a few uncomfortable coughs when the count's confessor was produced to deliver a blessing directed at the couple, but Raymond's glare gave the cleric the backbone to go through with it. After that, a banquet was held in the great hall. At the high table sat the newlyweds, Tancred and Judith, the witnesses, Balian and Matilda, and their host, Count Raymond. At his right hand, in a place of honor, was Fatima. Serving her, Esclarmonde, the head of the kitchen staff, had leaned in and whispered, "I always knew it, little one. You stood out from us all by the nobility of your bearing."

Fatima flushed, uncertain how to respond. At last, she looked into the expectant eyes and said, "Thank you, sister."

The servant took her hand and kissed it fervently.

Then she started in alarm when a large bearded man appeared beside her, smiling broadly. From his basket he produced a *fougasse*, which he laid on the table in front of Fatima.

"Thank you, Pascal," the girl said.

"Are we still partners, Lady Fatima?" the baker asked.

"Why, of course, Pascal. We must always work together."

Count Raymond watched, wide-eyed and puzzled, as the big man executed a bow, then walked from the hall.

"Who might that be, Daughter?" he ventured.

"Only time will tell, Father. Only time will tell."

CHAPTER SEVENTY-TWO

The giant bells of Saint John Lateran, Rome's oldest basilica, tolled in mighty solemnity. Beneath the great nave, a sea of dignitaries and churchmen watched the reliquary being deposited under the altar. The shinbone of Saint Giuseppe Martyr of Fiesole was being interred, on this, his first feast day. The pope, celebrating the mass, knew that it had taken considerable arm-twisting to get the Dominicans of Toulouse to relinquish even this, but the abbot had finally delivered. The pope also knew that the faster he got Giuseppe's relics made sacred, the faster his misdeeds would be forgotten.

Abbot Jean of Béthune, however, was not in attendance. In a palazzo near the Capitoline Hill, he stood trembling in an audience chamber. He had been summoned to Rome to explain himself.

"I had no choice, Your Eminence Romano," he said. "If I did not suppress the Holy Office, we would have been expelled from Toulouse."

His pleading was met with silence.

"It was the work of that devil," Jean added hastily.

A flicker of interest appeared in the narrowed eyes.

"Who?"

"Balian of Mallorca."

Cardinal Romano twisted the agate ring on his finger, thinking.

"The sorcerer of Saint-Germain-des-Prés?"

"I know not who he is or where he lives, but it was he who uncovered the killer, who influenced the Count of Toulouse, who freed the murderous Jewess."

"Did he kill Brendan?"

"No. But he knows of us. He knows of the Assembly. He asked me as much."

"So the Languedoc will become French," Romano said regretfully. His face darkened. "But I will get to that bitch Blanche in some other way."

He looked at the agate ring on his finger, a token of his past attachment to Blanche. A silence fell between them. Jean wanted nothing more than to leave this menacing presence.

"Balian of Mallorca... He will pay, mark our words... And so will the others."

Jean nodded meekly.

"Now, get out of our sight."

CHAPTER SEVENTY-THREE

The door to their cell creaked open on its hinges. A blazing torch was thrust into the darkness. The two bearded men illuminated on the floor squinted into the unaccustomed light—evening visitors to their prison in the Castel Sant'Angelo were few and far between. Indeed, it was only in the mornings, at two-month intervals, that a scribe arrived with the writing material for Kevin to write to his brother Brendan and tell him that they were in good health.

"Get up."

Kevin and Diarmaid rose unsteadily to their feet.

"Cardinal Romano has a message for you."

Cardinal Romano? Their captor? Perhaps news of Brendan?

That was their last thought. The two men facing them expertly raised their stilettos and slit the two Gaels' throats. They fell heavily to the floor, gurgling and gasping. The men with the bloodied knives stepped aside, to let pass a burly man in a leather apron. In his right hand he held a butcher's cleaver. There came two powerful thuds in quick succession, as metal cleaved flesh and bone.

The heads were taken out of the room to be affixed to pikes outside Cardinal Romano's palazzo. The crows performing their disgusting disfigurements would be a reminder to the restive Roman populace of the power of the prelate.

The headless bodies of the two Gaels were hefted up in the arms of the waiting soldiery. They climbed the stairs, then stepped out into the warm evening air. They stopped in the middle of the Ponte Sant'Angelo, a strong stone bridge spanning the Tiber since the time of the Old Romans.

At a whispered order, their burdens were released. Two loud splashes came from the turbid water below.

CHAPTER SEVENTY-FOUR

Then the Tiber flowed silently, dark as the night to come, toward the Mediterranean. At Ostia, picking its way along the muddy riverbank, a gray heron looked up and watched as two bodies floated out to sea.

abbot: Head of a monastery or convent

angel maker: Abortionist

apse: That part of a church, often semicircular and vaulted, where the altar sits; it is usually in the eastern end of the church, pointing toward Jerusalem.

butler: Servant who distributed ale and wine at a meal

Cathar: A Christian dissident who rejected the teachings of the Catholic Church and believed that there were two Gods, one Evil (who created matter and the world) and one Good, beyond the bounds of this Earth

Catharism: The belief system known as The Great Heresy of the Middle Ages

charivari: A boisterous celebration outside the home of newly-weds on their wedding night

choir: That part of a church immediately preceding the **apse**

clepsydra: Water clock

clerestory: From *clear story*; an upper level of a church wall pierced by windows

consolamentum: The sole Cathar sacrament; when performed, the recipient would become a **Good Man** or a **Good Woman**

crow: An epithet used to mock black-robed Dominican friars

ewerers: Servants who worked in pairs to wash the hands of guests before they dined; one would pour water from a pitcher (ewer); the other would catch the runoff with a bowl

excommunication: Expulsion from the church

Gael: A speaker of a particular Gaelic language, that is, Irish, Scottish, or Manx gibbet: Hanging gallows

Good Man/Good Woman: The Cathar clergy

helpmeet: A wife; Eve in Genesis 2:18

Holy Office: The Inquisition

hostler: A stable master or groom who takes care of the horses

infirmarer: The physician of a monastery or convent

interdict: An ecclesiastical punishment depriving a town or country of all the sacraments of the church

lauds: Dawn prayers in a monastery or convent

magister: A teacher

matins: Middle-of-the-night prayers in a monastery or convent

murmuration: A very large flock of starlings flying in a coordinated manner

necromancy: Black magic

Occitan: The language once spoken in the Languedoc, akin to Provençal

pantler: Servant who distributed the bread at a meal

prior: A monastic superior; an office lower than the **abbot**'s

provincial: The head of an order of friars in a given province

Saracen: Muslim

seneschal: French royal governor

strappado: A torture technique used in the Inquisition

solar: An upper-story room in a castle that served as living and sleeping quarters

trencher: A large, thick slice of bread that was used instead of a plate at medieval meals, hence the word *trencherman* for someone with a hearty appetite, a gourmand

triforium: An arched gallery running around an upper level of a church wall, often at the same level as the **clerestory**

trobairitz: A female troubadour of the Languedoc

Understanding of the Good: The Cathars' description of their religion

widdershins: Counterclockwise, used before the advent of clockfaces

HISTORICAL NOTE

The action takes place mainly in the Languedoc, that section of southern France stretching from the west bank of the river Rhône to the frontier of the province of Aquitaine, which is roughly 150 miles inland from the Atlantic port of Bordeaux. At the time, the Languedoc was and was not part of France. One part of it, centered in the city of Carcassonne, was absorbed into the French royal domain in the 1210s. The ruling family there, the Trencavels, had been deposed. Another more important portion of the Languedoc, centered in the lands around the city of Toulouse, resisted absorption into France for a bit longer. Its count, Raymond VII, signed a treaty in 1229 with Paris that essentially handed over his lands to France upon his death (which would come in 1249) and that of his daughter (1271).

The pretext for the annexation of the Languedoc was the fight against heresy. In the twelfth and thirteenth centuries the region became the homeland of the Great Heresy, what today we call Catharism. To combat this heresy, Pope Innocent III, in 1209, called for a crusade—in the heart of Christendom—against these dissident Christians who did not follow the teachings and accept the authority of Rome. The French barons answered the call, and for twenty years vicious battles were fought, known to history as the Albigensian Crusade, ostensibly to eliminate Catharism. *Ostensibly* is the operative word in that last sentence. The French adventure seekers sought new possessions and, when they obtained them, promptly abandoned the heretic hunting. The church, exasperated at the persistence of the heresy, then instituted the Inquisition in the Languedoc in the 1230s, which would eventually eliminate Catharism altogether over a period of one hundred years. For more on this history, consult my nonfiction book *The Perfect Heresy*.

In the story I have neither downplayed nor exaggerated the excesses of the Inquisition. For instance, many of the incendiary tropes used in the various sermons delivered by the characters are actual citations of Inquisition rhetoric. The torture methods, too, are backed up by documents, as are the arrest and incarceration of an entire village, which the Inquisition in Carcassonne did on several occasions. The horrendous incident of the old lady lashed to her bed and burned alive is, alas, not my invention either—it occurred in Toulouse in 1234. The horror of the mass mutilation at Bram is also a well-attested historical event. As for the assassinations in the story, their victims are fictional. However, two real-life inquisitors in the Languedoc were bludgeoned to death on the Feast of the Ascension 1242, in the village of Avignonet, hence the tip of my hat to that place in the narrative. Also, humiliating Dominicans with the call of the crow did, in fact, occur. During a famed revolt against the Inquisition in fourteenth-century Carcassonne (the subject of another of my nonfiction books, *The Friar of Carcassonne*), the townspeople harassed the friars with the derisive call. And the Dominicans were actually expelled for a time from Toulouse twice in the thirteenth century.

Aside from the rulers (Blanche, Louis, Raymond) and three others, the characters are fictional. There was a real Astruguetus, but what we know of him is confined to documents naming him as the first treasurer to the (French) Seneschal of Carcassonne. He was Astruguetus of Béziers; I changed his name to Astruguetus of Narbonne, as that was the Languedoc city with the largest Jewish population of the time. Robert de Sorbon, the founder of the Sorbonne, lived in Paris a bit later than I have placed him there. And Cardinal Romano had earlier in his career been the papal legate to Paris, which spurred rumors about his having been the lover of the widowed Queen Blanche.

As for the two principal fictitious people:

Balian of Mallorca. The detective is very loosely inspired by Arnau de Vilanova, a Catalan physician, alchemist, astrologer, agronomist, polyglot, and adviser to kings, whose career began shortly after the time of our story.

Matilda of Périgueux. Despite the damage done to the image of medieval womanhood by late Victorian prudes, a well-born woman with education, brains, and spirit could be the mistress of her own fate. Medieval history teems with such women: from the headstrong Crusader queens to notable patronesses of the arts and accomplished female troubadours and religious and healing figures. In the Languedoc, especially, where women inherited property and the Cathars viewed gender as irrelevant, a woman such as Matilda could well have existed. And certainly, disguising oneself as a man, as Matilda does, was not an infrequent gambit for medieval women longing for greater freedom of movement.

The two matters that might surprise, or strain credulity, come directly from the transcripts of Inquisition interrogations conducted in the Languedoc in the early fourteenth century. There was, indeed, a Muslim hermit–holy man advising Occitan villagers in the countryside at one time. And the peculiar method of birth control used at one point in the story, a pouch of herbs hanging between a woman's breasts, is described in those transcripts as well.

Last, at the time of our tale, the year 1242, the church had not yet codified the institution of marriage. So Count Raymond performing the marriage of Tancred and Judith is not beyond the bounds of possibility. And such mixed marriages between people of different faiths, although rare, were not unheard-of. See Stefan Hertmans' superb *The Convert*, an imagined reconstruction of one such medieval marriage based on well-documented historical facts.

ABOUT THE AUTHOR

Toronto-born Stephen O'Shea, journalist and translator formerly based in Paris and New York, is also the author of five nonfiction books dealing with European travel and history (more information at stephenosheaonline.com). The Sorcerer and the Assassin is his first work of fiction. He currently resides in Providence, Rhode Island.